THEY WERE COMING FOR HIM

THEY WERE COMING FOR HIM

BERTA VIAS MAHOU

Translated from the Spanish by
Cecilia Ross

Hispabooks Publishing, S. L.
Madrid, Spain
www.hispabooks.com

Originally published in Spain as *Venían a buscarlo a él* by Acantilado, 2010
First published in English by Hispabooks, 2016
English translation copyright © by Cecilia Ross
Design © simonpates - www.patesy.com
Cover image: Albert Camus's car crash. Villeblevin, France, January 4, 1960.

ISBN 978-84-943496-7-6 (trade paperback)
ISBN 978-84-943658-0-5 (ebook)
Legal Deposit: M-34134-2015

Esta obra ha sido publicada con una subvención
del Ministerio de Educación, Cultura y Deporte de España

For A.C.,
my A.C.

But again and again there comes a time in history when the man who dares to say that two and two make four is punished with death.

ALBERT CAMUS, *The Plague*

CONTENTS

A MEMORY DARK WITH SHADOWS

She said yes, or maybe it was no; she had to go back in time, through a memory dark with shadows, nothing was clear. The memory of the poor is less well-nourished than that of the rich, for they have fewer reference points in space, straying only rarely from their places of residence, and also fewer reference points in time, in a life that is all uniformity and grayness. They do, of course, have the memory of the heart, which is the surest, they say, but the heart grows worn with grief and toil, it forgets more rapidly under the weight of fatigue. Lost time is regained by the rich alone.

Really? Was that so? The rich didn't seem to have much of a memory, either. Just more documentation to prop it up. Jacques set down his pen, his eyes wandered around the room, and for a few moments he gazed at the portraits of Nietzsche and Dostoyevsky, who had accompanied him for some time now. His masters. In pain and in writing, in suffering overcome. Because he was not a believer and had no religion save for the religion of freedom and the struggle for justice and the sanctity of life, they were his patron saints. He rose from his desk, a tall drafting table, took a few steps over to the window, and leaned against its frame. A horrid silence, almost otherworldly, lay over everything out there. The snow fell increasingly thickly, and in the wind those floating bits of fluff, instead of drifting calmly, slowly downward, flew crosswise at one another beyond the glass, in a conniption. The rooftops all around him were already covered with a substantial blanket of it, and the entire world seemed to have come to a standstill.

They were orange, or red, in Spain. In Algeria they were whitewashed. Rooftop terraces where laundry was hung. In the summer the sun there would scorch the parched homes. The only way to live was in the shade of closed blinds, in a half-light filled with suspended particles each brighter and more colorful than the last. In Paris, though, the rooftops were black, or a gray color just as somber as the winter skies that covered the city for much of the year. Inaccessible, unresponsive. Their slate tiles had been damp at dawn and now were white. Shrouded in that light, the birds looked even darker. They shot past and disappeared, like projectiles on the trail of some invisible target, far off in the distance. Paris is a dingy sort of town, filled with pigeons and dark courtyards, he'd written several years back. The people here have waxen skin. And when night falls, they file into their houses. In my land, at sundown, everyone rushes eagerly out. People said this was one of the most beautiful cities in the world, but for him it was wearisome, and his most ardent wish would have been to return to his own land, a man's country, coarse, unforgettable. But that, for a combination of reasons, wasn't possible.

If he couldn't get himself out of there at the first opportunity, that city was going to do him in. It would crush him. And since he couldn't go back to Algeria, Jacques dreamt of the Luberon, the Lure Mountains, Lauris, Lourmarin. Of being able to go there one day. Of the smell of basil, rosemary, and thyme, of lavender in bloom. He dreamt of a modest house, roomy and comfortable. And a landscape he could gaze out on from his windows as one gazes out on the sea from atop a cliff. Leaving Paris. A longing few shared, and many couldn't even comprehend. Possibly only his friend René. One of the last remaining friends he had. He, for whom friendship had always held such importance. But René spent a substantial amount of time in Provence, while Jacques was still trapped in this capital city he detested. Perhaps because he was a monster, a barbarian. At least that's how he'd always seen himself, as one who'd betrayed his kin, left them behind, in a country that was being steadily and progressively gnawed away at by the cancer of violence.

Lost time is regained by the rich alone. He himself had come to represent a prime example. But what would have become of him if it hadn't been for the support of his high school teacher, that helping hand that had reached out to him then, expecting nothing in exchange, simply because he thought he deserved it more than others, that he would put the opportunity to better use? He would never have set about attempting to regain his lost time. Most likely, he would have done nothing more than waste it, resignedly, patiently, like so many other men and women throughout the ages and in so many different parts of the world. Like his mother. And yet it was back then that he'd known what happiness was. Poverty kept him from thinking that all was well under the sun and in history, while the sun taught him that history wasn't everything. Back then he lived in the present. Barefooted. Practically naked. Frolicking with the other boys through the dust-filled streets and along the beach. Now, the past stretched out behind him, the future seemed to shrink in inverse proportion to it, and the present was slipping away.

There, he'd gotten by with very few things, and even those were things he didn't possess. The sun, the sea, the wind, the stars. He recalled the nomads of Djelfa. Poor, destitute, offering every guest their all. Yes, he had grown up by the sea, far from that city he was looking at now through the window, that capital hunkered down in the interior of the world's smallest continent, and poverty had never felt to him like a hardship. He'd never heard any complaints or clamoring around him. They saw that life as natural. Later, he'd lost it, he'd lost the sea. And the sun. From that point on, all luxuries seemed gray. Poverty, intolerable. He did not belong among that race of people now surrounding him, that race of people who were all so preoccupied with money and so bored deep down inside. Who transformed their tables at this or that Left Bank café into courtrooms and themselves into judges, unsparing with various victims and magnanimous with certain tyrants, handing down sentences on matters they knew nothing about between sips of whisky, or coffee, and flippant, supposedly freethinking remarks.

How distant, in contrast, were the sun, the sea, the simple beach life. And how unattainable was peace. He longed for the solitude of a stone column. For that of an olive tree under a summer sky. That lesson in love and patience that had been imparted to him by the desolate desert expanses. He knew he would eventually end up buying a house. And furniture. And he would become a slave, despite living the life of a rich man, a slave bent on regaining his time. Like Proust, whom he imagined tossing and turning in his bed, inside a room lined floor to ceiling with corkboard, trying to shield himself from the noise, from the entire world, in search of words, like him. Searching for nothing. Or almost nothing. A slice of immortality. He imagined someone else, too, someone who had once been a friend of his, Jean Paul, whose father had, like his own, died young. Another dead man who hadn't had time enough to be a father, easily young enough to have been his son's son at this point. Just one of the commonalities he and Jean Paul still shared. Like literature.

Not even his own commitment to the poor, the persecuted, and the voiceless was the same anymore, not since a few years earlier when Jean Paul, *Monsieur Néant*, as he now called him, had had the gall, backed by the entire team at that snazzy journal of his, to say that if the working class wanted to leave the party, they had but one way out: to kick the bucket. Always falling back on threats whenever anyone dares to deviate even the slightest from the doctrine that's being pushed. All anti-Communists are dogs, he'd bark. That was the least he might say. And Jacques sitting there attempting to affect an air of bovine naturality and patience, but unsuccessfully, because what he really needed, what was still wanting there, was a revolution. The simultaneously urgent and gradual revolution of souls. I don't have time to go around writing for journals, he told himself, not even if it means getting to shoot down one of Jean Paul's arguments . . . I've only got so much of it left, and I want to put it into the new book.

Jean Paul, too, Monsieur Néant, too, in his devotion for books, had shut himself up from a young age in that imaginary world, the world of words, the words he read in books, the words he himself then wrote, the words he still had left to write. He, on the other hand, had gone a long while now without any of that, barely writing. He felt empty, tired. Though he knew a period of silence was sometimes necessary in order to then be able to write more, and perhaps even better. And now, beginning very recently, it seemed his memories were finally tugging at him, the weight of lost time, and a new book began to grow within his hands, a novel, although, as always, he was beset with doubts. No, not like always. His doubts now were even heavier. The craft of writing seemed to have nothing remotely craft-like about it. It was increasingly painful, increasingly difficult, ever more solitary. The unease, the scruples were ever greater. And ever more frequent the periods of fruitlessness, which threatened to become permanent each time they loomed into view, each time they took root, plunging him into a fit of anxiety only for their transience to eventually become plain once that mysterious fount began, finally, to flow once more.

If I had to write a book on morals, he'd quipped at an early point in his career, it would be a hundred pages long, and ninety-nine of them would be blank. And on the last one, I'd write, *I know of only one duty, and that is to love.* He hadn't ever really moved beyond that position. And he'd always felt the temptation, deep down, to throw in the towel on that endless effort. Despite the recognition. Or perhaps because of it. Because of the responsibility involved, which was increasingly weighty. Because of all the fuss surrounding him and his books. Because of his feeling of shame. At what? What could a man possibly feel ashamed of? Of his insistence on speaking the truth? Of his persistent quest for happiness? To his mind, that was an obligation for all human beings. Perhaps it was also fear. Fear of hurting others, specifically those he loved the most. Because how could you lessen the untruth, and even the hatred, the injustice, that's so often contained in words? And how could you repurpose words that are used by everyone, every day? How could he express all the love that he felt, love that pained him to the point of driving him to unbearable and ever more absolute silence?

Yes, there was no doubt in his mind, it was a path that led to silence. Nevertheless, he summoned his strength and wrenched himself away from his observatory at the window, the sight of the city greeting him daily with ever greater hostility, and he returned to his desk, to continue transcribing the words that were at long last bubbling up inside him. For the poor, time merely marks faint imprints along the road to death. Further, if one is to endure, one mustn't remember overmuch, one must bond oneself to each passing day, hour by hour, as his mother did . . . Jacques raised his head from his paper again and turned his gaze inward, losing himself in memories. When his mother lived in a room, she left no trace of herself, at most a handkerchief she would often tease and twist between her fingers and sometimes let lie in her lap while she waited for time to pass, for lunchtime to arrive. Or bedtime. Or a visitor. He was convinced that when she died, the traces of her time spent on this earth wouldn't be much more than that. A pair of shoes. A few items of clothing.

Or some newspaper page featuring a picture of her son, the younger of her two. Simple scraps of paper she felt such a swelling of pride for even now, when she couldn't make them out and had to wait for someone else to read them to her. She would brush her fingers across their surface, pretending she was trying to smooth them down, that they had gotten wrinkled or dusty, and on occasion she would show them off to one of the neighbor women. Gratified, discrete and innocent in her admiration. In his memory he saw her sitting in a chair out on the patio, directly in front of the door to the house, warming her bones in the sun, a newspaper spread out across her legs. It looked like a bedsheet in her hands, not just because of the size of its pages, but because of the defenselessness evident in every one of her gestures, the look in her eyes, her smile, her helplessness in the face of all those letters she didn't comprehend, although she did enjoy running a finger along them, staring at the pictures.

His books were likewise a mystery to her. She couldn't read them. Nor would she be able to read the book he was writing now, one he had decided to dedicate to her. *To you who will never be able to read this book*, Jacques had written on the first page. He, on the contrary, would leave an infinitude of pages behind him. Marks unlike those our shoes or our feet leave on the sand of a beach. These traces were doubtless less likely to disappear one day, even if someone might try to make them. Might take it upon himself to sweep away the vestiges of his journey through life. The things he had written. All those pages that were multiplying now before his eyes. All those pages filled with annotations, with ideas he was still intent on developing further, details he needed to research more fully, by picking the brains of his friends, his mother, and others who had lived through the same events, consulting books, rereading newspapers, pamphlets, and manifestos. They were filled with strike-throughs, too. Paths he'd ventured down, but left off shortly after.

Muslim brothers, all partisans of the FLN shall exterminate all Europeans, including children. Exceptions shall not be made. When he'd read that, his breath caught. It was a communiqué dated January 17 sanctioning a brutal strategy of indiscriminate attacks. Nothing new, really, since they'd already been killing children, in dozens of bombings in public places, and shootings in buses, and raids on farms, and torchings of churches and schools, and all without so much as batting an eye. But there was one difference. Now it was there for all to see, set down in ink and signed, right there on that handbill, and with it the door to apologies, to falling back on the rhetoric of unsought but inevitable accidents, of victim-blaming, was being definitively closed. It was a veritable declaration of all-out war. And just like that, the gears of violence ground to life once more.

In April, following the assassination of two French paratroopers, the dead men's comrades-in-arms had burst into an Arab bathhouse with guns blazing, out for blood, shooting any and everyone in their path, leaving some twenty or thirty dead and another twenty-something wounded. They unquestionably killed some of the terrorists that had gone there looking for a place to lie low while the police were after them, but the bathhouse also served at night as a shelter for a large number of homeless men. And no mercy was given to the poor. No mercy and not a single ounce of thought. Just as none was given by those colonists piling into their cars and carrying out raids in the Algerian highlands, shooting up the Arab peasants' *mechtas*. Or by the military commanders when they broadened the practice of summary executions under the cover of a highly lax Fugitive Law. And there'd been a fresh massacre just a few days ago. In Melouza, 338 Muslim civilians had been massacred at the hands of other Muslims. Shooting and knifing as they went, they'd castrated and slit the throats of every single man in the village, supporters of Messali Hadj, founder of the Star of North Africa, the seed of the entire anti-imperialist movement, now condemned by his own more radical offspring.

The FLN's propaganda machine would try to pin the bloodshed on the French army. For a long time they would remain unsuccessful, and that was no surprise. Torture and brutality were not the exclusive province of either side. Hatred feeds on hatred, in any culture. And when it reaches a certain fever pitch, it's called nationalism. Sometimes, like now, Jacques was tempted to give the whole thing up, for good. To give up writing and simply live, and love, a titanic undertaking, to make up for all the fear and the pain, the suffering and the anguish that filled so many lives, in so many places all over the world, but the urge to write, to fight back against lies and violence, against totalitarianism and injustice, would inevitably prevail. And it was creeping over him once more.

Yes, if one is to endure, one mustn't remember overmuch, one must bond oneself to each passing day, hour by hour, as his mother did . . . He, too, would become speechless in her presence, crippled, in his own way, and so he had to give up on ever learning anything from her. Even about that one incident that had made such a profound impression on him as a child and had pursued him his entire life, even in dreams. His father getting up at three in the morning to attend the execution of a famed criminal. He'd found out about it from his grandmother. Pirette was a hired hand at a farm in the Sahel, quite close to Algiers. He'd smashed in the skulls of his employers and the family's three children with a hammer.

THE BACILLUS OF THE PLAGUE

On the morning of June 3, as he was leaving his home, Doctor Bernard Rieux nearly tripped over a dead rat that was lying in the middle of the landing. He didn't mention it to the doorman. He could guess for himself what he'd say. That there weren't no rats in that house. Somebody must have brought it in from outside. Probably somebody's idea of a joke. Those are the words the doorman of the building where he'd lived in Oran had used years back. But later that same day, following his late afternoon coffee at the Metropole, as he stood once more in the entryway of the building and dug around for his keys before going up to his apartment, Doctor Rieux saw another large rat slink out from the far, shadowy end of the passage. The creature skittered away, and he stood there watching it for a moment. Then he started up the stairs. At least it wasn't bleeding and it hadn't keeled over right there at his feet. Was he about to have another plague on his hands?

Oh no, no, of course not. There weren't no rats in that house . . . Always the same cowardly eagerness to deny reality, to postpone the coming of the moment when there's no choice but to face up to a danger that's long been hovering over us. At that same time, the time of day when the office buildings and the houses of Algiers spill forth a chattering multitude that slowly but surely wends its way down to the boulevards, Marie Cardona could be found sitting, like every other afternoon, hands folded in her lap, motionless, at the balcony. She wasn't dozing, she was attentive to each and every one of the sounds floating up to her from the street. The sounds of the café across the way. Of the children streaming out of the school. Of the tram pulling into its stop. Or out of it. Empty at times. Other times crammed to the roof. Attentive, too, to the different wafts of scent, to the shifts in the sky, in the air, in the light. To the sounds of people's voices as they strolled past or paused in the shade of one of the many ficuses.

The poor, when they have any time, spend it watching life go by. In a house with practically no furnishings or belongings, it's not as if there's much to do, anyhow. Four chairs and a table, the parrot cage, a few pots and pans, a couple of beds, the kitchen, and a tiny bathroom. The walls were bare, and a single naked light bulb hung from the ceiling in each room. There wasn't even a clock to mark the passing of time. Lying in wait at the window to catch all the different sounds was enough. The shuttering of shops, the screeching of birds, the voices of neighbors, of passersby. Every afternoon, when Marie came home from working in another family's house, in the wealthy neighborhood, she would sit down right there, in a chair. The sky, though still blue, had taken on a pallid luster that would grow fainter as the evening wore on. And the breeze brought with it the smell of spices, of rocks and algae. She almost never spoke, until it was time to sleep. And even then she didn't say much. Bedtime, Antoine, but first you have to read me something. She enjoyed listening to her son read aloud. Or watching him when he'd become deeply engrossed, immersed in the lines of text in one of those books he was always bringing home from the public library.

And he liked for his mother to listen to him reading aloud, too. He got the feeling that the words in those books drew them even closer together, somehow, in the midst of her customary silence. And sometimes, although he didn't quite understand why it happened, some obscure chord would be struck within her and she would begin speaking. That's how he always remembered her. Seated at the balcony, silently, like someone in a box at the theater waiting for the second act to begin, while he sat kneeling on the floor beside the parrot cage, the sole extravagance in the entire house. It was made of wrought iron, painted white, and was very tall, although not quite as tall as him; he was fourteen years old now, trim as a bamboo stalk, and he was already five foot nine. Doctor Rieux had said he'd hit five eleven by the time he was fifteen. His skin was the color of wood, and it smelled the same, too, like a freshly sharpened pencil. Caligula's feathers, in contrast, were very light gray. The bird had been given to Marie some time ago by the owners of one of the houses she worked in, promptly after they'd realized that the beast was a perfect brute. They hadn't been able to make anything of him.

Mother, why does Caligula sometimes turn his back on strangers? Antoine would occasionally show up at the house with one of the neighborhood boys or a few of his classmates. And sometimes with Doctor Rieux, if he happened to run into him on the stairs coming home from the hospital. Everyone always wanted to see the bird, to try their hand at feeding him, but the parrot seemed determined to ignore them, having remained withdrawn for some time now in a state of unflinching silence. You know he doesn't do that with everyone who comes in here, his mother replied, still without turning around. Even though he knows almost all of them, he's grown to be quite a sullen bird. He usually only does that when it's a girl who stops by. Or a woman. They must make him jealous. And some of the better-looking boys, too. Or maybe he confuses them. The good-looking boys and the girls. Who knows. There was silence again. Perhaps Madame Cardona was expecting her son to raise some objection, but she quickly continued. The fact that Antoine had asked her something had been a perfect excuse to strike up a conversation.

He doesn't do it with you, because he knows you and loves you. A long time ago, Caligula talked a lot. And if a girl came by, he'd sometimes even squawk—*Girls!* His mother did a little imitation of the bird, affecting a sort of raspy, old-man voice. Then he would always make this one sound, to convey the deep disgust he must have been feeling. I don't know who he learned it from. You were very little then. Now he's a bit deaf, he barely ever speaks and most likely can't hardly see. He's probably tired of life. Or maybe he's been through some sort of trauma. Maybe that's why he's always yanking out his feathers. These parrots have a reputation for being very sensitive. Everything around them has to be in perfect order. Otherwise, they get neurotic and start behaving like absolute despots. Antoine gaped at his mother. It had been ages since she'd spoken so much. Caligula's not all that discourteous now. Here among commoners, among normal, everyday people, he's become rather refined. Since he doesn't speak, he can't berate us. Or maybe he respects us because we're poor. Or looks down on us and that's why he doesn't talk.

These double reasonings amused Antoine. No sooner had his mother put forth one suggestion than she was already contradicting it. Or asserting the opposite. He didn't know to what degree it was due to a deep-rooted feeling of self-doubt in her, or if it was her sense of prudence, her respect for others, that prevented her from saying anything she might later come to regret. Perhaps it was a code of conduct typical of high society and she, unlike the bird, had picked it up in one of those houses of hers. Maybe the parrot had only committed the worst of it to memory. That bird is far too smart, and that's why it behaves so stupidly, her employer had told her the day she had given it to her, gesturing at the same time for her to take the cage as well. And hasn't he ever done it to you? Hasn't he ever turned his back on you? Marie Cardona turned ever so slightly toward him this time and replied, smiling—I'm old now, Antoine. He didn't think so. He'd always thought her the most beautiful woman in the world. And so she always would be, despite her wistful demeanor. Or perhaps because of it. Sometimes she'd laugh, he'd be able to get her to laugh. And it was then, when she was happy, that he would imagine her when she was young.

It was then that he was able to think about how his mother had at one point been someone who'd gone out to the movies, gone for dips in the sea, how she'd had friends. But he made no objection. He merely repeated the parrot squawks his mother had let fly moments ago, putting on the same shrill, curmudgeonly voice. Caligula began rocking from side to side on his perch, rotating backward on his two wrinkled, fleshy legs, until he'd slowly spun around enough that he was facing away. Antoine broke into a laugh. Never become like that parrot, his mother told him then. Don't turn your back on anyone. Don't look down on those who aren't the same as you. He loved hearing her speak. Having her tell him things about when he was little. About when their parrot still spoke. Watch it! You could have taken a leg off, *madame*, the parrot had apparently used to say whenever his mother would take him out of the cage to let him stretch his wings. He'd fly from window to window and alight on the top edge of the sky-blue wooden shutter. Try to be a little more careful! You're such a clumsy girl, Marie. You're going to break the china one of these days. He must have picked up those last phrases in some rich person's home, because in Marie Cardona's there wasn't a single piece of delicate china, unless you counted the souls of the woman herself and her son.

And if a man ever came by, someone who might conceivably be considered a suitor, Caligula wasted no time confronting him. He had an unerring nose for love. Get out! he would squawk way back when at the slightest whiff of an ulterior motive on a man. We'll have none of you vultures around here! But it was long since he'd spoken, so now anyone could come in without the parrot troubling himself to give even a peep of protestation. They don't really speak. They reproduce the things they hear. And the more they hear something—a word, a phrase, a greeting—the more they repeat it. Just like most people. Maybe that's why he hardly speaks since he's been with us. Seizing upon the loquaciousness that appeared to have taken possession of his mother, Antoine told her that they'd been learning the names of the Frankish kings in their History class. By heart. All the different dynasties. Maybe if I recite them out loud, Caligula will learn them, too. He could help me study.

The Merovingians and the Carolingians. Chariberts, Childeberts, Childerics, Chilperics, Theuderics, Dagoberts, Sigeberts, Clovisses, Chlodomers, Meroveches, and Clothars. He rattled off the names in a single breath. He liked saying them like that, in the plural. Old-fashioned, pompous names. Arnulfs, Carlomans, and Lothairs. And the Pepins. They had to study the entire list, including the dates of all the different reigns and the battles in which France had expanded its territory. And what about Algeria? Not a word. About Africa, either. Be patient, Marie told him. It will come. Although it might just end up being worse. I'm afraid what's sometimes counted as history is nothing but a tangle of lies. Novels might deceive us less. Or poetry. I don't like history, Antoine declared, capitalizing on his mother's conjectures. It's nothing but Western prejudice. I don't care about the names of conquerors, or the names of powerful men. Or the names of the presidents of the French Republic, either, with their uniforms all pinned over with stars and ribbons. Or the Roman emperors. Or the Egyptian pharaohs. Anyone immortal.

Although he had to admit there were a few truly excellent ones. Names like Marcomir, Richimir, Priarius, and Malaric. To give just a few examples from the Franks. Is that why you came home from school early? The blood drained from Antoine's face, and he gulped. She had never struck him, and he felt an almost religious respect for her. And not just because of that. Yes, he'd skipped class. What he'd told her when he'd first gotten home wasn't true. That they'd been let out early because the teacher was sick. He'd left school an hour early so that he wouldn't have to sit through History. You have to go, Antoine, Marie told him sweetly. Even though it might not seem like it, it's a very important subject. You just have to learn not to take it too much to heart. Besides, sometimes we really believe we're right about something, and then it turns out we're not at all. Antoine looked at her with surprise, but he couldn't work up the courage to say anything. She didn't seem to know what else to say to him, either. Maybe she was thinking she'd said too much. Silence spread out into the room again, until suddenly Marie, in a serene, soft voice, declared— You have to care, even about what you don't care about at all. History will help you learn to distinguish good from evil, even though the two might sometimes seem the same.

27

And to not deceive people, she rushed to add, possibly to break the silence that had followed on that exceedingly transcendental declaration and was threatening to engulf the two of them again, although she must already be seriously questioning whether his continued study of the subject could really have any such effect. Antoine, you must never lose faith in humanity, or rather, in human beings, no matter how many times life seems to teach you that you should. Anyhow, she thought, her son was right. In the end, we only know those who are said to have written history, those who not only kill but spend their time amassing riches and frittering away the money that a great number of others could have used to live a little better on. The names of the poor, of the downtrodden, of the victims are to be found only, if at all, on an old, forgotten gravestone in some ordinary, anonymous cemetery. You can learn from it, she continued aloud. From history. It can serve as an example. A positive one and a negative one. Valor is one thing, but foolhardiness is another. It's the same with enthusiasm and fanaticism. Loyalty is one thing, and another very different thing is fidelity. You have to learn to distinguish. But I don't want you to become pessimistic. You're still very young.

And you may even be right. Perhaps an abundance of formal history instruction isn't right for you. A person has to live. And the streets are as good a school as any classroom. Antoine felt ashamed. He would not be skipping class again. But rather than keeping quiet, he carried on talking, to bury in speech the shame he felt over the two infractions he'd just committed. The lying, most particularly. And he told her that he preferred to know the names of the people that were like them, the people that worked or lived in the neighborhood. People who rose at dawn and toiled all day long, year after year, waging their own daily, silent battles against hatred. The name of the butcher. Gustave. The name of the fishmonger, a Maltese man who kept a stall at the market and had the same name as him. Antoine. And the baker. Louis. Or the fruit seller. Manolo. He was of Spanish descent, like his mother. A large, strong man with a waggish smile and a genial face who gazed down from behind his counter in a state of rapture at the sight of his mother's face. He always offered her a piece of fruit, and once he'd even presented her with a plant, a small potted mint that she'd set out on the balcony so that she could see it from her chair.

And there was the Galician man, too, one of the few of them in those parts, since the majority emigrated to America. The Spaniards that found their way to Algeria were almost all originally from the Mediterranean coast. That Galician man was a hero of Antoine's. Once, when he'd gone into the bar to ask to have a plate of noodles warmed for him because his mother's little gas burner wasn't working, Antoine spent the wait just standing there taking in the scene. After a few minutes, a badly dressed, disheveled Muslim woman about fifty years old had come in, hurried over to the bar, and asked for a glass of water. Of course, *madame*. The woman thanked him timidly, and the Galician man, with that candid smile of his, replied— It's a pleasure, *madame.* There were some disagreeable, unfriendly ones, too. Like the poultry seller. Daniel. A fat, preening man with flabby, pasty flesh and thick, black-rimmed glasses, whose indolent demeanor failed to disguise his perpetually sour mood and who was always locking horns with his employees, despite going out of his way to fawn all over the customers. Two-faced, like a coin. He had an assistant with whom Antoine was fascinated. A quiet Arab man, slender, with a soft fuzz of white hair ringing his otherwise bald head, which was a beautiful, shiny color, golden, like his skin.

Ibrahim. His name was Ibrahim. And he crisscrossed through the streets behind his pushcart stacked high with egg cartons and chopped-up chickens, never looking at anyone, hardly ever glancing off to the side, even, his eyes fixed on the ground, sadly, his thick eyebrows topping a face made beautiful by the symmetry of its features, by its almost complete lack of expression, rising impenetrably from the thin-striped, green-and-black apron that wrapped all the way around his body. Perhaps his sight was even worse than his boss's. Or he had no interest in the things he saw around him. Maybe they pained him and so he preferred not to look at them. Antoine had seen him just a few days earlier, walking along the street with his head in the clouds and his thoughts turned inward as usual, but this time he was digging around in his nose with great relish and a great, long index finger, and now he wasn't sure if he looked up to his idol all the more for having happened upon him in such a human posture, or if witnessing that maneuver from such a deeply admired sphinx disgusted him more than it would have coming from any other person. It was hot out, the air was dry. You could feel it on the skin of your entire body. But as soon as a good rain came, Ibrahim would go back to walking along immutably.

Regardless, his mother suddenly added, you're forgetting that there are plenty of other great names in history who aren't famous for their power. I know. Artists, thinkers, poets . . . Marie was about to contradict him, in order to correct her own words, but she thought better of it and said nothing. But in any case, what does please me is that you're willing to be critical. It's important to know how to say no, just as long as you never forget the importance of pity. His mother was like the Sibyl of Cumae. Almost always silent, she could reveal herself without warning as wiser than most. And he imagined her seated in a lush valley next to a smoking tripod at the entrance to a temple. So yes, she liked history. And mythology. Only a person who has suffered, he thought, can have the voice of an oracle. And he felt an overwhelming urge to hug his mother, but he didn't dare. Maybe we should give the bird a new name, Marie went on to suggest. She was right. After all, he hadn't spoken a word in ages, he wasn't capable of squawking, and he didn't even seem to know his name anymore. What do you think about René? Like Descartes? It's all right. Or François, a saint's name? It's also the name of a king . . . What about Benoît? Benito? Antoine burst out laughing. Like Mussolini? No. No way.

It was going to be tough coming up with a name that wasn't somehow sullied. Maybe even impossible. Everything in this life seemed to have two faces. What about Candide? Yes. Candide could be a good name. And the first part even sounded almost the same. No, though. They couldn't just up and change his name, just like that. A name ends up investing its bearer with a personality in a sense, whether it's an animal or a person. Look, Antoine, his mother said just then, turning back to the window. That was the time of day she liked best, when the sunlight was slowly fading and everything began cooling off. The breeze stirred up the scent of the trees, of the wood floors some of the houses had, or the different products people used for mopping up. Flaxseed soap. The smell of it made Antoine close his eyes and inhale deeply. Or vinegar mixed with a little water, which is what his mother used, because she, like the rich folks, abhorred bleach. At the moment, the pigeons were flying past the window. Afterward the swallows would venture out to hunt insects, and the air would be teeming with their cries. Later the streetlights would come on, and the lights of the other houses. Antoine went over to his mother and stood next to her. He liked all those lit-up rectangles. Most people waited until the last minute before turning on their lights, because electricity was a luxury. He would imagine what was going on inside everywhere, at that hour when the city looked like a model play set. There was no sadness there, or melodrama, or sickness. Perhaps nothing more than a gray, workaday life.

Or maybe not. Maybe it was all constant gaiety. Like in games. No. Even in games there was often bickering. People were leaving work now and flooding out onto the sidewalks. You could hear voices, laughter. The heat was intense. Just then, two young boys walked past in short-panted sailor suits, a bit stiff in their starched getups, along with a girl wearing a big pink bow and patent leather shoes. Their mother always dressed them like that, in their Sunday best, even when it was Monday. Trailing after them was the mother, a woman people in the neighborhood always referred to as a commode biddy. Antoine didn't know what that meant, and he didn't dare ask, because lots of people said it with a disparaging sneer. He'd look it up in a dictionary. In the library. Although, generally speaking, there was never usually an entry for the more upsetting things. The more colloquial things. None of his friends knew what it meant. The sound of voices and laughter rang out once more, coming from the tram stop. People would be waiting there for the next carriage, waiting to make their way home or down to the port area for a stroll and some fresh air. There was the sound of an ice-cream vendor on a megaphone, too, he must have been pedaling around the neighborhood with his cart hooked onto the back of his bicycle.

All of a sudden there was a loud boom, accompanied by sputtering sounds. As if the air were glittering with thousands of stars. Mom, look, fireworks, Antoine exclaimed, resting his hand on the window frame and leaning out to get a better look at the festivities that were apparently getting underway right there below them, but Marie lunged at him, yanked him back by the arm, and pulled him down onto the floor with her. Antoine caught a glimpse of several pigeons falling like wads of crumpled up paper being dropped onto a sidewalk. A few seconds later, another blast, stronger than the previous one, and the windowpanes shattered and crashed to the floor just an inch or so from where the two of them lay. A third explosion, this one slightly farther off, set his mother shaking as she huddled on top of him, shielding his body with hers. They remained frozen like that, barely breathing, but with all their senses on high alert, even though there wasn't a sound to be heard, as if life had come to a standstill.

It was only after several seconds had passed that they could finally hear any noise at all. And screaming. Quickly, the sound of ambulances, of police cars, began to drown out everything else. The mother sat up on her knees and hugged her son. He pressed himself against her. Then Marie stood up and went over to the front window. The glass had flown everywhere, and she walked on top of the fragments, crunching them beneath the soles of her sandals. She wanted to check that everything down in the street and all around her was still in its place. That the earth hadn't collapsed, but she couldn't bring herself to look out. She halted a foot or two from the balcony. In his cage, Caligula sat hunched over with his back to them, and he appeared to be trembling. Antoine, go look and see if your tree is OK. She wanted to get him away from there. Didn't want him to see what she was seeing. Right at that moment, someone stuck their head in at the door. It was Doctor Rieux, a physician who'd come over several years ago from Oran after losing his wife—a tuberculosis sufferer—

33

and his best friend to an epidemic. He'd always looked in on them whenever he could. He'd provided them on more than one occasion with medicine, food, and even clothing. And he probably didn't even have all that much money himself. There were too many people in need of help.

Hello, Antoine, Caligula said suddenly. The parrot had gotten his voice back. But was it maybe the doctor he was greeting? Or were those the only words he remembered having heard the whole time he'd been silent? The boy ran over to him. Hello, Antoine! the parrot repeated his greeting. Hello, Antoine! he chimed again. He must have been shaken up, too. There were three dropped feathers on the floor of the cage, lying alongside the folded paper birds Antoine had made for him. They'd been adamant to Marie about the bird liking toys, but Caligula never played. Those feathers, had they fallen off in the explosion? Or had he pulled them out himself? Is everybody here OK? the doctor asked. Don't worry, Marie just managed to stammer out in reply. Are you sure? Yes, yes. The doctor gave a hurried goodbye, closed the door, and then they heard him going down the stairs. He wasn't thinking anymore about the rats he'd seen there that morning and again in the afternoon, he was thinking about the three repairmen in the gas company uniforms, with the blue helmets, too, that he'd seen working near a lamppost just a short while earlier, when he'd finished his lunch and was having his coffee before heading back up to the apartment.

Had they not been workers from the Algerian Gas and Electric Company, then? He'd seen three men. One had used a key to unlock the small meter box on the iron base of one of the lampposts. A gigantic key that looked as if it belonged to some castle or fortress gate. Another had gone through the motions of tightening the connector bolts, but had quickly moved aside for a third man wearing a crossbody leather pouch, like all AGE employees. Bernard had seen him pull out a package. It was a truly Machiavellian idea. Placing explosives at the foot of a lamppost, right next to a tram stop. Somebody must have outfitted them with the key and the uniforms. And the helmets. There were plenty of individuals willing to bankroll such atrocities. People in the business of extorting Algerian Muslims in France. People who took the resulting money off to Switzerland. Who funneled it into the purchase of explosives and preparations for every one of those attacks, which were becoming increasingly frequent and savage. And a whole network of collaborators. Many of those in government, in the metropole as well as the colony, must have been bought off. On police forces, in city halls, among the ranks of ministers. And here, meanwhile, legs and arms get blasted off and go hurtling end over end through air, the doctor said to himself. And he thought about Kamel. About the many times they'd argued.

In November of the previous year, he recalled, a group of doctors had been arrested on charges of collaborating with the National Liberation Front, among them the Chief Health Officer of Algerian Gas and Electric. Doctor Liddi. The children! Bernard exclaimed the instant he set foot in the street. They must have been let out of school just then, too, mere minutes before the explosion. A drove of them, the majority walking merrily, or tiredly, but still whooping it up with their satchels in tow, off to their homes. Others would have been waiting for the tram. The doctor ran. They'd take the wounded to Mustapha Hospital, which is where he worked, just a few short steps away. And their relatives would already be standing there gripping the fence, waiting for word. For days they'd remain there, fists clenched in rage and impotence, while the doctors cut off an arm here, a leg there, a bunch of fingers over there. The air would be thick with dynamite. And panic would course through the Muslim neighborhoods, and fear of reprisals, of the blind, mindless repression that would heap violence upon violence. And mourning upon mourning.

Surrounded by the sound of ambulances once more, he thought. Always fighting with all his might against death. And death always two steps behind him. Right there in front of him. Violence is a highly contagious disease, he told himself. The virus propagates swiftly. And now others will be eager to respond in kind, they'll allow themselves to be swept up by their own warlike, defensive impulses. They'll start up the *ratonnades*, the hunts for Muslims, arbitrary and appalling, that always come after an attack. On both sides, the goal is to strip the other of its humanity. For its part, the FLN had recently put out a communiqué encouraging the killing of French people in Algeria, referring to them as dogs. Strike down all the dogs and all their young, they'd written boldly. And then they'd respond with systematized torture, and forced disappearances, combing the areas where Arabs lived, encouraging people to inform on one another, with surprise raids and death squads, applying the grievous and dangerous principle of collective responsibility. Arabs? Frenchmen? He didn't know what he was supposed to call people anymore. Not even all the so-called Arabs were Arab, or the Frenchmen French.

Perhaps it would have been more accurate to speak in terms of Muslim Algerians and Algerians of European descent. Or Muslims and non-Muslims. The labels were merely a convention people fell back on to make themselves understood, despite the fact that it was becoming ever more difficult to do so. Bernard Rieux finally arrived at the hospital. It wouldn't be long before the blood donors started showing up, waiting patiently for hours, inside the building and outside of it, as well, never minding that not all of them would ever end up making it as far as the blood collection hall, a sort of oversized aviary whose four glass walls reached all the way up to the ceiling. There, several nurses wearing caps and gloves, with bags covering their shoes and part of their legs and white handkerchiefs stretched over their noses and mouths, swung open windows on the walls' lower halves so that the volunteers, comfortably seated on what looked like deck chairs, could stick in their arms. Other nurses kept watch in the outer hallway, standing alongside the donors to make sure no clogs formed that might impede the passage of the rest of the hospital staff. In the center of the hall stood the metal trays, each with its syringe, needle, and tubes. Mustapha was the largest hospital in all of North Africa. And the most modern. A city within a city. Pumping blood.

Antoine had gone over to the back window. It was the only windowpane in the house that hadn't been shattered, and his gaze was transfixed on the courtyard he so loved whiling away his time in, sitting and reading at the foot of that strong tree that rose from the center of it, stretching up past the rooftops. Every windowsill had several chunks of stale bread sitting out on it that the residents left there for the rats. That way they didn't come inside their homes, where food was kept under the beds because the refrigerator was an American luxury for most. Mother! Antoine suddenly shouted. Mother, he echoed. Marie turned toward him. In the tree in the courtyard . . . in the tree there's . . . It was as though he'd developed a stutter. There's a horror, he managed to articulate at last. His mother ran to him and clasped his shoulders. Silence then overwhelmed the two of them. Antoine pointed at the plane tree that took up nearly the entirety of their building's courtyard. Yes, Marie had just spotted it, but she was incapable of uttering a sound. A leg dangled from one of the branches on the tree. A little boy's leg.

If they were in Calcutta, surrounded by dark faces, shiny, jasmine-scented hair, black antelopian eyes, and gaunt bodies draped in cloths of red or orange or sky blue, hemmed in on all sides by carts hitched to oxen and buffalo, it could have been that a crow had flown into the courtyard with that leg. Or with some singed bits of entrails. Or a half-charred bone from down at the Nimtala burning ground, where the bodies of the Hindustanis smoldered away in a murky atmosphere only faintly cloaked by the smells of sandalwood and other precious woods with which they are burned. Similarly, in Bombay, or in Yazd, or in Kerman, it could have been that a vulture had deposited that raw leg there in their courtyard, or even on any of the various families' balconies, after carrying it back from one of those famed towers of silence, where the bodies of the Parsis and the Iranian Zoroastrians slowly rot in the sun, the rain, and the wind, laid out in circles like the circles of Hell.

There, too, it would have been a natural phenomenon. But here, in this North African city, less than five minutes had passed since three detonations had sounded and they'd all dropped to the floor. The windowpanes had shattered. And down in the street, right beneath their front window, chaos now reigned. Here, in this North African city, somebody had gone and set up that attack just as calm and cool as can be. Marie hugged her son, and at that very moment she realized that the reason he was still alive was that he had decided to skip class that day. This is the plague, she whispered then into his ear, like someone sharing a secret no one else can know. The plague we are fated to endure. Antoine could feel her heart racing wildly, but she went on speaking. The bacillus of the plague never really dies or disappears for good. It can lie dormant for decades deep inside drawers, folded into stacks of clothes. It can bide its time in bedrooms, in cellars, inside trunks, on handkerchiefs, in among old papers.

So, his mother read, too. And just as avidly as he did. She'd memorized whole paragraphs. Maybe she was picking up the books he got from the library and reading them at night, while he was asleep. Maybe she had insomnia. Curled up inside each one of us, in the darkest recess of our being, Marie concluded. And this plague, she suddenly added, the one that's ravaging the country as we speak, is the worst. It's the one that's driven human beings to raise their hands against other human beings just like them. His own life was not unconnected to that plague. Antoine's father had died before he was born. He'd been imprisoned. Over in Barberousse. And one morning, as day broke, he was executed. Marie hadn't told him the truth about it. Another one of her contradictions. Convinced of the importance of historical awareness, she was nevertheless unable to tell him the truth about his own past. His father had shot an Arab man to death. One particularly hot afternoon at a beach on the outskirts of Algiers. He was put on trial and sentenced to die by the guillotine. She'd attended the proceedings and had even gone out to the jail, that imposing, dismal building perched atop the city, right at the edge of the Kasbah, although she hadn't been allowed in to see him. One morning, so early it was almost still night, they'd led him out to the scaffold.

If a man didn't, and shouldn't, have the right to kill another, why did society? she'd wondered on many an occasion. A society that had ordered him to the scaffold largely because he hadn't shed any tears at his mother's burial, because he hadn't wanted to look at her once she'd been placed inside her coffin, because he'd smoked a couple of cigarettes and even dozed off during her vigil. Because he'd put her in a home. It was shortly after his mother's death that Meursault had killed another man. And all those people—judges, journalists, and most of those in attendance at the trial—were concerned not with the crime that had been committed but with these minutiae that had nothing to do with them, and the dead Arab man seemed to be of no importance to them. Not a single word had been spoken about him. Just as Meursault was of no importance to them. Marie subsequently lost her job. She was a typist at a company where Antoine's father had been employed for a time. She was ostracized in the neighborhood where she lived, as well, so she had to move to a new one. And that's how she'd come to work cleaning other people's houses. She hadn't told her son the truth of the matter. She'd never been able to work up the courage. She still couldn't. He thought she was a war widow, like the mothers of so many other children in his school and in their neighborhood.

She hadn't told him the truth. And Antoine's teacher said that's why the boy had nightmares, because traumatic family events, even if they'd taken place in the grandparents' or the parents' generation, before the child was born, would eventually, if not brought out into the open, if not discussed at any point, resurface in just that fashion, in the dreams of those who had not actually witnessed the scenes themselves, scenes at times sad, and at times monstrous. Marie wasn't so sure. If Antoine was already having nightmares without knowing the truth, with no inkling as to what his father had done and what had then been done to him, the nightmares he would experience if he knew everything would be even worse, like hers, which she never spoke of, though there were times they assailed her both day and night. And she would imagine her son in a trance, on his knees and trembling before Caligula's cage, rocked by waking visions like the one they'd seen that very afternoon. Once again, reality had turned out to be not so very different from that young boy's dreams.

None of the neighbors will speak about what's dangling from one of the branches on the tree in the courtyard. Nobody will alert the police. That's the muzzle of fear. And the leg will rot on the branch and shrivel in the sun. Then one day it will drop down and get mixed in with the trash piling up on the ground. Or maybe a seagull will peck out a chunk of it and one of those rats there aren't none of in the building will eat whatever other flesh is still left clinging to the bone. Maybe Doctor Rieux will see it before then and insist on taking it down or calling the police. Maybe he'll never see it, ever occupied as he is in the unending task of doing his part for others.

A MYSTERIOUS BOND

They'd found the occupants' remains mutilated, blood up to the ceilings, and, huddled beneath one of the beds, the youngest child, still breathing and soon to be dead like the rest, but who'd had just enough strength to daub onto the whitewashed wall, with a finger dripping with blood—*It was Pirette*. A manhunt ensued, and the murderer was tracked down in the middle of the countryside, half dazed. Appalled, the public clamored for the death penalty, it was granted, and the execution took place at Barberousse prison, in the presence of a considerable multitude. Jacques's father awoke before dawn to witness the exemplary punishment of a crime that, according to Grandmother, had incensed him. In fact, no one ever knew what happened. The execution had apparently gone off without a hitch, but Jacques's father had returned home livid, gotten into bed, climbed back out again several times to vomit, and gone to lay down once more. Afterward, he never wanted to talk about what he'd seen. And on the night he heard the story, Jacques himself, curled tightly into a ball and scrunched over to the edge of the mattress so as not to have to touch his brother, with whom he shared a bed, choked back a heave of horror as he replayed in his mind the details he'd been told or had imagined. And those images pursued him in the darkness, reappearing infrequently but regularly in a singular nightmare that was different each time but whose substance was always the same—they were coming for him, for Jacques, coming to execute him.

He paused for a few moments to take a couple of deep breaths. It was difficult for him to recall it, and even difficult to go on breathing when he did. It was an obsession for him. An episode of his father's life that he himself had never experienced but that had nevertheless left a mark like few others. He'd dealt with it in previous books. In fact, it was present in almost all of his writings, in some more directly than in others, but always at the heart of them, in the background, and now that he was delving into his own history, he wished to return to it, not simply as something that had affected another person but as an integral element of his own development, his sensibilities, his way of thinking, something that might even be a determining factor in his own destiny. Jacques forced himself to breathe even more deeply, and only then did he have the strength to continue writing about the incident he'd learned of only long after the fact, his father having passed away when he himself was barely a year old.

And for a long time, when he awoke, he would shake off his fear and his anguish and return, with a flood of relief, to that comforting reality in which there was, strictly speaking, no conceivable chance of his being executed. But later, after he'd come of age, when the events he'd seen unfolding around him had ultimately persuaded him that an execution was, in fact, a foreseeable outcome and not in the least farfetched, reality ceased to provide him with any measure of relief from his dreams and instead merely fed in him, during a very particular stretch of years, that selfsame feeling of anguish that had so affected his father and eventually been passed down to him, his one clear, undeniable bequest. Although in the case of that dead stranger at Saint-Brieuc (who, after all, would also never have thought he was going to die a violent death), it constituted for him a mysterious bond, one linking them directly rather than going through his mother, who'd heard the whole story, seen the vomiting, and then forgotten all about that morning, and who was now unaware that times had changed. For her, the times were always the same, and misfortune might rear its head at any moment, without warning. Grandmother, on the other hand, had a more accurate view of things. You're going to end up on the gallows, she warned Jacques regularly.

He set his pen on the desk and brought both hands up to his neck. It was aching unbearably again, and he could hardly move. It was as if someone had shoved an iron broomstick up his spine. Some days the stick was positioned vertically, exactly paralleling his backbone, but other days it seemed to run him through from shoulder to shoulder, as if he'd been impaled on a cross. He was stiff, and he felt as if his vertebrae might pop straight out of him any day now. He began massaging with his fingers, stretching his neck backward and from side to side. There was so much tension all concentrated in that one spot. His spine cracked every time he turned his head. From all that writing and reading, with his head perpetually tilted forward and his neck bent down? That's why he went out of his way to work standing up, without a chair, at that tall desk he had at home, that drafting table his teacher had given him as a gift, the same kind he'd always seen him use. But he could only work like that there. Here, in his office at the publishing house, he had to sit at a desk, a normal desk, just like everyone else. Or was it age? In a few months he'd be forty-five, although he often felt much older.

It was the marked-for-death syndrome. He'd coined the term himself. And a few days ago he'd mentioned it to his friend René, who'd stopped by to see him one afternoon at his apartment and let out a jocular guffaw in response to Jacques's melodramatic air. The knight of the sad countenance, he'd called him, clapping him on the shoulder with one of those immense lumberjack hands of his, but the look on the poet's face transformed completely when Jacques explained to him just what the syndrome entailed. It was the pain of all those who'd been sentenced to death, of every single man and woman to date who'd had their head cleaved off in a public square in any one of a number of European cities or on some African beach, at the sea's edge, in front of a frenzied crowd. Even in a waking state, without the need for any sort of dream, he could envision the forty-five-pound blade dropping from twenty feet up, see that massive knife piercing through flesh, slicing through nerves, splintering vertebrae, crushing each and every bone, every fiber, every vein. And René's complexion, as he described it all to him, went ashen.

How could a justice system do such a thing? There would be no lasting peace, either in the hearts of individuals or in societal customs, until death was outlawed, he himself had recently written. Now he allowed his eyes to wander off the sheet of paper where just moments earlier he'd been transcribing that nightmare of his that had been haunting him since childhood. Tuesday. June 4, 1957. The Algerian newspaper sat folded on his desk. It was left there for him every morning along with several other papers, most of them French, and a magazine or two, but he usually went over his mail first, trying to put off for as long as possible that daily reading that was proving more and more difficult for him. He'd have liked to go out onto the roof and have a smoke while surveying the Paris rooftops. All he'd have to do would be to stand up and open the large window behind him that delimited the gabled space. The other walls were covered in books. His desk was, too. He wasn't a neat person, and in spite of harboring a feeling of indifference toward the vast majority of objects, he was incapable of getting rid of anything.

Steeling himself, he reached out an arm and picked up the newspaper. He still didn't feel up to the task of unfolding it, much less reading it. Lately he hardly even dared to look at it, because he knew his native country, and perhaps even his city, would be splashed all over it, and it wasn't exactly the bearer of good news. As mouthpieces of hatred and blindness, newspapers almost never were. Comforting realities seemed to have been permanently banished from their pages, and, to an even greater degree, from the land of his birth. And practically every day, the post and the telephone would apprise him of even more of the latest terrible news. In a single morning, he might receive a letter from an Arab school teacher relating how several men in his hometown had been lined up before a firing squad without so much as a trial, and a call from a friend whose French employees had been murdered and mutilated at their work site. His hands trembled in anguish. There it was. In two-inch letters. You didn't need an especially keen eye for catastrophes, you didn't even need to turn a single page before you happened upon one. The spring there was shaping up to be a bloody one. More than eight hundred acts of violence were being registered every month, and on a near-daily basis he would come across a story that would plunge him into the most profound depths of despair. For some time now, that country had been a lump in his throat.

And once more, in spite of all his effort, his superhuman determination to not lose hope, to persist in the belief that the whole thing could somehow, some day, be resolved, what he read in the paper, what he was able to imagine beyond the words printed there on the page, reminded him that he was still living in a world where murder was a commonplace occurrence, where the use of violence seemed to be rapidly gaining legitimacy, a world where human life was viewed as something trivial. In his mind, it was clear that if a person didn't want to be killed, that person shouldn't kill anyone else, either, and that he must stand not only against war but against terrorism, as well, and against repression, which is so often blind and irrational, against the death penalty, against any and all forms of violence. For it was vital that it come to be seen, inevitable though it may be, as completely unjustifiable. He had dedicated his entire life and a good portion of his life's work to combating this particular ill, but he was increasingly on his own.

It was twenty years ago now that he and a small handful of other Frenchmen had petitioned for citizenship and equal rights for Algerian Muslims, but their request had gone unheeded. And he'd been kicked out of the party, because they read this as him espousing a nationalist cause that was not his own, just as none were. Any person who didn't toe the official line set down by Moscow—and backing the Arabs was not among Stalin's objectives at the time—was looked upon as a counterrevolutionary. And transformed, unwillingly, into a dissident. He'd even been summoned to appear before the local party courts. It has become necessary to purge the party of a number of Trotskyist provocateurs, in the words of the final report that was sent on to Moscow and listed the names of Jacques and one of his comrades. But now the directives had been modified, and the number of PCA militants being arrested for acts of terrorism in support of the FLN was growing exponentially. It was true, he'd been saying the same thing for years, and he wasn't about to endorse either of the two sides, which were now crossing swords more and more frequently, or to offer even a single excuse for such abominable slaughtering. That's why he chose to keep silent.

Now he found himself being reproached for that silence, despite the fact that what many actually wanted was for him to keep his mouth shut. His pen was a weapon that could just as soon pacify as inflame people's spirits. He'd received more threats, most likely, than any single other individual. Attempting to denounce the nationalist apparatus, of either side, would have been like trying to stand up to the Church in the fourteenth century. Jacques set the newspaper back down on the desk. There, in the city where he'd grown up, where he'd gone to school and first taken up employment, where he could return now only for short periods of time, that city where his mother, his brother, and his brother's family still lived, along with many of his friends and thousands upon thousands of innocent people, in that city he loved so dearly, violence had broken out yet again. *Three time bombs affixed to lampposts went off at 6:30 p.m. in close proximity to a tram stop. The death toll currently stands at 8, with another 88 wounded. The explosive devices had been put in place at approximately 1:30 p.m. by terrorists disguised as electrical repairmen. Several suspects have been arrested.*

Among the dead were a fourteen-year-old girl, Vincente Mas, a boy of ten, Jean Baylé, and another boy of six, Georges Saint-Jean. Their photos had been included. A high number of women among the victims. And Muslims. Fatma Zohra Chadil, Mohamed Chehili, Abbés Nefou, Kamel Hamdini, Chérif Bensadi, Zoubida Rouassia, Mohamed Bentata, Mohamed Medahi, Mohamed Messaoudi, Sid Ahmed Bendouche, Hamid

Kadri, Fatma Sahnoun, Mohamed Aoudia, Zekkla Amouni . . . Bombs made no distinctions. They behaved as irrationally as the individuals who'd planted them there a few hours prior to the explosions had rationally. Individuals who had perhaps even stuck around to see how things played out. Seated at an outdoor café. Or calmly smoking a cigarette while leaning against one of the houses across the street from where the children were let out of school. They would have flicked the butts of their Bastos to the ground, and after stamping them out, they might even have moved to blend in with the crowd that would subsequently be seen running to the scene to help. Or to try and get a better look. Or in with the fleeing, terrified stampede. And the count would continue to rise the next day. More people always died. The number of amputees among the wounded would be bone-chilling. Algeria was mutilation country. The bloodthirsty cut. And the doctors cut, too.

Jacques remembered his childhood. His mother at the window, in silence, keeping watch over all the changes of light, every sound. And he imagined other mothers. And their children. Marie Cardona. Antoine. They could easily be himself and his mother. Years ago. He imagined a long procession of similar scenes, endlessly repeating. And he saw a small boy's leg dangling from a branch in the middle of the courtyard of some nondescript apartment building. Then he recalled that painting by Picasso. He'd painted it twenty years ago in the same city he himself had ended up in. That oversized canvas depicting the misery of war had become quite the symbol. A flat, black-and-white world, like a newspaper world. Hunks of flesh, the disfigured bodies of men, women, and children. Pain in its purest state. But was there any work of art that reflected—in the same way Picasso's had for the Spanish Civil War—the horrors of a terrorist attack like the one that had taken place in Algiers the day before? And if no such work existed, why not? The consequences were the same. Blood, pain, death, interminable agony, lifelong traumas and nightmares. And the exodus of many thousands of people. No, paintings weren't made to be hung as decorations, it would seem Picasso had said. They were offensive and defensive instruments of war, to be used against the enemy. Perhaps that painting was a universal icon.

A lot of people thought there must be zillions of colonists in Algeria all sporting riding crops and puffing cigars and zooming around in Cadillacs, when in fact the vast majority of the Europeans who lived there were poor. They'd been working in the country for several generations. They'd come ashore believing it to be some sort of promised land, but all they'd found were pain and death and the very same poverty they'd been fleeing from. And yet they'd stayed, working ten hours a day, seven days a week in exchange for piddling wages, and they transformed wilds and swamps, crags and marshlands into arable fields. Many of them had French first and last names. Many others, perhaps even more, had a French first name and a Spanish last name, like his mother. Or Italian, Maltese, or Greek names. There were Jewish ones, too. The men were named Pierre, Robert, Michel, Albert, Jean, and Adolphe, but many of them had last names like Rey, Ortega, Lucas, Font, Guerra, Martínez, López, or Escudero. The women were named Delphine, Lucille, Catherine, Claudette, Hélène, Marie, and Gilberte, but their last names were Salazar, Ferrando, Soldevilla, Ruiz, or Cardona.

Sinners twice over, as far as the holy men of the *Rive Gauche* were concerned. They were Westerners and pariahs. And as such, they were the objects of both the hatred rightly heaped on colonizers and the lofty disdain reserved for the poor, for the uncouth. All those people seemed to be of absolutely no importance to anyone. They weren't from anywhere, not from Algeria, not from France, not from Spain, not from Italy, and not from Greece or Malta, either. Just like he himself, who at times no longer knew where he was from. Where could he possibly be from in a world like that? The only thing he knew for sure is that he wasn't from there. That he would always live in exile. Like all those men and women, each of them suffering in solitude. Just as the Jews had suffered, right in the heart of Europe, just a scant few years ago. They were the *petits blancs*. Just like him, growing up as he had in the Algerian district of Belcourt. People who were for the most part somewhat less poor than the majority of Arabs, but still unable to visit the metropole unless it was to make war, to die for the French, who would afterward want nothing to do with them. With all those Fernándezes, all those Lópezes and Seguras trying to pass themselves off as Frenchmen.

Qu'est-ce que c'est que tous ces Fernandez, ces Lopez et autres Segura qui se voudraient français? To the Europeans, they were African. And to the Africans, they were European. And second-class, not to say worthless, Europeans at that, in the eyes of many of their Hexagonal compatriots. They were nothing. And they would eventually be stripped of their land, not in the sense of property, which was something the vast majority of them did not possess, but in the most profound sense, in the sense of roots. They would be left adrift. Or left for dead. Tossed into caskets, feeding nutrients back into that land they loved so dearly. The suitcase or the coffin. That was the choice they'd eventually have to make. Those exact words had been popping up on walls all over Algeria for years now. *La valise ou le cercueil.* Most would flee. Some toting exquisite leather luggage, hermetically sealed. Plenty of others would be lugging pasteboard cases fastened with ropes. Or make their escape with crude bundles of clothing knotted inside sheets or mats and flung over their backs. They'd cram themselves onto packet boats—the *Ville d'Oran*, the *Ville d'Argel*, the *Kaoirouan*, the *Mansour*—and pull away from the coast with their hearts in their throats.

Some would cover their eyes to hide their crying. Old men, their faces furrowed with wrinkles, their skin hardened from years of sun. Wearing berets. Gripping walking sticks. It wouldn't be only the women, leading their children by the wrist to get them away from that place, who cried. Old women, with kerchiefs knotted under their chins. Or buns pinned up with seashell combs, worn from years of use. And scattered among them, Arabs dressed in the European fashion, wearing turbans, keeping their bindles close like the rest. They would never again see the land where their ancestors, going five or six generations back, had been born, the land where they'd lived for years and years, the land that was now drifting further and further away. White, like a festoon of sea-foam stretched along the horizon. Others would stay. Many of them to die. Their throats would be slit. Or they'd be stabbed. The children would have their skulls shattered. Smashed in. They'd be hung upside down by the ankles and thwacked headfirst against a white wall. Like ripe tomatoes. The young of the dogs. And in France, nobody wanted anything to do with them. They'd even greet them in the port of Marseille with shouts and placards telling them to turn around and head back out to sea. Try Brazil. Or Argentina, they'd shout.

They would never grant citizenship rights to the Arabs, never grant them the equality they deserved and that might provide the beginnings of a solution. And now independence and every man for himself seemed to a lot of people like the only way out, even though what it was, in fact, was just the easiest and the quickest way out for themselves. What would we do with all those ragheads running around in the Parliament? some in government had dared to ask. There were a lot of them. And who really wanted Colombey-les-deux-Églises turning into Colombey-les-deux-Mosquées? more than one had remarked. And another thing, others were wondering, if we really have to fork out reparations for all these Ortegas and Barrals going around claiming to be French, where the devil are we supposed to get the money? He'd spoken to the President of the Republic himself. He knew what he was thinking. He knew what he was saying. The same thing as most people in metropolitan France. In the entire Republic. Now that Algeria was costing France more than it was bringing in, let them fend for themselves. They could end up drafting my own son! Drafting a Durand, a de la Villiere, a Bernard, a Gaillard. Just to defend a million well-to-do colonists . . .

Not all French Algerians were bloodthirsty beasts, despite all the noise from some who were demanding sanctions in retribution for the attacks they'd suffered. *Frapper vite et fort.* Just as not all Arabs were murderous maniacs, either. In any case, indiscriminate killing was not the way to secure an independence that might one day prove peaceful. He'd heard about a group of thirty Arab students aged eleven and twelve who'd been asked by their teacher to write an essay in response to the following question: What would you do if you were invisible? Every single one of them confessed a desire to take up arms and kill the French, the paratroopers, the representatives of the metropolitan government. What possible future could there be given this sort of starting point? Was the last remaining possibility simply to keep your mouth shut so as not to cause any harm? Every word uttered in Paris could end up costing many lives across the sea.

There, ground down by poverty and hunger, most people languished under the effects of a pain none spoke of. That's what he'd set out to capture in his book, but he was afraid of failing in his task, of not figuring out the right way to go about it, of not having enough time. He was sick, tired, and alone. He found himself thinking about his childhood more and more frequently, with a painful sense of nostalgia, a feeling that somehow seemed to herald the end of a life. And he thought about death. Maybe he wouldn't be able to finish it. Maybe someone would stop him. At times he felt overwhelmed with panic, like in the nightmare that had bedeviled his dreams since boyhood. But once more Jacques gritted his teeth and took up his pen again. He didn't have much time. And he had to use it wisely. He slept fewer and fewer hours every night. He shut himself in more and more. Alone, with his words. He, who was not a solitary person. Who enjoyed the company of others. And listening to what they had to say, even though it might not bear the slightest resemblance to what he himself thought. It was the only way a person could come close to understanding reality in a world that was hell-bent on seeing things in black and white.

Now would come the reprisals. The mass, knee-jerk detentions had already begun. And presently they'd commence with the executions in Barberousse prison, high up, above the Kasbah. With the hour still bordering on night. Surreptitiously. Executions that were ostensibly meant to serve as a warning to others but were nevertheless carried out under cover of darkness and practically in secret. The other prisoners would rattle the bars on their cells and sing out in chorus at the top of their lungs, while the appointed men filed, faltering, out to the courtyard. Jacques brought a hand up to his neck. He couldn't shake the pain. And at night, as soon as he closed his eyes, those condemned men would haunt him, shuffling past with the heads they'd just lost to the guillotine's blade, their hands hooking them firmly by their open mouths. Their hair had been cut off on the eve of their execution. They'd begged for mercy, for someone to put a stop to that supremely cowardly conception of justice that would never succeed in doing away with crime. Jacques walked over to the window with his arms in the air and both hands on his neck. He tilted his head down slightly, massaging continually, and looked outside. Twilight was falling over the city.

Absolute silence, a stillness that was never present at any other moment during the day, was settling over every last inch of Paris, as if everyone had paused to marvel at that spectacle that was reprised, with infinite variations and permutations, each evening. The clouds had been tinged pink, and orange, and red. It's the blood of all those who've been marked for death, seeping out into the sky, he thought. And his grandmother's words echoed inside him. You're going to end up on the gallows, she was always warning him. And why not? It wasn't so preposterous a notion anymore. She didn't know it for certain, but being the kind of person she was, nothing would have surprised her. Standing there upright, in her long, black prophetess dress, uneducated and stubborn, she, more than anyone else, had been a dominating force in Jacques's childhood. Although she, at least, had never known resignation.

SONS OF CAIN

The city on the sea opened out under the sky like a mouth, with its white façades and their wood-slatted windows and doors painted blue. A small ice-cream cart was parked at the edge of the sidewalk, its two large wheels and its back legs resting on the curb. The vendor, clad in an impeccably white coat, had sat down on a chair to rest, holding his ice-cream spade out in front of him vertically with both hands. Next to him, a woman wearing an apron over a flowered dress was holding a two- or three-year-old girl in her arms. Their assistant, clothed in a dark-colored djellaba, had also stopped to take a break, although he took it crouching on his knees some distance away. The little cart was made of wood and painted white, and it had several French inscriptions on it. *Glaces. Sorbets. Citronnades.* The name *La Ibense* was plastered up all over town. It was a business run by a family from Alicante who'd arrived in Algeria ages ago to sell ice cream, making their way through Oran, Tlemcen, and Médéa before finally putting into port there in the capital. At that hour of the evening, having covered a good portion of the city's streets and selling ice cream up and down its various beaches, they were now back at their ice-cream parlor, its walls decorated with paintings of penguins, located directly next to one of

Algiers's many funeral homes, mortuaries being one of the most lucrative businesses in the city.

At a café table, slightly removed from everyone else, two Algerian men sat sipping tea from small glass cups that glittered with gold filigree. All around them, people were drinking a whitish, slightly cloudy concoction. The tables were covered with colorful dishes. *Kemia.* Lupini beans, chickpeas, fennel-marinated olives, cornmeal, eggplant . . . A lot of people were playing dice or cards. The heat in Algeria in the month of June can be extreme, even more so if the wind is blowing from the south, off the Sahara. Some combat it with cool drinks, others with warm brews. Saddok knew the café owner and had reserved several tables together so as to be able to speak more comfortably. Kamel, meanwhile, had just pulled out the paper and spread it open on the marble tabletop. Three kids were killed in Monday's attack, he remarked. A fourteen-year-old girl. A ten-year-old boy. And the littlest one was just six. You've got to get these little weasels while they're still young, Saddok grumbled, and then he raised his eyes. There in the heights, you could see the Kasbah rearing up, white and jumbled. And the cypresses in El-Kettar Cemetery.

They're almost never colonists, or even the children of colonists. Not to mention the fact that there are always Muslims among the victims. And women. So if you look at it, we're not so very different from those we've decided to fight against. This whole thing is getting out of hand. On the contrary, that's the whole idea. Precisely that. Action and reaction. Saddok was unyielding, he seemed utterly free from doubt. A boss shouldn't have any doubts. But was he capable of feeling them? Following a period of outraged protestation over all the suffering being inflicted, he had come to accept crime with an air of indifference befitting of the gods. Kamel, on the other hand, was a man who allowed himself to question the course of history. And he enjoyed getting the chance to do it in front of one of his superiors. We have to capture the attention of the entire world, Saddok continued. It is only through injustice that we will be able to obtain justice. From the moment you kill a person, you can no longer hold back, Kamel replied. You become a machine. A beast in pursuit of the slightest whiff of blood.

He liked sitting there. Seeing the throngs of women in sandals and lightweight, brightly colored clothing walking up and down the street. That's why they went there. To be admired. And this was one of the best viewing spots in the city, along with the beach. And you could go there any day of the week, although there were more people out on Sundays, because in Algeria almost nobody stayed home on Sunday. A shoe shiner approached them, carrying his brass box on one shoulder. The metal gleamed in the sunlight. The rivets dotting the edges of each of the different compartments—for creams, brushes, and rags—all flashed brightly. As did the thick glass of the various tall jars, perfectly proportioned to fit snugly into every last nook and cranny inside the box. Saddok waved him away, and the shoe shiner moved on to a tourist couple sitting a few tables over. He took out several brushes, three types of rags, and a jar of polish cut with gasoline.

Why did you want to see me? Kamel inquired, his eyes still glued on the procedure unfolding at the other table. He enjoyed watching the displays of men like that who were devoted to their trade, but at that very moment the waiter arrived carrying a tray with a fresh pitcher of tea. And so he was captivated by another trade. Steam was rising out of the heavy embossed-metal pitcher. A thick rag had been wrapped around the handle to protect against burns. The young waiter, dressed all in white, poured the greenish-yellow liquid out smoothly, so that the tea fizzled when it touched the mint leaves and the sugar, which dissolved instantly. For a brief moment, that potent aroma rose above all others, above a medley that had been dominated up until a second before by the smell of asphalt cracking in the sun. The scent of aniseed disappeared, along with the faint odor issuing from a nearby butcher's. *Boucherie Chevaline Arregle et Parrin.* With that painted wooden horse's head hanging above the sign. A frothy spume floated up to the topmost layer of liquid, its bubbles shimmering with the several colors of the rainbow, in tiny prisms, and a fine film of steam formed on the surface of the glass and then instantly evaporated, so that now, newly transparent, it shone even more brightly.

Saddok and Kamel raised their small glasses, carefully placing their thumbs on the upper rim and their middle fingers under the base of the cups. And there they sat sipping. They could spend hours like that without ordering anything else, refilling their glasses, savoring the taste and breathing in the smell of the mint and the sugar. Of the toasted pine nuts they often added into the mix. The fighting is going to escalate soon. Not just here—in the metropole, as well. We have to defend ourselves there against the cruelty they're meting out here. That's why, beginning now, we want you in France. You're a well-educated person, you've studied. You speak perfect French, you have no accent at all. Just like a real "frog." Like a purebred Frenchman. Look, Kamel interrupted, isn't that Kid Avion? He liked making him think that he wasn't listening to him, that he was paying more attention to what was going on around him. A lottery ticket vendor had just begun weaving through the café tables. No, that's not him, Kamel answered his own question aloud, but he reminds me of him. Before becoming a boxer, that's how Kid got his start, selling lottery tickets at outdoor cafés. Did you know that? Saddok didn't reply, he didn't even glance in the man's direction. He might have ended up the same way, Kamel went on in a melancholy tone. Although now that I think about it, it's not all that bad a life. Either way, I see you're not much of a boxing fan.

Saddok must have despised the entire human race, not just the colonists, with whom he was permanently at war. Was there nothing in the world capable of rousing his enthusiasm, other than the cause he was fighting for? I don't think you would have brought me all the way out here unless you had something genuinely important to tell me. Yes, it's a very special job. Involving a man of a certain degree of public importance. This time Saddok did glance around to make sure no one was watching them, to make sure no one was listening in. But that was merely an affectation, a way of putting on airs. Nobody cared what they were talking about. Those empty tables all around them were an equally ridiculous and unnecessary precaution. That buffer zone. It must have been a question of mannerisms, a fairly well-established habit among those belonging to the organization, independently of the position they held in its intricate hierarchy. Secrecy was all part of the game.

Saddok stuck his hand into one of his jacket pockets and produced a photograph that appeared to have been clipped from a newspaper or a magazine. It was a little wrinkled, and there were several people in it. Kamel reached for it, to get a better look. He saw three men sitting around a café table, a tiny, metal-rimmed table crowded with an assortment of small platters, several empty glasses, an ice bucket, a pack of cigarettes, and a glass pitcher. The face of one of the three men, the only one looking at the camera, was marked with a large, red circle. Somebody had drawn it on with a thick pencil. The man was slim, he had a pale complexion, light brown hair, a bony, slightly asymmetrical face, a wide forehead, and a pensive gaze. He looked about thirty. He wore his coat with the collar flipped up and a white scarf tucked into it. He was holding a cigarette in one hand, under the table. His other hand was raised and open, as was his mouth, and he appeared to be speaking. A second man, huskier, wearing a suit and tie, a cigarette dangling from his lips, was looking over at the next table. A third man, in an overcoat, had his back to the camera.

Another man to dispose of. Kamel inspected the image more closely, looking for that second glimmer, like the shoe shiner after rubbing his cloth over the leather one extra time. He, too, was a professional, determined to peer deep into the dark recesses of things, of every matter. And he glimpsed a crack beneath that countenance suffused with kindliness, a crack rent open by the feelings of despondency and anxiety that, from the looks of it, had taken up permanent residence within the man. Saddok cleared his throat, no doubt attempting to jolt him from his abstraction, impatient to hear his assessment. He has the eyes of the sand men, was all Kamel replied. What the hell is that supposed to mean? Saddok disliked the lyrical flourishes Kamel sometimes slipped into conversations, the enigmatic air of some of his remarks, and also the fact that he didn't answer his questions right away and instead just sat there in silence, as if weighing up each and every one of the words that would go into his response.

That he's a brother, he replied at last with a solemn gesture. Saddok's eyes flashed almost feverishly, but he pretended not to have heard him and went on with the objective details of his briefing. He's living in Paris currently, but he travels frequently and changes his residence often. He's a restless man. He works from several locations at once. Sometimes until very late at night. I know perfectly well who this is. What do you take me for? Kamel remonstrated, dropping the photograph back down on the marble surface. And you know, it wouldn't have killed you to have gotten a more recent picture. This one is over ten years old. Saddok overlooked the nitpicky comment. Yes, yes, I know. You're not just educated, you read the papers and you know absolutely everyone. He wasn't wrong. Kamel had an ear to the ground everywhere. Or practically everywhere. That's why he was such a valuable asset to the organization, despite his often arrogant or even defiant attitude. That's why he hadn't needed to ask about the reasoning behind that particular choice of target. Ben Bella had spelled the whole thing out in '55. Written it in his own hand. He'd seen the document himself, with his own eyes. All individuals capable of playing a meaningful intermediary role had to be eliminated. Close the door to the third way.

Liquider toutes les personalités qui voudraient jouer à l'interlocuteur valable. It was in the interest of certain intellectuals, and not just from an ideological point of view, that such individuals be eliminated. He really is good, Saddok mused. You didn't have to explain hardly anything to him. Just give him his instructions. The others carried out their assignments with little to no understanding of what they were doing. But not this one. That's why he never failed, because his brain always went that one extra step. He might even have known that Saddok and the man in the photograph had been friends, long ago, when the two were both militants in the same party. Later, they'd grown apart. But Kamel didn't bring it up, and Saddok let out a small exhalation of relief. Deep down in his soul, he knew it was a betrayal. We need a code name, he continued, unyielding. It'll be the same name we use for the operation itself. Their names, Saddok's and Kamel's, were also monikers used exclusively for the conducting of secret affairs, and they would change them again as many times as was necessary.

Golan. We'll call him Golan, Kamel said after a few seconds' pause. The only people he really looked down on were the Jews, who'd settled in Algeria long before the French. And even before the Arabs, in fact. Those repulsive *goumis*, he thought to himself. All right, said Saddok, and as he scanned the outdoor space, his eyes came to rest on the café's exterior wall, where, in keeping with a custom popular among many of the cafés in Algiers, dozens of cages had been hung, with canaries chirping and flapping in all directions inside their pint-sized enclosures. And there in the middle of all the cages was a poster ad for Orangina, featuring a redheaded woman dressed in nothing but a skirt and a headdress both fashioned out of large green leaves, like an Indian maiden with flames coming out of her hair, and she was leaping up into the air while hugging a gigantic orange. *Nouvelle Boisson Gazeuse*. Saddok liked those birds, and he'd even crumbled up a bit of bread to take over and feed to them, but when he caught sight of that giddy redhead, he recoiled. Operation's off to a bad start, Kamel declared, laughing. He knew a lot of people considered redheads to be harbingers of bad luck. The mark of Cain. He wasn't superstitious, but he delighted in the fact that others did have that weakness, which allowed him to poke fun at their expense.

Actually, it's only men with red hair that bring bad luck. Never redheaded women, he added mockingly. So it turned out, there was something after all besides the cause they were fighting for that was capable of piquing Saddok's interest, something that spoke to his heart. It was the birds that had made him choose that café, not just the fact that he knew the owner and he felt more at ease there than in other places. The birds drew his gaze. They even brought out a touch of generosity in him. Kamel studied him. It didn't take him more than an instant to sketch his portrait. Stiff carriage, black nails, and a bitter expression always crouching somewhere on his face. Sometimes in his eyes. Other times on his lips. And almost always on his nose, which he used to sniff over every object and every person that came within two yards of him, it seemed. I love birds, and violets, and the cool mouths of young girls, he imagined Saddok professing with rapture. It can be refreshing from time to time. After all, I'm an idealist . . . Kamel smiled. No, he's not very interested in women, he noted. Not even the flesh-and-blood ones, much less the paper variety. He himself, on the other hand, could fall in love at the drop of a hat, even with a picture on a poster. Bad sign. This guy hardly even glances at women when they walk by. Only if they get too close.

It'll be an easy job, he said at last, accepting with apparent docility the mission that was being entrusted to him. It's just one man. And a peaceable man, at that. We'll simply wait for him to come to Algeria. After all, his family is still living here. He's sure to show up soon enough. Maybe to take part in some public ceremony. And he conjured up the scene, regaling Saddok with different possible variations of the event. A blow to the back of the neck with the butt of a rifle, and his body turns up on some random street corner. A nice ending for someone who participated in the Resistance. A knife to the back. On a deserted street, at night. Or while he's strolling along one of the nearby beaches, taking the final drags off his cigarette. Or a slit straight across the throat. Saddok shook his head. No, no. Nothing like that. It has to look like an accident. That's why we have to wait for just the right moment.

Lay all the groundwork ahead of time. Everything down to the last detail. Oh, yes, naturally, we're very delicate assassins, after all. Kamel saw Saddok's expression contort and his eyes shoot daggers at him. It was a joke, he said. We're not.

Didn't you just say we have to capture the attention of the entire world? Kamel always liked getting the opportunity to contradict the person he was speaking with. It was one of his strategies. One of his quirks. It allowed him to get more information out of people than they were willing to give. And we will. But in this case we have to be discreet. He's an important man, as you know. And we don't want to go around dropping Grade A martyrs like that right into the other side's lap. You'll receive further instructions after you've met up with your contact in Marseille. In the meantime, the two of you will have other missions to dispatch. Kamel took a few sips of his tea. Who is he? Saddok put up a hand to ask for the check. Your contact? he asked. You don't know him. A young Algerian fellow trained in France. At a technical school near Paris. He knows all there is to know about mechanics, and he's a professional driver. Ah, there it was, Kamel's only defect. He didn't know how to drive. He was aware that it was an issue, but deep down he loved having a chauffer. It made him feel important. Not even he was completely free from that appetite he'd always found so ridiculous in others.

So he's a rookie. That's all I need to know. He didn't just like to contradict people, he liked inciting them. He didn't want the bosses to think that everything was simple and straightforward. That they had everything under control and that nothing could possibly escape them. It'll be an easy job, as you said, but only when the time is right. Until then, you need to exercise caution. A great deal of caution. Saddok pretended he hadn't heard Kamel's comment about the contact he'd been assigned and didn't know anything about. It wasn't worth it. He needed someone who could get the man from place to place once he was on the mainland. Not to mention cars broke down a lot. They overheated easily. That's why it was important to have a mechanic on hand, as well. And this guy could do both things. Only a short while back, an operation of theirs involving a couple of time bombs had to be aborted when an engine seized up. The unit members had been forced to get rid of the devices by detonating them somewhere else, out of the way.

In any case, Saddok added, you'll only go active when we're completely sure. So we shouldn't take any risks, Kamel grumbled again, appearing none too thrilled with his new mission. And yet I'm starting to miss that feeling of risk. In Russia, in the early days of the century, we'd have waited for our target to come around a corner and then tossed a bomb up between his legs. Kamel was a romantic. Even when it came to blowing other people to smithereens, he preferred his actions to have a certain flair. All that gray matter knocking around inside his head, and now suddenly he's turning his nose up at premeditation and the idea of the perfect crime? Perhaps he was simply repeating expressions he'd heard from the lips of some stage actor in a theater somewhere. The words of one righteously indignant individual flying in the face of the particular, inexorable path justice had been set on as a result of a group of other righteously indignant individuals deciding to take it into their own hands. Saddok never knew if he was reciting something he'd read or if he was saying what he actually thought. Or maybe both.

You'd better talk quieter. Someone might hear you. Kamel ignored Saddok's warning. I miss the risk of staring into my victims' eyes, Kamel went on. The chance that someone might see us. I sometimes feel guilty. And cowardly. Even more so if children or women die. And in a way, it feels like we're not accomplishing anything. And nobody's going to remember us, either. Conquerors occasionally wax melancholic. Kamel did it far too often. On the other hand, he thought, if he was capable of all those things, what was there that could possibly act as a check on him? Fear of his own death? It was that blasted desire for immortality, plain and simple. The allure of playing God. Now *there's* a beautiful woman, look, he exclaimed just then, craning his neck to get a better view of the target his retinas had just locked onto. He was blind now to everything else. And for once, Saddok showed slight signs of interest, too. Where? Over there, look, the one walking next to the boy with the parrot on his shoulder. Saddok followed his gaze. Kamel never used a finger to point. And it was obvious Saddok was fascinated with this latest winged, plumed specimen, because he began making a variety of little noises to try and draw its attention.

A woman and a tall, thin boy with a gray parrot on his left shoulder were walking past at that precise instant. *Glaces, sorbets, citronnades*, Antoine read as soon as he spotted the small cart with its metal lids glittering in the sun. Mother, will you buy me an ice cream? He must have been thirsty. From the moment he'd first seen that leg dangling there from the tree in their building's courtyard, he hadn't eaten, had barely drunk, and he hadn't spoken a single word, unlike the parrot, which despite not saying much—he just kept screeching out greetings, repeating Antoine's name over and over again—was constantly making all sorts of noises. Antoine appeared upset with himself. Perhaps he felt guilty for having come out of the whole thing unscathed while others had lost their lives or were lying in the hospital. And so he'd fallen into a sort of a trance, until just then, when the sight of the ice-cream cart seemed to jolt him awake. The look in Marie's eyes as she turned to him said it all. She needn't have spoken a word, but she wanted to explain. I can't, Antoine. She smiled in an attempt to soften her refusal. Not until Madame Praneuf pays me . . . She owed her the entire last month. Her employer was always late with the wages, and she was too embarrassed to remind her.

I can't, Antoine. She wasn't speaking loudly, but the Alicante woman had excellent ears. She quickly deposited her daughter on the ground and gestured at the boy to come over. And what flavor would this fine, handsome boy like? My husband's treating. Aren't you, Miguel? Antoine blushed but still managed to request a vanilla ice cream on the spot. The man set down his spade, flipped open one of the cart's stainless steel domes, and then dug in the scoop to serve him. Say thank you, Antoine, Madame Cardona admonished her son, whose tongue was already poised and hovering above that cold, creamy surface, when Caligula, who'd just caught sight of the ice-cream lady's daughter standing there in her white dress, two bows tied in her hair, let out a mighty squawk. He flapped as far away as he was able and perched on the edge of one of the tables over at the café, the very same table where two Arab men dressed in the European fashion were sitting, somewhat removed from everyone else. Antoine shoved his ice cream into his mother's hands and bolted after his pet, trying to catch him. Marie went after him. Saddok stretched out a hand and tried to pet those lovely gray feathers, but the parrot—before his master could reach him, and before that stranger could touch him—sprang into the air and landed a well-aimed peck smack on the face of the other man at the table, whom he'd been eyeballing the entire time.

Vicious varmint, the younger man snapped, standing up and clutching his nose with one hand, while the other hand wavered, uncertain which item to grab out of his jacket. He settled on the handkerchief, which he shook open with that same free hand and pinched tightly over his face. It changed colors in a matter of seconds. Blasted bird! he exclaimed, this time from under the cloth square. And he clenched his other fist, endeavoring to control his fury. He didn't like having attention drawn to himself. Antoine made a signal to call the bird back to him. His name is Caligula. His mother, catching up to him at that precise moment, put a hand on his shoulder. Hush, Antoine, she spoke softly, almost in a whisper, tugging firmly on the back of his shirt collar to try to get him out of there. Hush. Or we'll get into trouble. Her instinct was to apologize, but she thought better of it and instead did everything in her power to get her son to walk away. She knew that if he did, the parrot would fly back to his master's shoulder. I'm going to get a scar, Kamel muttered from beneath his handkerchief. Oh, don't exaggerate. Stick a bandage on it, you might even catch more girls. Maybe they'll mistake you for Kid Avion, Saddok took the opportunity to slip in a joke, but when he saw the amount of blood the handkerchief was soaking up, he knew they'd have no choice but to go to the hospital.

Let's go to Mustapha. I'll track down Doctor Rieux, Kamel said. They'd often argued over the direction that the movement he'd become involved with was taking. I hate death and iniquity, he'd bellowed at him once, fuming uncontrollably. But he was a generous man, and when it came to matters concerning the health of Kamel or Kamel's mother, he'd always been willing to help out. It was thanks to him that he'd been able to study, unlike most of his compatriots. Saddok

70

picked the photo up off the table and folded it back up carefully, painstakingly returning it to the way it had been before he'd taken it out. Then he began tearing it into smaller and smaller pieces, which he subsequently slipped into his jacket pocket. Meanwhile, Marie, Antoine, and the parrot were hurrying away. Those men are dangerous, Antoine. And as she said it, she envisioned grabbing one of them by the lapels and screaming into his face just exactly what he was. Murderer. That pair stank of carrion. But instead she quickened her step. Come on. Quickly now. Antoine pulled up suddenly. Didn't you tell me not to turn my back on people who are different from me? But you have to learn to distinguish. All that reading, and you still can't see where the evil lies. Just the other day, you yourself said that the bacillus of the plague is everywhere. Marie said nothing.

She couldn't rightly consider herself an expert, either. She'd fallen in love with a man who'd shot another man dead. Bam. Just like that. And he couldn't even claim that he'd done it in self-defense. And she'd had a kid with him, even. Did you see that photograph they had out on the table? Marie hadn't noticed, but Antoine was able to describe it in full detail. A result of his photographic memory. He could locate whatever passage he liked, with astonishing speed, from any book he'd ever read. Any picture whatsoever, too. It was a snapshot showing a group of men sitting around a café table. One of their faces had a big red circle around it. I know who it is. He's a famous writer. You recited a passage from one of his books the other day by heart. I brought it home from the library. His mother stared blankly at him. Perhaps she'd become lost in her memories, in some past moment, but then suddenly she lifted both of her hands and placed them on her son's shoulders, staring at him steadily, though her eyes seemed to see nothing.

Her movement instantly caused Caligula to slip to one side and nearly fall. There's always so much I want to say that I never end up saying any of it, she declared. Antoine smiled, and then his mother worked up the courage to speak.

I can't stand it here. I know I've never wanted to leave, but it's obvious we have to get out. What do you think about the South of France? Marie's gaze grew vacant again, as though she were waiting for some answer or some sign, as if her son could decide for her. Madame Vibert is leaving for France next month. Her husband and three children are staying behind for now, but she offered to take us with her. She could find me a job. Antoine knew now what a *commode biddy* was, and his eyes grew wide as saucers. He'd looked it up in the dictionary, which furnished a definition for the first word only: a cabinet housing a washbasin and sometimes a water jug, soap, and other items used for personal ablutions. He didn't understand how that could have anything to do with Madame Vibert, but a short while later he happened to overhear a conversation among several of the neighborhood women. Now he knew that she worked in a brothel. She used to be quite a knockout, he heard the woman from the first floor say. But age is unforgiving, another one of them had replied, and now she's nothing more than an old commode biddy. One of them must have looked at her quizzically, because she quickly added— She's does the cleaning at the Étoile d'Or.

OBSCURE FEUDS

Jacques couldn't remember what had prompted the drama. Obscure feuds sometimes divided the family, and the truth of the matter was that nobody could have possibly puzzled out their origins, especially because, since none of them had any capacity for memory, they no longer remembered the first causes, so they simply perpetuated the resulting outcomes, which they'd long ago chewed over and come to accept once and for all. The only thing Jacques remembered about that day was his uncle Ernest standing up at the table, the meal not yet finished, and bellowing insults that were all completely incomprehensible, all except for *Mozabite*, directed at his brother, who'd remained seated and gone right on eating.

There was a loud noise. Like a door slamming shut, but that was impossible, he was alone. There was no one else there. He'd been living in that rented apartment for some time now, without his wife and children, whom he visited often. Might he have left a window open, and now the wind had just blown it closed? Or was it an echo from the past? Perhaps that bang had come from within himself? Jacques set down the pen he'd been writing with and rested his elbows on the table. Then he hung his head in his hands. The pain, that excruciating pain, was flooding into his soul once more. And with it, there reappeared in his memory certain scenes from a couple of years ago. He felt incapable of enduring yet again the suffering he'd gone through then. But from time to time, there were still a few shards that would reignite and sparkle for an instant or sink themselves a little further in.

How often do I find myself almost unable to breathe? he thought. He had a condition, an imperfectly cured case of tuberculosis he'd been fighting off from a very young age. And deep inside him, once again, a torrent of rebukes burst forth, like hail on an old roof already pockmarked by previous storms. Reproofs no one need utter aloud. He was perfectly capable of torturing himself to no end. A feeling of guilt could grow into something of a disease. And the memory of that day when his wife had gotten too close to the balcony swelled afresh, filling his entire space. He'd hugged her close and managed to get her back inside the house, but in the end he'd had no choice but to take her to the hospital, where she remained for a long time. There, crying, he'd spoken of María. Over and over. Like a man sentenced to die, his mind was capable of housing only a single thought. Always the same one. Always slumping under its own weight. And her sisters and her mother had blamed everything on him. On his infidelities. A culprit had to be identified, and there had to be just one. A guilty party. Who better than him?

It was a task that appeared at times to have been granted even more importance than the task of finding a solution for their problems. Even more importance than the disorder his wife was doubtless struggling with. More than trying to cure it. And the whole thing had been repeated on several occasions. One of those times—and they didn't know if she'd been trying to escape from the clinic she'd been placed in or was actually trying to kill herself—she'd even fractured her pelvis.

And then her sickness was twofold. There was an emotional component, barely visible even to her most immediate family, despite the fact that there was a serious risk of it straying into the realm of mental infirmity at the slightest provocation, and a physical element, as well. After that, her overall condition would always worsen whenever she found herself facing any sort of adversity, no matter how trifling. Like when their daughter had fallen ill, even though it had turned out to be a simple case of scarlet fever. But she'd reacted as though their child might perish at any moment.

Jacques didn't feel strong enough to revisit all that. To relive the nightmare, a nightmare that had been a recurring one for him throughout his entire existence. The nightmare of his first wife, a drug addict who was so strung out most of the time that he'd had no choice but to leave her. Things were different now. There were the twins, for one. Besides, she wasn't like the first woman he'd married. No. His wife was completely in the right. Was she? Yes. And also no. Like him. A woman, if given over to all the upheavals of irrationality and robbed of her ability to exercise even the slightest self-control, can, every so often, act like a terrorist. A trigger for desperation, the feeling that there's no other way out. And so, indifferent to justice, to reason, they ended up behaving as though they believed any course of action they might choose to follow in pursuit of their objectives was valid. That the ends justified the means. And a large portion of society did the same. Maybe they thought they had no other choice. That they had to do what they were doing at any cost, even if that meant risking their own integrity and the integrity of others.

And yet . . . Yes. Weakened, glutted with medications, trembling like a spiderweb out in the rain, she'd dropped to just under ninety pounds. She'd been transfigured into a sack of bones and nerves, with bulging eyes. Her body quivered, and every tendon, every artery, and every vein stood out on her skin, which was growing paler by the day, and sadder. To him, the doctor prescribed freedom and self-interest. I love life too much not to be egotistical, he would say to convince himself, to clear his head of his constant doubts, and for a long time he found all inspiration lacking, found himself lacking the necessary spirits or strength to do anything. The malice demonstrated by his adversaries didn't help, either. All that hurtful sniggering in the hallways of his own publishing house. All those invectives that were more personal insult than textual analysis. More hostile cross-examination than literary criticism. The majority of them were united by a common fear of what others might think. And they did their best to ensure that nobody could possibly suspect they might espouse the same ideas as that man they'd been so weak-minded as to ever have felt affection for. Their greatest fear was to be viewed as reactionaries. So they became incapable of thinking for themselves.

Dostoyevsky had described it in diabolical terms in one of his texts. As though it were an easy-to-follow recipe for an explosive cocktail: Convince four members of a group to denounce the fifth, on the pretext that he's veered too far from the collective doctrine, or even to off him on the grounds he's a snitch. The blood will unite them. The orthodox Left could ostracize a person with more deftness than the Greeks themselves. Excommunicate better than any pope. And ever since Jacques had spoken out publicly against the concentration camps uncovered in Stalinist Russia, the sidelong glances and the spontaneous tittering had been on the rise. Despite putting on a tough front, he had to acknowledge the great pain it caused him to be spurned by the vast majority of those who'd once been his friends and comrades in the fight for liberty and equality. He still remembered the first time he heard people laughing behind his back. It was as if he'd heard a volley of shots being fired into the air. A volley of shots that could have rent the heavens, his whole life, asunder.

Sometimes he wondered if he might not be losing his mind, but luckily, his remaining friends assured him his concerns were no delusion. René, Emmanuel, Michel. Or his teacher from back in high school. Not many more. His good friends. María. Catherine. Mi. And his wife. She, too, was among the small number of people who were making an effort to understand him. He'd fallen into disgrace. Because none of it could even be discussed. Jean Paul himself had issued his own personal anathema. We must not allow Billancourt to become disheartened. For a long time, the Renault factory there represented the largest concentration of workers in France. The upshot being, once again, that the truth must not be spoken, for fear of jeopardizing the working class's morale. Every bit as paternalistic as Papa Stalin. You can't talk about the purging of artists in Russia, because that would benefit the reactionaries. It was always the same. Doggedly denying reality in order to safeguard ideology. With that unique way they had of looking on certain crimes with their right eye, to denounce them, and on others with their left, to hide them. A cross-eyed sort of morality.

And almost everyone kept their mouth shut. For fear of going against the current, for fear of swimming against the tide of history. Under no circumstances must one engage in self-criticism, or concede one's own faults. Once a person has shaken off, unblinkingly, the moral dilemma of whether taking another man's life is a permissible act, the question of the permissibility of lying becomes mere child's play. And so, having started from a theory grounded in the notion of authenticity, and its antithesis, bad faith, we wind up at systematic mendacity. Consequently, on returning from a trip to Stalin's U.S.S.R., in 1954, one could declare unblushingly that the people there were absolutely free to engage in critical analysis. For a long time, Jacques hadn't even been able to work. He hadn't managed to set down a single line. And he was still scared it might happen again. Every time he heard a door slam, he'd jump and immediately relive the whole thing. Back then, he would often go out to soccer games or to stroll around the muggy, squally streets of Paris. Later he would visit friends, lacking the strength to do anything for himself. And knowing full well he had no right to bring up his own personal misfortunes, he would sit there in silence and listen to everything they said, but without paying any attention, just to hear somebody speak.

Back then, he'd thought that if his wife recovered, which he desperately hoped she would, he would try for a separation, availing himself of his energy, availing himself also of his pessimism, a quality so useful in certain of life's circumstances. They were living apart from one another now. And Jacques was slowly getting back to writing. The whole thing was his fault. But he still didn't deserve that. Just as no one in this world deserves the noose. He wasn't with María anymore, but he would be as soon as their paths crossed again. Catherine had come along next, another of the actresses he worked with. And then recently there was Mi, a buoyant, youthful blonde. And there was a time there when he'd been seeing all four of them at once, with their knowledge. A constellation of women. He was incapable of making a clean break from any of them, and from time to time one might appear to grow dimmer, only to then shine out again. More brightly than before. And yet he'd felt empty. Perhaps he wasn't ready for a love like his wife's, a singular love. To have the ability to make somebody the happiest person in the world and at the same time the most miserable. Did that capacity lie within a given person's self? Or was it that others were eager to impress it upon him? Out of weakness? Because they were suffering from some sort of imbalance? Or perhaps just the opposite, because they were much stronger?

Sometimes he would get to thinking that he'd ended up hurting every single one of the beings he'd come into contact with over the course of his life. Had he made no one happy? Were there so few people out there that shared his apparently inexhaustible gift? The ability to be happy in almost any circumstances? He required almost nothing. Killing for love. What a contradiction in terms. Killing one's self. Killing another. And at a certain point, loving another human being implied killing everyone else. Why did so many people seem to not understand what he'd long felt when gazing upon a landscape, next to the sea, alongside a scattering of rocks? Down in Tipasa, he'd grasped what that feeling called glory must be. The right to love limitlessly. There was not, there could not be, a singular love. That curious feeling of bliss spilling out of the sky and down to the sea had taught him to love all creatures. Yes, but for that to happen, he had to be alone. Completely alone.

Why did so many people insist on defending such a complex sentiment as love by just any old means? How did they expect to secure any fundamental rights through the use of force, of violence? Standing against everyone else. Oftentimes against even themselves. And yet, if you stopped to think about it, how little we need in order to be happy. A barefooted boy, out in the sunshine, with all the time in the world to simply kick a ball around, could be perfectly happy. Why were most adults incapable of returning to that state? Why did they expend so much effort transforming life into a never-ending game? Why did they stick so stubbornly to their unnuanced sensibilities? In all aspects of life, there seemed to exist only good and evil, the victor and the vanquished. Black and white. Not just in a boxing match or a soccer game. You had to be right if you weren't wrong. And it was always the other guy who was wrong.

But thinking about death was enough to make him refrain from casting reproaches. And anyway, it was time to get a move on. A person couldn't just sit there going around in circles on that millstone of unhappiness, of self-inflicted torture through feelings. Oh, how he'd loved her. How he loved her still. And admired her. He would never stop admiring her, never stop loving her. Despite the pain I myself brought upon her, unintentionally. That's why she didn't understand him. She would never understand him. All she could see was that he didn't love her in the way she wanted him to love her. How can you talk about love, when you're incapable of loving? she'd asked him once. It wasn't an accusation. He hadn't interpreted it as such, at any rate, but rather as a desperate attempt to make sense of him. Sometimes it feels as though no heart lies within our breast. And other times it's as if we had several of them all pounding away in there at once. Now he and his wife lived like brother and sister. Like a brother and sister who don't live together but who tell each other the truth, who respect each other, who have no need to deceive or to lie to one another.

Freedom and self-interest. That's what the doctor had prescribed him. That's why he had to press on with his novel, the one he intended would represent the initiation of his third period. Maybe then he would understand everyone else.

Maybe then he, too, would understand. First there'd been the absurdist period. That's what had reaped for him, through the publication not only of narrative pieces but also a play and even an essay, the greatest number of professional successes. After that had come his rebellious stage, the one that had brought him so much suffering and disenchantment, so many losses. Distanced him from so many people, friends and strangers alike. Now it was the time for love. He wanted to regain his past, his childhood, that simple world he'd had to leave behind but would never forget, the one he felt he had betrayed. In a sense, those three periods were like the three metamorphoses of the spirit that Zarathustra had spoken about.

From the camel, patiently toting its load—like Sisyphus, or like the Danaides, condemned to an eternity spent pouring water into a leaky vessel—to the lion, bravely daring to say no. The rebellious man clamoring for a version of individualism steeped in solidarity. And from that to the boy, ready for endless play. The first man. Jacques went over to the window and looked out at the dark sky and the stars. The Great Bear. The Arabs saw in that configuration of stars a caravan. Charles's Wain, serving from antiquity as a guide for travelers and seafarers, helping them to locate Polaris and, by it, to know which way was north. He'd discovered those same stars on Mi's back. A constellation of freckles. Those inconceivably remote pinpricks of light put Jacques in mind of a recent episode. Something that was supposed to turn a writer's world upside down. A radical twist of his fate. He still hadn't completely gotten over what had happened. It was something that for others would have constituted their greatest ambition but in him, from the very first, had touched off overwhelming feelings of suffocation and claustrophobia, along with insomnia, anxiety attacks, and fits of panic.

An enormous star blazed like a torch in the center of the great hall. This was just a few weeks back. And he'd been made the star of one of the most important events, or so it was said, for Western culture. Between dinners, interviews, and meetings with other authors, he'd been kept constantly busy over the course of those several days. But what were the greatest moments of his brief stay in Stockholm? His walk, alone, along the snow-covered piers, wrapped inside a long, dark coat, his head likewise muffled in black. Stealing away from the city center, where the shop windows were stacked ceiling-high with books of his in languages unintelligible to him, and stopping at a carnival stall to buy a stuffed bear for his children. And later, it was only during one of the breaks in the middle of that aseptic, stiff ceremony, in which he'd had to make a titanic effort not to appear out of place, that Jacques felt himself at ease.

Surrounded by his friends—Michel, Janine, Claude, Simone, and his wife—the men all dressed in black, sporting tuxedos and white bow ties, and the women in long, pale-colored dresses that made them look like bottles of champagne or some more translucent, effervescent draught still, Jacques smoked his cigarette with a deep sense of satisfaction. That precise instant, laughing and chatting, free from all the spotlights shining at him and the applause that had gone on ringing in his ears for a good several minutes, was a moment he would never forget. His wife looked radiant, almost completely recovered after all that suffering, and was beaming at him tenderly. He'd insisted that she accompany him. She'd stuck it out through the worst of it with him, and so she had every right to revel in the accolades. And her generous eyes and her smile had always been there, ready to take him in whenever he'd turned to her. The following day, Jacques found himself confronted with the diametric reverse. With a glare of hatred on a brother's face.

During a talk held at the University of Stockholm, a young Arab man reproached him for his silence on the subject of Algeria. He hadn't spoken a word about it for the past year and eight months, and he had his reasons, very carefully considered ones. Jacques had chosen to remain silent in order to avoid sowing further divisions, to avoid any escalation of suffering, although he'd never ceased taking action on the issue. And he never would. Many of that young man's friends were still alive thanks to Jacques having intervened in ways those present were utterly unaware of. Thanks to the petitions for clemency he'd penned in support of whole slews of individuals who'd been sentenced to death. Many of whom were undoubtedly guilty, but he was convinced that no person deserved death. I have always condemned terror, Jacques told that young man, an Algerian like himself. But I must also condemn that brand of terrorism now operating blindly in the streets of Algiers and planting bombs on tramways. My mother or another one of my family members might be on one of those trams. If that's justice, then I prefer my mother.

That last sentence was the spark. It would travel the world full circle, get twisted by this person or that along the way, and he would be blasted for it relentlessly. Planting bombs at bus stops, on trams, in cafés, or in casinos was not his idea of justice. It was what he'd been fighting against his entire life. But his pronouncement, taken out of context, lent itself readily to misrepresentation. Perhaps sentiments were already so inflamed that it wouldn't have mattered what he'd said. The hysterical mechanisms of manipulation were capable of flipping any argument on its head. Love before justice! cried one Russian revolutionary as the curtain fell after one of his plays. Yes. He was absolutely convinced. Love and justice should not be divorced from one another. But there were plenty of people out there who were bent on misunderstanding him. On keeping him from speaking out, if necessary. I'm going to have more enemies now, he'd thought, immediately upon receiving the news that he was being awarded that prize he didn't feel he deserved in the slightest. As he saw it, he was still at the beginning of his career. Not to mention the fact that there were others more worthy of praise.

He wasn't wrong. He had many more enemies now. Jacques saw his reflection in the glass. His long, slightly asymmetrical face, a cigarette hanging, as there almost always was, from his lips. That stern, sorrowful air. How could he possibly seduce anybody looking like that? And yet he was a huge hit with women. It was a mystery, even to him. He moved away from the window. He needed to go out for a walk. He couldn't stay indoors for so long. Maybe I should go knock on René's door and see if he wants to come out and watch the sunset, he thought, but his friend wouldn't be home at that hour, and the Seine at year's end, its bridges ablaze with Christmas lights, and those massive barges carving a silent path through the water, out among the naked trees and that frigid, inhospitable air, was something he couldn't stand. It made him think of his wife, skinny, shrunken, and trembling, a bundle of nerves, when one November just a few years back, she'd crossed through those same streets with a silent scream, oblivious to the traffic on all sides of her.

That scream represented guilt, downfall. The guilt and downfall of Jacques, who'd feared she might end up throwing herself headfirst, without fully comprehending what she was doing, into that wide, cold current. It was the scream of a fragile, desperate creature, and from time to time it reverberated inside his conscience. The children, Bidasse and Mandarine, had eyed her fearfully, still unable to understand, confronted with a mystery of superhuman proportions. When it comes down to it, the only thing children want is to play. To play all day long. And all year long. And for others to do the same. We have so much to learn from their attitude toward life. Jacques put on his overcoat, flipped up the collar, and lit another cigarette, still unsure whether or not to go out. To walk around that city that had grown so hostile toward him. He'd rather be on the banks of the Tagus, in the middle of a vast, wide-open plain, surrounded by the silence of twilight and boundless solitude. The red water, slowly deepening to silver, and finally to black. Out among olive trees, holly oaks, and dry fields of wheat and sunflowers, beneath clouds of gray and blue, and orange and pink.

But instead of heading for the door, he walked back to the window, and while leaning against that dark, cold surface, he allowed himself to be transported by the thought that he was actually in Provence, and he became immersed in the imagined contemplation of that panorama that was so reminiscent of his own land and what he pictured of Spain, the land where his mother's family was from. And he saw her, too, his mother, forever seated before a window. Not just in Algiers, but also when she'd come to visit him in Paris. And when he'd taken her on vacation to the South of France, to see if she could be persuaded to come and stay with him permanently. But his mother, surveying the traffic and the pedestrian shuffle, both much less picturesque than in Algiers, longed for the noise of the trams and the commotion of the crowds. What do you want me to say? There aren't any Arabs, she'd said. And she chose not to remain in France. Jacques understood her perfectly.

THE GUARDIANS OF HONOR

Beneath the wide-striped awnings of white and yellow lay piles of loquats, oranges and mandarins, apricots, and melons. All around, a throng of men, women, and children bustled and buzzed, like a swarm of flies. Let's go to the bar with the *agitateurs*, Khaled instructed. His partner looked at him in surprise but didn't dare question him. He knew, from the few hours they'd spent together in that city since their first introduction, that he disliked responding to even the most mundane of queries. You had to wait for the moment when he'd elect to reveal the information you were looking for of his own accord. Assuming that moment ever came. Or else content yourself with not knowing anything. They'd met at the port, down where the boats coming and going from points all across the Mediterranean weighed and casted anchor. It was one of Khaled's favorite spots, and although he'd arrived from Algiers no more than a week ago, he already appeared to have a better handle on the place than most. A few hours spent walking around, a few days wandering the streets of any city was all he needed to acquire a level of knowledge that could rival that of the locals. Surprises, he thought, could be found lurking in practically any dark little corner, the gold among the dross. Or the absurd. Beautiful women who would age ere long. Or be dead the very next day.

They made for the marina, walking past a series of market stalls. Hamid took in the scene around him. It was a gorgeous day, although the two of them, as usual, were dressed rather warmly. Generally speaking, their compatriots were in the habit of wearing lots of clothes. Occasionally, because they were hiding something, but for the most part it was because, being poor, they felt no compunction about piling on everything they owned at once. Quite the opposite. It was more practical. Down at the waterfront, they'd seen a long line of people who'd just docked in from Algeria and were waiting for the bus that would carry them to the outskirts of town. Some were old men with tottering heads. They had on multiple layers of clothing and were each carrying a bag with a handful of personal belongings inside. They wore very fine wool caps, mostly black or white, which made them look darker than they were. A matte, ashy coating lay on their skin. Khaled had gone over to help one of the men up the steps of the bus. He appeared stuck, unable to move either forward or back. He'd given him a hand and even accompanied him inside to assist him to his seat.

Somebody like that has got to feel vulnerable, Hamid thought to himself, while admiring an open watermelon. The stall keeper, a plumpish woman with an abundance of hair, a dark, tousled mane, had just sliced the fruit in half with a knife longer than her arm. *Ne touchez pas les fruits.* Hamid inhaled deeply, willing his nose to capture the scent of that bright, wet red fruit. Those droplets, doubtless sweet and fresh, were making him salivate more than usual. And blind now to everything else, even the other mounds of fruit filling the stall, he raised his arm slowly and stretched out his hand inch by inch toward the target. And he touched it. Hamid's fingertips brushed the forbidden fruit. Instantly, the stall keeper began screeching at him. Don't you know how to read? *Sale bicot!* Just what you'd expect from an Arab! Khaled, who'd been monitoring the scene in anticipation of its ending in some sort of outburst, had leaned in close and whispered to his partner— Do you want me to bite her ear off? Hamid had blinked at him, dumbfounded, but Khaled had already brought out a few coins from his pants pocket. The woman had stifled her demonstrations at the first whiff of money.

And Hamid, taking up the half watermelon in his arms, caressing its hard, cool rind, had set off with his companion once more. He wasn't used to getting gifts. Afterward, he'd stopped for a moment and taken out his own knife, which he used to cut off bits of the watermelon as they walked along. He'd already eaten more than half of it when Khaled halted at one of the many outdoor bars spanning the length of the marina and gestured with his eyes for him to follow. They picked out a corner and sat down at a table. The boat masts were clustered in a dense forest that bobbed in time to the ocean breeze and the gentle rocking of the salt water. Mizzens, foremasts, and gangways keened and creaked like stars trembling and tinkling in the heavens. It was like an organ recital. That spot might rightly be considered Marseille's second cathedral. An open-air cathedral, filled with light in constant motion. Overhead, they could hear the squalls of the gulls flying above them and reflected in the small, glass tabletop. A host of swallows darkened its surface every now and then. Or were they starlings? Khaled watched closely. No, they were swallows. The clouds, too, treading heavily on the heels of one another, paraded across the sky.

Khaled ordered a pastis and gestured for Hamid to tell the waiter what he wanted to drink. After hesitating a moment,

Hamid ordered tea. Green tea, with spearmint leaves and pine nuts. A model student, Khaled had thought to himself immediately after setting eyes on him for the first time. Naïve, easily enthused, even by the most inconsequential nonsense. The darling of all the female teachers. And even the male ones. Impeccably behaved, seemingly on the ball, hardworking, even, but dumb as a post. A lot of his colleagues were the same way. Or *brothers*, as they called each other. A wellspring of ignorance. A bunch of dunces. Even those who'd gone to school, since the majority of them had no studies whatsoever. Not even at the most basic level. They could barely read and write. This guy, on the other hand, had been lucky enough to study in France. In the metropole. At a mechanic school, granted, but that was better than nothing.

The waiter brought over the glasses, the bottle of Berger, the jug of cold water, and the steaming teapot. So it wasn't a bar where political agitators got together to hatch plots in an atmosphere of the utmost secrecy. In that establishment, the pastis and absinthe, tea and champagne, and even the sparkling water were all served in glasses with *agitateurs*, swizzle sticks for stirring your ice, mixing your drink, or getting rid of the bubbles, and these stirrers were in the shape of women. Naked, see-through women, exceedingly slender, their hair almost as long as their legs, which plunged down the length of the stem into the glass and were lost beneath the liquid's surface. Khaled enjoyed caressing those soft bodies, running his fingertips over their outlines, their contours, every dimple, every swelling. There were red ones, green ones, pink, yellow, and blue. Even a few black ones, which, naturally, weren't see-through. Their hair hung down their backs. And they lounged inside glasses and cups with their arms folded behind their heads, so that their breasts bobbed up over the rim and their bottoms were either dipped in drink or brushing up against the sides of the glass, depending on the size of the cup.

It was no easy thing making off with one of those stirrers. There was always a waiter standing by outside in case any of the bar's patrons required something further. Or maybe they were posted there in order to keep a better watch over that plastic harem that most of Marseille's male inhabitants and many of its foreign visitors so coveted. In other places, the tops of the swizzle sticks were shaped simply like palm trees. Elephants. Hearts. Stars. Or were nothing more than unadorned wooden or plastic sticks. Khaled poured a little more water into his glass, and the red lady swiveled around, quavering like a weather vane, like a streamer in the wind, but then he grabbed her by the hair and stirred the liquid around a little. He picked up the glass, leaned back in his chair, and, with his first sip, squinted up at the sky. Hamid focused on his tea, which couldn't hold a candle to the stuff in his own country. Next time, he'd order something with alcohol in it. His partner had done it without a flicker of shame, without a moment's hesitation.

In the animal world, just as in our own, there's a division of labor, Khaled thought to himself, as he followed the paths of the birds on high. There are seagulls that head out first thing in the morning to the garbage dump, in punctual flocks, like so many clutches of office workers, factory or construction hands, shop assistants, and bus drivers. They return in the evening, in punctual flocks once more. There are others, though, that spend all day wheeling and frolicking along the cliffs or over the harbor, trailing ripples across the salt-sea expanse, from time to time diving in after a fish, tracing lines and complicated patterns in the air. They travel not in flocks but as a scattering, each alone. Sometimes in small groups.

Or in pairs. These seagulls are the artists. Some are painters, he mused. Others, actresses. And others, writers. They work alone, but they need to be seen. They, too, like to be the center of attention. To feel themselves gods. Immortal.

High up, atop a limestone crest rising some 525 feet from the ground, the basilica of Notre-Dame de la Garde jutted skyward. A massive sculpture of the Virgin, bathed in gold, crowned the nearly two-hundred-foot-tall bell tower. The metal was shimmering just then in the sunlight, contrasting sharply with the white marble—likewise blinding—and the blue of the sky and the green of the verdant hillside. He'd been up there the previous afternoon, and not just to take in the view of the city and the sea from that privileged height. He'd gone inside the church, as well, seen its images of saints and virgins. Of men, almost always depicted in the act of being tortured and with hardly any clothes on, and of women, wearing far too many, like in his homeland. The veil hides everything, he reflected. Wealth, poverty, sex, infidelity, homeliness. A women with one eye pointing up and the other eye pointing down, or with a mark like a slash wound in the center of her forehead, could conceal herself quite nicely beneath that suggestive cloth and charm a man much better looking than herself. He thought about his mother. The few times he'd seen her uncovered, a shiver always ran down his spine.

The church reminded him of the Notre-Dame d'Afrique. In Bab el Oued, in the northern part of Algiers, an abrupt, leafy slope led to the top of a 407-foot bluff where the basilica stood, commanding a view of the sea and an endless expanse of white houses. Khaled had gone inside once, and behind the altar, he'd read the following words, inscribed in French, Arabic, and Kabyle: Our Lady of Africa, pray for us and for the Muslims. It was like standing before a mirage, as if there at the edge of the sea that separated those two continents there were a mirror, reflecting the opposite shore, even though the domes of the Algiers sanctuary were encrusted with mosaics of blue and gold. Khaled looked around him, surveying all the tables and then all the different outdoor bars stretching down the pier.

So many unattached men, he thought. Out together. Especially when it's Arab men. Like the two of us. How fine it would be to be sitting here with a couple of girls, instead of that randomly assigned partner he'd been slated to work alongside for the next coming while. He observed him carefully. He wasn't handsome. He wasn't smart. He was just another Algerian. Dark skin, coarse, even squab features, square face. He felt no desire whatsoever to converse with him. Or with anyone. Only to look at beautiful things. Women, landscapes. Occasionally he went to the movie theater. Everything there was beautiful. In movies, everything happened for a reason. Nothing in them seemed to be the product of chance, or fancy. Nothing in them was left to fate, even the briefest sequence of action had its rationale, and he loved those stories that came full circle, where the ending was foreshadowed in the beginning, where the opening scenes or the first snippets of dialogue as the screen flickered to life shone through clearly again at the finish. Those stories in which destinies were always fulfilled. And then there were the actresses, too.

Men like us, Khaled reflected, have short careers ahead of us. That's why we have to rush headlong across this earth. That's why he liked women so much. Our clandestine existence forces us to live as loners. We cannot have a family or lead normal lives. At that moment, a car pulled to a stop nearby. It had to be them. They'd arranged to meet there at noon. Khaled looked at his wristwatch. That morning's contact was impeccably punctual. The man driving remained at the wheel, while a mannerly looking woman stepped out of the passenger side. You often came across that sort of woman among the ranks of those volunteering for operations such as this. She might be a nurse at a Catholic hospital. Mouthwatering, he thought. Her skin was so white, without a single freckle, without a single blemish, that he felt the urge to run his tongue over it as if she were a scoop of vanilla ice cream. Khaled saw that the waiter was staring at the woman, too, and took the occasion to slip his stirrer into his jacket pocket. A long, tall woman, see-through red, smooth-bodied and curly-haired, bedded down next to his gun.

The presumptive nurse continued her walk toward them. She had enormous green eyes. Cat eyes. Flashing. And there it was. The inevitable suitcase. Old, oversized, imitation leather, battered and scratched, covered in half-torn stickers. It must have been heavy, judging from the strain apparent in the woman's arm and neck muscles. In all of her muscles. But the smile on her face never faltered. The latches are doubtless in working order, Khaled thought to himself, but there always had to be a nylon strap or something of the kind to make doubly sure the thing wouldn't pop open unexpectedly. He'd already carried out several of these types of missions, enough that he was now capable of gleaning a great deal of information about his contacts and all the various operational details at a single glance. And the remainder, he guessed at. And whether those guesses were right or wrong, the fantasizing amused him. The driver must be a colleague of hers. A doctor at the hospital. Eventually they'll get married and have four or five kids. Then they'll forget all about the things they did when they were young. She'll become a robotic drudge, churning out crocheted doilies. And they'll waste away on the couch, watching television or listening to the radio. Until they finally die. *Rumi* swine, he muttered through clenched teeth.

Was he becoming like Saddok? Did he, too, despise practically the entirety of human race? Now she'll sit down with us for a few minutes, we won't exchange a single word, because we don't have anything to talk about, because we aren't supposed to, then she'll stand up and leave the suitcase behind. As if she's forgotten it. That was the plan. The woman was now standing beside them and looking at Khaled admiringly. Maybe even a little desirously, he thought, and he brought his hand up to his face, trying to hide the scar that ran from the bridge of his nose over to his right cheekbone. He was used to it. Ever since he was young, women had been devouring him with their eyes like that. And when she finally took her seat next to them, a billow of perfume enveloped them. Khaled and Hamid breathed in deeply, and gulped. She smelled of lavender oil. Of the countryside. The way the women of that land smelled. It was a delicate, subtle fragrance, not like the balm of the women in their own country, which was much stronger and more penetrating, slightly acidic, and thick. Khaled liked that smell, too, but these more refined scents drove him wild.

Inside, there'll be a STEN, an old-fashioned revolver taken from some Resistance stash, a new model Beretta, automatic, 9 mm, a Spanish Astra, same caliber, several magazines, and a half a dozen grenades—he went over the list quickly in his head. That's the plan, although there are occasionally changes. People can't always get ahold of the items they want or that have been requested, and then they improvise. Sometimes for the better. But other times, it can end up being a complete fiasco. All the weapons would be carefully wrapped in newsprint and folded inside old clothes. Scraps of sheets. Tattered shirts. And every last crack and cranny inside would be stuffed tight with more wads of paper. There'd be a little money, as well. There was always a little money. Khaled pulled an envelope from one of his jacket pockets and set it on the glass tabletop. It contained two photographs. One of him. The other of Hamid. The woman leaned forward slightly, picked up the envelope, and slipped it inside her purse. Shortly, in a meeting very like that morning's, they would receive two shiny new ID cards. The suitcase woman stood up, and after stealing a last glance at Khaled, she walked away and got into the car.

Hey, hey, he then exclaimed. Get a load of that *cagole*! Hamid gaped at him. That sudden burst of enthusiasm from such a reserved man stunned him. He'd straightened up in his chair and was looking as if he'd been hypnotized. So there *was* something in this world that could make him lose his cool. What are you talking about? He'd never in his life heard the word. *Cagole*. This guy sure did know a lot of French. More than he himself did, and he'd studied in the metropole. Khaled gestured with his head, cocking it to one side to steer his attention in the proper direction. His young partner looked and saw a gorgeous woman walking toward them, twirling her purse around like a toy. Spinning it in circles by its long, thin strap. Were women the only thing that could get him talking, make him break that intractable silence he must have held to be one of the foremost marks of virility? Hamid observed him out of the corner of his eyes. He looked like a fox or a hunting hound that's just caught the scent of its prey. His body tense, frozen, only his nostrils moved, quivering slightly. Rising and falling, pumping air he seemed to be struggling to take in, like the gills on a fish out of water. What's a *cagole*? he asked, seizing on the other man's trance.

You see that neckline? Hamid looked at her red, strapless shirt. And that tight, red skirt, and those heels? She had a tiny scarf knotted around her neck, too. Bright red colored. Pure ornament, considering the size of the thing, the temperature, and the rest of her outfit. You don't see women like that anywhere but here, Khaled went on. Pure attitude and a cloud of perfume. How do you know that? I know everything about women. He did not go on to explain that he'd begun using the word to refer to the women who worked in the Marseille date factories, selecting pieces of fruit off a long table called a *cagoulo*. And, by extension, to any woman with over-the-top clothing and makeup. *Vive les filles des calanques*, Khaled declared in a somewhat louder voice just as that representative of the daughters of the Sormiou Coves walked past the bar's outdoor seating area. And the woman, swinging her hips a bit more gustily, winked at him with one of her big black eyes. Hamid thought he could hear the rustling of her eyelashes brushing against one another. It's like they're coming to life and fluttering like birds, Khaled sighed, then he let out a loud whistle.

After they'd gotten up and left the bar, the two men headed to their own car, which they'd left parked there early that morning. Once they'd locked the suitcase and the rest of the watermelon in the trunk, Hamid stepped around to the door, but Khaled signaled with his hand that they should continue to stroll around some more. It won't be safe, he warned weakly, but as he said it, he realized it was completely ridiculous. If Khaled got it into his head that he wanted to walk, he was going to walk, and then he'd have only two choices. Stay in the car and wait for him, or accompany him on another lap, so they sauntered along the marina, toward the sea, weaving their way through the pushcarts and stalls whose vast assortment of wares brightened the pier alongside the various sailing and fishing vessels. There were cakes of soap. Strangely colored.

Dirty looking, almost. Postcards, mostly featuring views of the city. And secondhand books, and radios, and watches. In one particular wagon stall, under a yellow shade, there were sunflower seeds, lupini beans, almonds, salt-sprinkled toasted chickpeas, and peanuts. Another sold seafood. Squid, sardines, scrod, red mullet. Their silver scales and their green and pink veins glittering in the sun.

Further on, a Berber man had arrayed a collection of metal objects on a blanket and was sitting on the ground with his leather slippers neatly beside him. Another was selling Arabic pastries filled with honey and pistachios and shaped to look like small baskets, carefully folded handkerchiefs, and miniature hummingbird nests. Look, Khaled exclaimed, without making any discernible gesture in one particular direction or another. Another pretty woman? Hamid followed his eyes and saw a black rat scurrying across the tram tracks toward the far end of the pier to throw itself into the water. Did you know these rats can bite clean through a lead pipe? And they're so dexterous, they can carry an egg all the way back to their nest without breaking it. So they're hungry little buggers and decent acrobats to boot, Hamid joked. Khaled, without so much as cracking a smile, continued his own train of thought—Let's lay the cards on the table, shall we? Why wouldn't he have done that back at the bar, instead of spending all this time walking around enjoying the view? He probably preferred walking and talking. Maybe he thought no one would be able to overhear them that way. In any event, members of this sort of unit didn't ever talk much. You had to watch what you said. Even with it being just the two of them, and despite the fact that each might have said of the other that he was one of them, a brother. They were just one tiny cell. An insignificant cog on an enormous gear assembly in a highly complicated network.

Like two flies trapped in a spiderweb. And a single misstep is all it would take. But the truth is it didn't matter whether you spoke loudly or in a whisper as you walked along. The greatest threat was always your own partner. Encouraging people to snitch on one another had a sanitizing effect on the group. Khaled glanced at this "brother" of his and felt a surge of contempt when he thought about having to put up with another one still, as they generally operated in units of three. At times he felt as if he were part of some sort of religious order. As it was, they lived most of the time like monks. They had no possessions. They went through life with nothing but the clothes on their backs. The revolutionary is a doomed man, he reminded himself. He has no personal interests, no private pursuits, no feelings, no attachments, no property. Not even a name. His entire being is consumed by a single purpose, a single thought, a single passion. The revolution. That was the opening paragraph of the *Catechism of a Revolutionary*. Though written almost a century prior in reference to Russian anarchists, it was an apt description of the reality members of terrorist outfits experienced.

It seems our guy is writing something that could end up compromising the organization, Khaled resumed. Nevertheless, the latest incoming order is that we wait. He's been given some prestigious award, and the whole world's eyes are on him. It's not a good time for us to put anything in motion. At any rate, according to our informants' reports, it seems Golan intends to retire to the countryside. To the South of France, not far from here. If that's the case, in a few months' time, or a year at most, everything will be much easier. Although we can also make our move in the capital, if need be. It was such a thrilling thing to be deciding the fates of others. It was like playing God. And that exciting, sometimes dangerous amusement was, without a doubt, what might bring them closest to immortality. Who is it? Who's hiding behind the name of Golan? As soon as he said it, Hamid realized he shouldn't have asked. Whenever he opened his mouth, Khaled would clam up for a while. He wouldn't answer him. Or he'd talk about something completely different.

And sure enough, he fell silent for a few minutes, brooding, slowing his pace. Death is inescapable, he said at last, without taking his eyes off the ground. Do you know the story of the rich merchant's servant? Hamid looked at him in surprise. He couldn't believe he was deigning to speak to him like that, that he was bothering to pay him any attention at all. He did know the story, of course, but he let the other man tell it. One day at the Baghdad market, a servant man bumps into Death, who draws himself up into what he takes to be a threatening pose, whereupon he runs as swiftly as he can to his master, and asks him for a good, fast horse, with which to flee to Isfahan. Later on, at the same market, the merchant also runs into Death, and he asks him why he greeted his servant so threateningly. Death replies—It was a gesture of shock. I was surprised to see him here, for I was to bear him off to Isfahan this very day. Hamid looked at him uncomprehendingly. What did that mean? That they were infallible? That nobody could escape once the organization had decided to eliminate them? Be that as it may, Khaled declared, as if thinking aloud, I'd rather meet Death on my horse than in my bed.

In the meantime, they were to turn their attention to cash collection. Here in Marseille there are a lot of slow payers, enthusiasm doesn't run high. So just like Death, we'll linger here awhile in the market. We have to make sure they understand that they can't fall behind on their payments. If they want their luck to change, for the whole world to change, these guys have to kick in their share, too. These guys especially. *Charriot magique. Toute en musique. Bienvenue chez papa Omri. Specialiste du thé à la menthe avec pignons,* Khaled read aloud. The magic wagon was decked with flowers. Papa Omri, a graying beard on his chin and a thermos in one hand, walked along with a cornet hanging around his neck. He used it to herald his arrival. Music was coming from the wagon, too. There was a transistor radio wedged in among the thermoses and the huge number of paper cups crammed onto the upper shelf of the cart, whose lower half and every other available surface was covered with flags from all different countries. There was the French flag, and the Algerian flag, but also the Swiss flag, the Canadian flag, the German flag, and the Spanish flag. A little Arab tune was playing just then, and it made the sun and the fresh air blowing in off the harbor seem all that much more pleasant.

Hamid headed over to the cart, hoping for a sip of tea that would whisk him away to his homeland. Papa Omri was serving two very young girls in sundresses and leather sandals. The wind teased the fabric of their dresses, ruffling it across their thighs. And as they walked away with their cardboard cups balanced between their fingertips, blowing coolly into the tea so as to be able to drink it as soon as possible, the wagon master pretended to call them, imitating the ringing of a phone and bringing something up to his ear. The young girls turned back around, bemused. How could he be getting a call there, outside? Papa Omri held out the fake telephone to one of them—it was really just an empty cigarette packet with a curly black wire hanging from one end—and with a roguish glint in his eye, he said—*C'est pour madame.* The girl he was pointing at, a little brunette thing about sixteen years old with blond streaks in her bountiful hair, a slender frame, and very round, dark eyes, had a look of wonder on her face, but she let out a giggle at the same time. Khaled's tongue went dry and his heart started racing. It doesn't do to point, he muttered to himself.

It's as if they were food, Hamid thought, seeing him like that. His nostrils were pulsating rhythmically again. It was as if the whole city were a fruit stand in Khaled's eyes. *Comment s'appelez vous?* Papa Omri enquired. *Claire*, the girl replied. *Clara. En français, Claire. Ah, vous est espagnol? Oui. C'est un cadeau pour vous.* Papa Omri leaned forward, bowing. Look, Khaled whispered with almost religious admiration, the girl has a book under her arm. I want to know what she's reading. *Et vous? Comment s'appelez vous?* Omri asked. *Olga.* The two girls laughed in unison. They're laughing at how badly he speaks French, Khaled groused, as the girls walked back over to the cart and Papa Omri stuck his hand into a box, pulling out two bright red lollipops and handing one to each girl. Smiling, Olga and Clara turned to head back downtown. Hamid saw both of them look at Khaled. Out of the corner of their eyes, but very intently. Women always turned to look at him, with barely contained exhilaration, but he only paid attention to a few. And from the very first, he'd been transfixed by this Clara girl, so that he no longer desired anyone else, at least not for those several moments.

You see? That there's the perfect example of one of your good, colonized Arabs, he said suddenly. Papa Omri heard the comment, detected the threat, and started walking, pushing his wagon ahead of him. And as he hurried away, with quick, short steps, Khaled smiled. The apple of the well-meaning colonist's eye. He doesn't seem like a bad guy, Hamid replied. Idiot birds, they're all a bunch of idiot birds. Farm fowl. Toting their own little cages around. At that precise instant, a woman and a tall boy with a gray parrot on his left shoulder walked past. Khaled, who'd begun trailing after the man with the cart, who in turn was following the two young girls with their tea, stopped short and stared at them. Some other woman's driven him out of his mind again, thought Hamid vaguely, relieved that they'd so quickly given up their pursuit of Papa Omri. It can't be, Khaled hissed under his breath. The woman and that boy are following me. They could be working for the Messalists. Both of them. Or at least her. Maybe they're police informants. They must be with the French intelligence service. Hamid couldn't believe what he was hearing, and for the first time, he decided to speak up. Are you nuts? Have you lost your mind? A woman and a kid with a parrot?

Had his partner gone mad? And what about this famed intelligence of his? Had it dissolved into thin air and been replaced with some childish delusion? They're the reason I have this scar, Khaled explained further, touching his hand to his cheek. Or rather, the parrot is. The bird did this to me. At a café. In Algiers. And now they show up here, in Marseille. They're following me. There's no doubt in my mind. Hamid burst out laughing. You mean to tell me that scar isn't from a bullet? Or some knife fight—He cut his chaffing short, because Khaled had just shot him a frigid glare. Let's go, let's just go, he insisted, trying to pacify him. Why couldn't another beautiful woman walk by and make his partner forget all about those two and spare him the tongue-lashing he was surely about to receive? Then, pulling him aside by the arm to prevent him from running after that completely innocent-looking pair, he added—Anyhow, it's better than having a wart . . . For a moment, the two of them stood in silence, looking straight into each other's eyes. Hamid had crossed a line.

You're going to lose that Clara girl. Khaled blinked at him in bewilderment, as if he could no longer even remember who that was. As if he could only hold a single thought in his head at a time. Every time I look in the mirror or catch sight of myself in the reflection of a shop window or any random, passing car, I'm reminded of that parrot. And I always will be, until the day I die. Come on, brother, let's go back to the car, Hamid said, and he rested a hand on his shoulder in an attempt to calm him. Khaled's face grew even darker. He removed his hand. We shouldn't leave the suitcase unattended so long, he added, almost in a whisper. What would you have said to them, anyway? You have no proof. How could they be spies if they didn't even see you? What would you know? You're the one who doesn't see anything. Besides, Khaled didn't need any proof. You just have to threaten them, he snarled. Frighten them. Fear is our greatest ally.

THEY WERE AND THEY ARE
GREATHER THAN I

Rescue this poor family from the fate of the poor, which is to disappear from history without a trace. The Speechless Ones. They were and they are greater than I.

He'd been thinking about her when he set that down on a page of the notebook he was still jotting ideas in. Not just about his own family. His mother. His uncle Ernest. Or the men at the cooperage in Algiers where his uncle and occasionally also his brother worked, those men he enjoyed observing at their toil. Lending a hand, when they'd let him. He still had a photo he'd taken with them when he was six. Their faces grimy, their clothes well worn and patched, all of them in long smocks and mustaches. Surrounded by hammers, barrels, and wooden hoops. And on the floor, a layer of sawdust. The only one smiling, the one seen draping an arm over his shoulders, was his brother Lucien. He'd also been thinking about his father, who'd died in battle shortly after arriving on the continent. The speechless ones. There were so many of them. Men and women condemned to disappearance, a disappearance just like everyone else's—immutable—but in their case it was a silent one, as well. Carina had recently begun working for him, and every time he ran into her with a rag in her hand, in this room or that, he would get embarrassed. Or when he'd catch sight of her down on her hands and knees, scrubbing the wooden floorboards inside the house or the terracotta tiles out on the patio. She always looked up and smiled at him. It was enough to take a person's breath away.

The embarrassment he felt went far beyond mere unfamiliarity, faltering confidence, or nervousness in the face of her beauty. It was a similar feeling, in a way, to the one that had been coming over him regularly ever since he'd become the owner of that house. And every single one of the objects inside it. Of everything apart from a table, a few chairs, and a bed. The most rudimentary items. Because he'd finally found it. He'd found his house. The place he hoped to retire. He spent as much time there as he could now, and he hoped to live there permanently one day in the not-too-distant future, far from the noise and the tumult of the cities. Property, Proudhon posited, was theft. In point of fact, the phrase was coined by Brissot, another revolutionary who'd died on the guillotine. Property is death, he himself had written just a few years back. And he considered that having such a beautiful home, even if it was only a ramshackle house in the countryside, and even if he was set to turn fifty soon, was a sin. That recent impulse to acquire a place of his own, a refuge, must have been influenced at least in part by the persecution he felt he was being subjected to lately.

Cart yourself off to the Galapagos Islands, Monsieur Néant had written to him several years earlier, with a healthy dose of contempt. That's the way with these philosophical commissars, always battling mercilessly for total domination in the name of liberating humanity. But he didn't need to go that far. All he needed was to get out of Paris. All he needed was to feel the light of Provence, which is where René was, too, his friend

René. Jacques felt better knowing he was so close by and that the only thing separating them was a few miles of country road through fields of flowers and trees. The two of them had rediscovered in that place the path that could lead to innocence. Or they knew they could search for it there, at least. In the landscape. In the people. In people like Carina, utterly lacking in adulteration, utterly lacking in duplicity, who were capable of forgiving not only others but also themselves.

Whenever she heard him coming, Carina would lift up her big, dark brown, dancing eyes with a tiny glimmer of apprehension, like a doe, and she would greet him, smilingly, in that sweet, argentine voice of hers. Good morning, Monsieur Terrasse. Good afternoon, Monsieur Terrasse. Jacques might do an extra lap through the house just to see her again, her smile, her flowered dress, and her apron, her dark skin, and her long black hair, just to hear her voice, unsure, perhaps, whether the proper response was to greet him anew every time she saw him or, rather, if it was better to say nothing, to avoid repeating her greeting so many times. But she was incapable of that. Whenever she saw someone, whoever it might be, a man, a woman, or even a child—especially if it was a child—she couldn't help but greet them, regardless of whether she had already done the same not five minutes earlier. Good morning, Monsieur Terrasse. Good afternoon. Why did he feel such embarrassment? Why was he still sheepish and silent? Because she reminded him—he, who was in danger of growing too far removed from that first life of his, from real life—of where he came from?

Those speechless people were not only in Algeria, in Africa. They were here, too, in France, in the metropole. All over Europe. And they would never stop existing. They would spread out all over the world, moving from one place to the next. Or remain forever in the same spot, leading obscure lives, experiencing modest emotions, leaving faint traces. Barely a scratch. Like his mother. That young girl had captivated him from the very first. She was born in Spain, where she'd lived with her parents until the age of fourteen. And as soon as Jacques learned she was Spanish, his mind was made up. He had a weak spot for the country of his descent, which he'd been to only once, more than twenty years ago, when he was twenty-two. He'd never gone back there. And he never would, not until the Franco regime was a thing of the past. Spanish citizens. Franco is dead . . . Jacques dreamt of one day hearing those words, although he'd prefer for him to be overthrown. Tossed out on his backside.

And when he'd learned her name, he'd fallen to fantasizing. Carina Ortiz. Carina was the name of a constellation. The keel of the ancient Argo Navis. The constellation's brightest star, Alfa Carinae, was the second most luminous stellar body in the entire firmament. Another lodestar for seafarers, Jacques reflected. A reminder of a perilous journey undertaken by a hero tasked with an impossible errand. And when he'd first seen her, when he'd first seen Carina, with that gaze of hers that radiated innocence, kind-heartedness, and shyness, but with an unmistakable sparkle that hinted at sprightliness and perhaps even a propensity to mischief, he knew instantly that she was going to be perfect. The perfect person to work in his or any other person's home. Or anywhere. The perfect person to do anything she set her mind to. Applying herself unhurriedly, almost soundlessly, never in half measures. As soon as he saw her, he was convinced not only that she wouldn't be a bother but that seeing her arrive every morning would brighten his day, although he also suspected she would have a detrimental effect on his already so hard-to-come-by sleep. That his nighttime visions of her would make rest all but impossible.

Jacques wasn't particularly concerned whether she ironed well or not, whether she knew how to cook or make the beds. Whether the house was clean. Which it was. She demonstrated a great deal of care in all things. She'd even bring in flowers she picked along her way and arrange a few in every room. Anemones. White ones, pink ones, lilac ones, blue ones. The windflower, Jacques mused. The most delicate and short-lived of all. And the first thing he'd done was to hand her the keys. The next, to give her a raise. If money was good for anything, it was for paying people well. Now he took pleasure in hearing her knock each morning at the door before stepping inside, so softly it hardly made a sound. The way she sometimes rang the little bell beside the worn stone steps leading up to the porch. After that, and only after that, when she was sure someone had heard her or that no one was home, would she go ahead and stick in her key and turn it in the lock. Her sweet, open expression cut your heart in two, like a razor blade. Although she spoke scarcely a word, her character shone through immediately in her eyes, charming all and sundry. His wife held her in high esteem, as well. As did the children. Whenever Bidasse and Mandarine came to stay at the Lourmarin house, they never let her out of their sight.

Jacques had taken to reading aloud to her from different books. Occasionally even from some piece of writing of his own. She followed every single word, with wide, round eyes, and when something she was hearing moved her, she would repeat it to herself, in a voice so soft it was barely more than a faint movement of her lips. She always told the truth. I don't understand a word of it, but I like it. And she'd smile. Other times she'd begin crying, but then she'd laugh, perhaps embarrassed at her own feelings. When he spoke with her, Jacques—who'd come there for the purpose of shutting himself up to write and getting away from Paris, from the interviews, from the obligations, and seeking out the temperance and the solitude he needed to progress with his writing—didn't feel quite so alone. Temperance was easy for him to manage. It was something he'd practiced instinctively his whole life, at the beginning with the instinct of a man who has no other choice, and later with that of a man who no longer cares. Solitude was a different matter, though. He missed working as part of a team. In the theater, at the paper. Alongside other men and women.

He set his manuscript to one side and went to look for Carina, and he found her making up his bedroom. Jacques, following his usual custom, had risen very early, before sunrise, to take his daily walk, and he'd forgotten to make the bed before he left. Good morning, Monsieur Terrasse, she said, even though she'd already greeted him when she'd arrived and had even sat down with him for a cup of coffee. Jacques went over to where she was and, without saying a word, began helping her. Carina protested. That's not necessary, Monsieur Terrasse. This bed of yours is very narrow. I'll have it made up in two shakes. And as she spoke, she blushed and then laughed. It's easier with two sets of hands. Also, don't call me *monsieur*, use my name. I've asked you several times. Otherwise I'm going to have to start addressing you in kind, as *Madame Ortiz*. And Carina laughed again. Very well, Monsieur Jacques, she teased back.

When the bed was finished, the young woman went into the laundry room. Jacques followed her there but stopped before going in and stood leaning against the doorframe while she plugged in the iron and spread out a blanket next to the

110

pile of clothes she'd taken off the line a little earlier. That was when Jacques best liked chatting with her, making her laugh, because he knew she didn't like to be idle. She considered it improper to interrupt her tasks, and speaking, for her, was a form of not working. How is the book coming on? she asked him, as she laid out and then folded each item of clothing after plucking it from the pile. There's a long way to go yet. I don't know if I'm going to have all the time I need for it, especially because I'm hoping to write a second part. The story of a man who, as a result of his steadfast refusal to rationalize the practice of assassination, to legitimize means with ends, as well as his conviction that violence is every bit as unjustifiable as— What?

The two of them burst out laughing. He wasn't in Stockholm, delivering his acceptance speech before the Swedish Academy, or in the editorial department of some newspaper, trying to fire up his coworkers and put out an issue with the power to transform hearts and minds the world over. Jacques tried again. It's going to be the story of a chance but inescapable fate. The fate of a man who's taken a stand against violence, the death penalty, and terrorism, had his life threatened as a result, and even goes on to die in an attack that's arranged to look like a straightforward accident. But before I get to that, I have to finish the other part. He'd been working on it for a long time, trying to recover the memory of the poor, of his kin, the few remaining traces of all those humble, simple people he'd known in his childhood and youth. Whom he'd loved above all else.

On the one hand, there was all the beauty. But there were also the downtrodden. And he'd set himself the knotty task of not being unfaithful to either. To the memory of people like Carina, who was now staring at him in fright. Isn't there anyone you can go to for protection? Jacques shook his head. No, I don't think so. Besides, it's only a hypothesis, he added. You can't fool me. You've been looking worried for days. There might not be sufficient cause, Jacques continued. Just a tidy collection of threat-filled missives, although I'll admit there's so many of them that I've sometimes thought I should be walking around in a fifteenth-century suit of armor. And a couple of warnings, too. But no, it's nothing the police can really do anything about. And besides, I wouldn't like to live that way, kept under constant watch. Jacques had recently received a letter from Marseille. A teenaged boy newly arrived from Algiers, just like himself all those many years ago, had written to warn him of the danger he was apparently in. The boy, who'd just turned fifteen, had included a photograph of himself. He must have been five foot eleven, and he had a parrot perched on his left shoulder, but he'd inscribed it with his first name only. Antoine. Maybe he was scared.

A month after receiving the letter, Jacques had dreamt about him, dreamt that he was in danger and asking him for help. Immediately upon waking, he remembered that there'd been a story in the newspaper that very day about an attack carried out in a café in Marseille. A straightforward revenge attack, according to the press. He didn't know why, but he'd instantly thought of the boy. The topic—organized violence— was becoming an obsession for him, one he could hardly discuss with anyone. The boy had written in his letter of a chance encounter with a couple of hit men. Of a photo of him, of Jacques, that it seems he'd caught a glimpse of where it lay on a café table, of his face with a red circle drawn around it. He'd recognized him at once, because, being something of a bookworm, he'd seen his portrait at the public library. The photograph he described to him was a real one. It had been taken in 1945 at a table outside the café Aux Deux Magots, in Paris. The one sitting next to him smoking, a strapping man in a suit and tie, was Pierre Galindo, one of his friends from back in his Oran days. The third man, who was wearing an overcoat and sitting with his back to the camera, was Paul Bodin, a special reporter with *Combat* who'd been assigned to Brussels. A fellow Resistance member.

Jacques didn't know what to think. One minute he'd be completely untroubled by all these threats, and the next he'd be consumed by fear, by an irrational feeling of distress. To calm this anxiety, which he didn't care to acknowledge, he took out a pack of Gitanes from his pants pocket, stuck one between his lips, and lit it with a match he held cupped inside both hands. They were indoors, so there wasn't any wind at all, but he was in the habit of lighting up like that. Ah, cigarettes, he breathed, looking at the packet before putting it back into his pocket. It was blue, with the silhouette of a Gypsy woman waving goodbye from inside a fog of gray and white tobacco swirls. These things are pure poison. But I can't quit. They make me cough, make my throat raw, and it's getting harder and harder for me to breathe properly. Carina smiled. Not to mention you hardly sleep, you don't eat enough, and you work too much, she remarked with the sort of sweetness that comes from selfless concern.

I'm a weak man. My doctor laughs every time he sees me. To keep himself from crying. And he's absolutely right. Tobacco's not for you, he tells me, patting me on the back at the end of every examination. But he knows I'm a lost cause. It was true. He shouldn't be smoking. And yet he was powerless to stop. If somebody didn't stick a gun to his forehead quick, the tobacco would get him soon enough. His lungs were destroyed. How does a person know when his final day has

113

come? A writer is a man ahead of his times, he thought, still finding himself unable to quite shake off the idea that someone might actually try to kill him. There were plenty of precedents. Of writers who'd managed to glimpse beyond the horizon that's visible to most of their contemporaries. Dostoyevsky, Nietzsche, Kafka. Might he be able to predict, to describe, even, his own death? Perhaps writers would, like Oedipus, be well-served by an extra eye. And being as he was a connoisseur of the theater, his thoughts turned to that tragic hero, the victim of a hostile transcendence whose ire he'd unleashed with his—perhaps imprudent—exploit.

Everything he'd predicted would happen in Algeria was coming to pass. And there was still more to come. If soccer taught me anything, he remembered having written at one point, it's that the ball never comes at you from where you'd expect. Yes, the blow might come from any direction. From head on, which was clearly the preferable option, as it afforded the possibility of mounting a defense. But it could also come from behind. And just as easily from the left as from the right. From the French Algerian ultras, say. Jacques had been the target of a number of increasingly aggressive attacks. Having his work censured wasn't what bothered him; he had his own reservations about it himself, persistent, profound reservations. Moreover, those people were completely within their right. But he often got the impression that what he was actually dealing with was a thoroughgoing campaign directed against his person, the explosion of a long-repressed feeling of hatred. And the number of threats he'd received in recent years was so great that his urge to get out of Paris had grown quite acute.

There'd been direct threats, too, spoken to his face. From the bravest ones. Others had been transmitted to him over the phone. By voices he couldn't recognize. Perhaps because they'd been distorted. Or because the people calling were total strangers. Still others had come to him by mail. Anonymous letters. There were even a few letterpress-printed ones. He had a whole drawer full of the things. There were almost as many of them as there were of the letters he'd written in the hopes of staying the executions of all those many individuals who'd been sentenced to death, one of whom had later come out against him. For not even that favor, the greatest that can be done for another human being, had been enough to stop the man from turning around and berating him in the most humiliating terms. Thankfully, when he went there, to that house, to write, it was as if all those voices somehow fell away, as if they were silenced forever. The reproaches, the malicious, ill-intentioned abuse. Any intimidating letters addressed to the Paris office were collected by Suzanne, his secretary. He didn't even want to see them anymore.

Jacques looked off into a distance that was nonexistent from where he stood, since the blinds were half closed and almost nothing could be seen through them. Anyhow, he said, at least I've finally found the cemetery I'm to be buried in. And nodding his head to one side, after taking a final drag off his cigarette, he gestured toward the town's burial ground. It will do very well for me. Besides, he added, trying to lighten the effect of what he'd just said, I'm starting to look a bit like a cadaver already. There's this insect that's been buzzing around me for a week that looks like some sort of gutter flower. Carina set down the iron and turned around. The row of cypresses was just visible beyond the wooden blinds. Their support stakes, the ones that were still in place, that is, since several had long since gone missing, swayed from side to side in time to the breeze. Jacques noticed that the brown velvet of the girl's eyes was now moist. Had she already buried someone? She was very young, although that didn't necessarily signify anything. The first thing some people learn of is suffering.

Carina smiled sadly. You don't have to answer if you don't want to. No, on the contrary. It will do me good. It's more painful when I'm alone. And she picked up the iron again and went on with her work, going back over a pillowcase and folding it carefully, then suddenly she began to speak, slowly, calmly, as if in a dream. One Saturday afternoon, when I was thirteen years old, my brother Héctor and I had been doing our homework and we started kidding around, looking up bad words in the dictionary to make ourselves laugh. My mother was very angry. The next day was Sunday. Héctor would go off to the fields with my father to graze the cattle, and when Monday came around and it was time to go to school, his homework would be incomplete. So she scolded us, and we got back to work, but we quickly grew distracted and started playing with the dictionary again. I asked Héctor to look up the word "cemetery." And then, every word we could think of that was in any way connected to death. We were always looking for things we thought would be forbidden. And so we frittered away the day and barely did any of our work.

When we woke up the next morning, it was a foul, cloudy day. The wind was blowing, and it had a damp smell to it. My father was supposed to spend the day tending to the animals, but he didn't want to take my brother along with him that morning. Héctor was only ten years old, but he'd already taught him everything. How to ride horses, how to train them for racing. How to feed them. How to take the cows out to graze and then bring them back home. He even accompanied him on days when he went to buy or sell livestock. There's a storm coming, my father told him simply, but Héctor pressed him. And he got his way. My father let him go with him.

Then Héctor insisted on saying goodbye to everybody, one by one. My grandma Selunga, my father's mother, was deaf, and since she couldn't hear him, Héctor got off his horse, touched her, and said—Grandma, I'm going. She still didn't hear him. Grandma, I'm going! When Grandmother realized that her grandson was trying to say goodbye to her, she exclaimed— All right, it's not as if you're going away forever. You never know, Grandma, he replied, and he gave her a very big kiss, so that she would not only feel it but would be able to smell him, as well.

I went out to the road to see them off. And when Héctor turned to look, I did a funny little dance for him. He always loved seeing me dance. He waved at me. That was the last time I saw him alive. Up on his horse, waving goodbye. Carina took a deep breath and set the iron upright on the work surface. Jacques, not daring to say a word, kept his eyes fixed on her unwaveringly. Every one of her movements was painfully beautiful. No Paris women moved like that. None of them spoke with such sweetness. That same afternoon, the storm broke. We were all very scared at home, because everything went black, and the thunderclaps burst above our heads. Lightning lit up the whole house. We knew the two of them were still out there, but we said nothing. We could barely bring ourselves to look at one another. And in the evening, one of the neighbors came over on his tractor, looking for my mother. She went out to see what he wanted and then came back into the house crying. I have to go, she told me, because he says something's happened to Father, but I know it's Héctor, because if something had happened to Father, Héctor would have asked to come home and stay with you girls.

She was right. My brother never left our side if our parents had to be somewhere. My mother went, and I was left there

117

with Carmela, who was six, and Mariana, who was still a baby. Grandmother hadn't realized there was anything going on. She hadn't even noticed the storm. I was so distraught, I finally went up onto the roof of the house to see if I could spot anyone coming. I climbed the ladder up to the attic, pushed aside a few stacks of things, opened a little window, and then used a stool to get out onto the roof. Finally, after a long wait, a truck appeared, carrying several neighbors and my aunt Rosa, my father's sister. I ran down, and my aunt, right as she walked in, told me to go get some clothes for my brother. But why? Where's he going? Aunt Rosa said to me then—Héctor's been struck dead by lightning. What? I answered. But he was supposed to come give the lambs their milk . . . We had two little goats who'd lost their mother, and the two of us were in charge of giving them their bottles. Then I broke into tears. I went to his closet, and I picked out a little shirt with red and white stripes. And a pair of corduroy pants. Afterward, I went to get my little sisters ready.

Jacques listened attentively while she told him all this. Her eyes were still calm, if a little more agleam. I remember almost nothing of the journey to the house where everyone was waiting for us. Only that when we passed the spot where it happened, my aunt told me—Look, that's where the lightning hit him. No one else heard that. She told it to me in a whisper. The first thing I saw when we arrived were two men crying against a wall. One of them was my father. I threw myself at him, and he hugged me. He told me I had to be strong. That Héctor was in Heaven now. My father tried to buck me up, but he couldn't, because he'd seen it all. There were a lot of people there. All the men who worked on the farmstead. And their families, too. My mother was waiting inside, next to my brother, who was laid out on a bed and looked as if he were sleeping. Like he was smiling. My mother took my hand and said to me very calmly—Come closer, Carina. Touch him. Don't be afraid. In the sweetest of voices.

It was the first time I'd seen a dead person. My brother was cold. And I didn't understand a thing. Then my mother lifted up his little shirt, the same one I'd chosen from his closet, they'd already dressed him in it. Carina paused, she took another deep breath, but then she went right on speaking, in that calm voice that must have sounded very like her mother's. A bolt of lightning came down from the sky and shot all the way through his chest, my mother said. Héctor had a line running across his torso. There was no blood. Just that tiny, little line, which was very dark. The lightning had burned everything inside him. The doctor said he hadn't suffered. Neither had the horse. Then I see him in the coffin. I wanted to cry, but my aunts told us not to, so that my parents wouldn't see us. But that was so damaging for me. And my sisters. I was so tired, I kept falling asleep. Carmela and Mariana slept at my side. And whenever I could, I would go up to the casket and I would look at him, and touch him, though they didn't let us in to where the deathwatch was very much.

The next day, to move him to the cemetery, we had to take the tractor and several trucks. Everything was muddy, and one of the men, one of my uncles or some neighbor, I don't recall, must have lifted me up onto the tractor. Inside the church is when I couldn't bear it any longer. When they put the lid over him. First they placed an aluminum lid on top of him and sealed it shut. That's when I lost hold of myself. Then they took him over to the niche. Don't cry, don't make a fuss, don't say his name, my aunts instructed me. But every night I would go to bed and I would talk to him. And I'd ask him— Héctor, where are you? Nobody explained anything to us. And one night I had a dream. In the dream, Héctor appeared before me on his horse and told me to get on, he wanted to show me something. I got on and saw that we were heading down to the cemetery. Why are you bringing me down here, *negrito*? I asked him. That's what I used to call him. Even though his skin was no darker than mine. Come on, come on, I want to show you something, he said. Then he brought me over to a grave, and he explained to me—This is where I am now. We aren't going to see each other anymore, but I'm always going to be right here, and we'll be together, even though you won't see me.

I never talked about it with my parents. I heard about what happened from Orencio, a friend of my father's who'd come across them on the road shortly beforehand. The two were on their horses. Héctor out in front. My father behind. Orencio joined them and then rushed ahead to open the door to the corral where they were going to put the animals. The weather had turned really ugly. It had been raining for a while, and everything was muddy. Suddenly Orencio felt everything light up behind him, and in that same instant he heard a very loud thunderclap. Never had a storm fallen so fiercely upon him. He turned around and saw the boy and the horse lying on the ground. He threw himself to the ground, as well, trying to help, but he couldn't see a thing. Everything was dark, and the lightning kept blinding him. He crawled over to where the boy lay, and touched him.

Le petit cheval dans le mauvais temps. Qu'il avait donc du courage. C'était un petit cheval blanc. Tous derrière et lui devant . . . Jacques must have heard that poem a hundred times before, set to music by Brassens and sung in that smooth, throaty voice of his to a beat that jounced along like the trotting of a horse. *Il n'y avait jamais de beau temps dans ce pauvre paysage. Il n'y avait jamais de printemps, ni derrière ni devant . . . Mais un jour, danse le mauvais temps, un jour qu'il était si sage, il est mort par un éclair blanc. Tous derrière et lui devant* . . . What a coincidence. What a whole lot of coincidences. The horse, the boy, the bad weather, the lightning. Ever since she'd begun speaking, he'd been feeling he'd heard the story before. But perhaps it was a common occurrence in the countryside. And yet, yes, for a moment he wondered whether Carina might not be making the whole thing up. But why? Jacques felt dirty for having even dared to think such a thing, and he looked at her. The edges of Carina's eyes were growing redder by the minute. Why would anyone lie like that? And not only that, how could she possibly simulate sadness so well? She wasn't one of his actresses, up on a stage.

I'm a monster, he thought, but that didn't stop him from asking—What color was the horse? She looked him straight in the eye. White. Jacques inhaled sharply. He gulped. With big, black spots, Carina added. The two of them stood there in silence for a few seconds, but she quickly resumed her story. We didn't go back to the house for a week. The first to return was my mother, and she asked me to accompany her to pick up Héctor's clothes. She told me not to be scared, that I could speak to him. At that point, we were already staying at the house my parents still live in now with my sisters. They brought us there shortly after Héctor's accident, it's a less remote place. The other house was so out of the way that we had to travel several miles by horse to attend our school classes. Héctor always worked the reins. Carina stopped. She took a deep breath. Jacques could hardly believe she was speaking this much at once. All on her own. It was the first time anything like that had ever happened.

When Carmela started going to school, too, and it got very cold, they'd hook up a little wagon for us. And when it snowed or started to rain, my mother would wrap us up in a blanket, covering us entirely, even our heads. The horses weren't ours, they belonged to the master, and even though Héctor was very young, he took excellent care of them. A few weeks after he died, my mother decided to go to the school and sit at his little bench. And chat with his best friend. After that, we began talking about him, not surreptitiously but all together, out in the open. Soon afterward, my mother worked up the courage to open Héctor's backpack, and she took out his exercise folder. There was a single sheet of paper inside, on which he'd written a list of our names and, next to them, what he liked about each one of us. He was not of this world, my father said. He'd written the list the day before going out to the fields with him. He must have done it while we were goofing off together and not doing our homework. Next to each name, he'd written, *I love you very much.* The same thing for each person. With the exact same words. I don't know if he sensed something. Maybe he wrote it without thinking.

My father wanted to have a plaque put in to mark the site of the accident, but the master, the proprietor of the farmstead at the time, wouldn't let him. He said it was a transit area for the livestock and might create a hazard. Now there's a new master, he came to the place a few years ago, and right when he arrived, as soon as he heard about what had happened, he asked my father to tell him everything. After listening to him, he gave him permission to install the plaque. It's just a marker, really, with his name and the years of his birth and death. Very small, right up against the side of the corral. Jacques imagined his own gravesite, in the cemetery of that town he'd finally found his way to. A simple stone marker with his name on it and the years of his birth and his death: 1913-1960. Yes, come next year, he might well be dead. Covered all over with wildflowers. With lilies, which grew so readily in that county. With different aromatic plants. Bay laurel, rosemary. Just then, the bells rang out.

Then strange things began to happen, Carina went on. The dog that had always tagged after Héctor went out every morning and spent the entire day lying on the spot where the accident had occurred. He only ever returned to the house at night, and one fine day, shortly afterward, he died. So did the two chickens that had belonged to him. Two guinea fowls, as my mother used to call them. Their feathers were gray, they looked as though they were covered in sequins. He'd taken care of them, fed them. I sometimes have queer dreams. And a few weeks before all this, I dreamed . . . Her voice cracked, but Jacques smiled, and she mustered the strength to continue. In the countryside, the women say that if a person dreams of murky, swirling, cloudy waters, something bad is going to happen. A few weeks before Héctor died, I dreamed that I was under water, very dark, turbid water, filled with gigantic branches, and roots, and mud. I couldn't swim, and I couldn't get out. But a voice kept telling me to keep swimming, because I had to save someone. You have to save him, it kept repeating. I obeyed and dove in a little further. Then I found something down there and pulled it out. It was a cross. There was someone on the cross, but I don't know who it was. It was years before I told anyone. Was it a sign? My mother says my dreams are omens.

Carina lowered her eyelids, took a deep breath in, and appeared to be attempting to collect herself in order to go on, as if she were trying to find her way out of that snarl of roiling waters from her dream. At that point, I became very angry with God. I felt a great deal of misdoubt. No, He doesn't exist, I told myself. How could He allow something like that to happen to a child? I didn't want to attend the masses that were held for him. I've never gone to any of the masses any of the times I've been back. They still hold one every year on his birthday. And another on the anniversary of his death. I prefer to walk down to the cemetery and bring him a flower. On my own. The poor devoid of hatred, thought Jacques. And he saw that a tangle had formed on the young girl's forehead. A knot of furious determination right between her eyebrows. The poor devoid of hatred. Those who are not compelled to rise up against their brethren, those who would never visit harm upon their fellow creatures. But it was necessary to rise up, he thought. And he recalled that shortly after coming to work for him at the house, she'd told him that she'd run into trouble with the Francoist police. It was the reason she'd fled Spain. It was something she had never wanted to explain, but it made her all the more irresistible in his eyes. And now he imagined her lying upon the ground, years ago, beating the cold, hard dirt with clenched fists, over and over again, pummeling the earth because she couldn't reach the heavens, demanding an answer of the immutable rock there beneath her. Why? Why? For her, justice had long since ceased to exist.

Jacques thought back to the lamppost attack. A few years ago. In Algiers. The faces of the three children who'd been killed. And he thought, too, about the scads of photographs of mutilated children he'd seen since then. Boys and girls who would have to live with that constant memory in their minds, in their dreams, day and night, the aftereffects shouldered by body and soul alike, and a glittering of sadness in their eyes very like the one he'd been seeing on Carina's face for the last several minutes. We're naught but bodies marked for death. All of us. And that should be enough to bring us together. He was convinced that the idea of death was the only thing capable of teaching people what truly matters in life. Which is almost nothing. It was something Carina's parents and sisters, those upstanding people with no greater aspiration than to partake mutually of whatever affection they might be able to show one another, had grasped early on.

We only have one photograph of Héctor, and it's been all eaten up by mold, she remarked suddenly. It must have gotten wet and then some paper got stuck on top of it. It's of him and me sitting on top of an enormous wheel. A tractor wheel. Both of our faces are covered in little green and orangish circles. But you can see his sun-kissed skin. His black hair. His sweet little face, frowning slightly because he was always so responsible by nature. Carina lowered her head and breathed in deeply. Then she picked up the iron again and started running it over the sleeve of one of Jacques's shirts. Forgive me, Carina, he thought silently. Forgive me for having listened to your story and not hardly spoken a word. She raised her eyes again and looked at him steadily, but Jacques realized her gaze was actually focused off in the distance. She was somewhere else. In another time. Eight years ago. You're one of the most extraordinary people I've ever known, he murmured. Was he falling in love? Again? How many times had this happened to him? No. He had no right. She's too young. Too good.

Carina's eyes were still on him, but a wide smile now lit up her face. And stepping over to him, she whispered—I don't know if I'm extraordinary, but I . . . She stopped for a second, perhaps intimidated by the potential consequences of what she was doing. But I do know, she repeated, working up her courage, then she faltered again for a brief instant before rushing through the rest of her sentence. That I'm very lucky to have met you. Jacques smiled, too, and could do nothing to stop himself from leaning in a little closer, despite the fact that

an evil little voice started humming away inside him again—
He never saw the Spring arise to gild the dreary landscape
o'er. *He never saw the sunny skies, either behind or before* . . . The
young girl lowered her eyelids. He would have liked for that
instant to last an eternity. Each standing so close to the other.
Raising one arm, Jacques brushed her oval face with the back
of his hand and felt her shiver. His breath caught. He felt all
the strength draining from him and his knees beginning to
buckle, when all at once she opened her eyes, which appeared
to him even blacker than ever, and brushed her lips against his
so lightly, it was as if she was afraid a kiss of hers might poison
him.

Carina then turned and dashed out of the room. He didn't
dare follow her. Only after a few moments had passed did he
walk away, too, lost in thought. The speechless ones. How
he enjoyed listening to them on the rare occasions when they
chose to speak. The rare occasions when they'd open their
hearts, as Carina had just done, often to a stranger, and allow
themselves, almost without noticing, to be carried away by
all the words that had been building up inside them. They
were the truly poor ones. The ones who had no voice. The
Speechless Ones, he repeated inwardly. They were and they
are greater than I.

IN THE NAME OF HISTORY

Cormery had only ever lost his wits once. Night had fallen after a scorching day there in that corner of the Atlas range where their detachment had made camp at the top of a small hill sheltered by a rocky gorge. Cormery and Levesque were supposed to relieve the watch detail that was posted at the foot of the gorge. Nobody had answered their calls. And behind a prickly-pear bush, they found their comrade with his head tipped back, staring at an odd angle straight up at the moon. At first they didn't recognize it as being his head, the silhouette was somehow off. It was simple, though. He'd had his throat slit. And in his mouth, that livid swelling was his phallus, in its entirety. Then they saw his body, his legs spread wide, his Zouave pantaloons torn open, and in the center of that opening, beneath the dim reflection of the moon, a pooled seepage. A hundred yards further on, behind a boulder, lay the second watchman, splayed out in the same fashion. The alarm was sounded, the number of sentries doubled.

At dawn, back at the camp, Cormery declared that those who had done this were no men. Levesque pondered and then replied that to such minds as theirs, it was precisely how men should act—they were in their own land and making use of whatever means were available to them. Cormery persisted

127

stubbornly. That may be. But it's wrong. A man doesn't do that. Levesque said that as they saw it, in certain circumstances, a man must allow himself everything, and destroy everything. Then Cormery shouted, as if overcome by a fit of rage—No, a man controls himself. That's what a man is. Otherwise . . . Then he calmed himself. I, he added hoarsely, am poor, I leave the orphanage, they stick me in this uniform, they drag me off to war, but I control myself. There are Frenchmen who don't control themselves, said Levesque. Then they aren't men, either, Cormery replied. Then suddenly he bellowed—A damn filthy race! Every last one of them, every last one of them . . . And he ducked inside his tent, white as a sheet.

Jacques rested his elbows on the table, letting his arms slip across it, pushing off to the sides the papers and the books that were littered all over it, and slowly hunched himself over. The sun was setting, and he was feeling depleted, too drained of strength to continue. He'd been writing for hours, nonstop, trying to capture one of the few episodes of his father's life he had any knowledge of, one he had always considered exemplary, because it provided a perfect illustration of what he believed it meant to be a man. His conviction that ends could not justify any and all means. But he closed his eyes and tried to think about something else. So many hours spent trying to fall asleep at night, and then sometimes during the day he might drop off in a matter of seconds. How does a person coax himself to sleep? By thinking about something beautiful? A landscape we'd like to return to? A woman? Or the light that always brings us joy? By imagining ourselves floating in the cool salt water of an estuary, amid pine trees rustling in the breeze and goats clop-clopping over rocks? Or by trying to clear our minds of all thought? Jacques felt himself sinking into the darkness of his closed eyes, becoming lost in the labyrinth of his thoughts.

A hearse flew along at top speed, careening around every curve, nearly tipping off the cliffs that fell away to one side of that winding seaside highway. A Cadillac Eldorado Corbillard, specially outfitted for the transportation of bodies to their places of interment. The rear spoilers, each equipped with two pointed taillights that appeared to be shooting out flames, gave it the semblance of a spaceship, despite the fact that part of the roof and most of the interior were covered in funerary trimmings. Six silver-plated ornaments shaped like urns topped the chassis, while black silk curtains with an embroidered lily in the center of each panel festooned the rear and side windows. Lamps fashioned to look like torches occupied the spaces between the drapes of the side curtains, keeping watch over the departed. They'd set out before daybreak from the city of Marseille and were now turning onto the so-called Ridge Route, between Cassis and La Ciotat. A splendid day was dawning, and the two front windows were wide open. A long, pinewood box lay in the back, as if it had been left there by mistake, knocking up against the vehicle's walls. It was a plain, unembellished coffin.

The driver steered the car with one hand. His other arm was resting on the edge of the windowsill, and every so often he would grab the bottle he held stuck between his legs on the seat and take a swig or offer it to his companion, who invariably turned it down. The sunlight on the horizon was blinding. An odd light, too intense for that time of day and year. If I die, I want you to toss me into the sea, just as if I were a fish. Rouget had said that a few hours before the strike, and Hilal was determined to carry out his wishes to the letter. A dead man's will must not go unfulfilled. Superstitious by nature, he had from the outset disapproved of a redheaded man taking part in the operation, let alone as a member of his own unit, but he didn't have much say in the matter. Another one on about this, Khalîl thought to himself when Hilal had confided his misgivings, although the man's ignorance was somewhat of a mitigating factor. *Zim boum-boum: hier au soir et zim boum-boum, dans la rue Bab-Azoun et zim boum-boum, on a trouvé et zim boum-boum, une jeune fille assassinée . . .*

Hilal sang loudly as he drank. *Camus and Soda*, it said on the label, next to a horseman depicted from the waist up with his arm dangling at his side, just like his own, although the figure on the label was holding a riding hat instead of a bottle. Scotch Fashion, 43°. It was a cognac that could be found all over the world, and he'd picked it out at the shop on the sole strength of its name and the fact that it had a little horse and rider figurine hanging from the cap. The idea of mixing it with soda was revolting, but they'd seen an oldish-looking poster on the wall showing a boxer toasting his victory with a French king, standing at the foot of the ring. It was in black and white, except for the brandy in their glasses, which was tinted golden. Khalîl had been taken with the print. It's Georges Carpentier. The Gentleman of the Ring, he exclaimed the instant he saw it. *L'enfant prodige.* His father was a miner, and he wanted Georges to follow in his footsteps, but since he was a scrawny sort of kid, he decided to send him to a gym. The boy took such a shine to it and showed such promise that the coach had no choice but to ask his parents for permission to let him train properly and become a boxer. He offered to pay them all the money the boy would have earned in that same stretch of years had he been working in the mine.

And who's the king? Hilal had inquired. *Le bon roi Henri,* Khalîl replied. A brave and gallant king who changed his religion on six separate occasions. From Catholicism to Protantism and back again, threatened at times by his father, at others by his stepbrother—then king of France—and finally put under pressure by the majority of his own subjects once he himself ascended to the throne. Neither of the two sides must have been all that happy with him, because they tried to assassinate him a good number of times, and in the end they were successful. A king who went out of his way to ensure that towns and cities taken in times of siege weren't sacked and that their inhabitants were treated with respect. A man magnanimous with his foes. Go in there and buy a bottle, he'd told him suddenly. This poster's put me in a good mood. Hilal had stolen the car in the early hours of the morning, before the crack of dawn, after assisting in a disciplining operation the night before. Marseille was another city with an abundance of funeral parlors. Very poorly guarded ones, he smiled to himself in satisfaction. *Mourrez!* read a sign at the entrance. *Nous ferons le reste.*

Khalîl wasn't overly thrilled with the choice of vehicle, and he remained lost in thought as he rode along in the passenger seat, but at least he'd conceded to the whims of another for once. Not out of respect for the dead man, whom he couldn't have cared less about, but in order to give a little freer rein to the feeling of euphoria that always followed such assignments. Binge drinking like some mangy *Rumi*, the poor devil, he thought. And exposing his underbelly so pathetically like that. He might almost have felt sorry for him, if it weren't for the fact he felt so disgusted by him. At least this way he had him at his mercy. On the other hand, he did love danger. He was a hard man to frighten. Periodically, and silently, as was his wont, he shot hostile glances at Hilal, though he trusted his skill as a driver even when slightly drunk. All of a sudden, the bottle, which his partner had apparently just drained of its last drops, went flying out the window and smashed against the pavement. There was a loud shattering noise, and the spot where it had fallen was covered in shards of glass. It's a pity this is where you ended up. Hilal turned to him, grinning. You could have been famous. Gone into writing. Been a poet. Or a movie actor. It's not just that you're smart, you've got that great physique . . .

Khalîl stared daggers at him. The alcohol was emboldening him to excess. It was one thing to have a little anisette once in a while, as he himself occasionally did, but it was quite another to fall prey to inebriation, to lose control. His patience was wearing thin. *Et la police et zim boum-boum, toujours pleine de malice et zim boum-boum, collait des affiches et zim boum-boum, sur lesquelles on lisait: hier au soir . . .* Khalîl switched on the radio to see if he could get that stupid dunce to quit prattling on and singing, but as soon as it came on, there was a new melody, so he changed the station. During those few instants, Halil commenced with the new song and then broke into a fit of laughter. Khalîl turned the dial again. The news. Of course. Why hadn't he thought of that in the first place? It was the surest way to put an end to that ridiculous warbling. Or some cultural broadcast.

We now bring you an interview recorded for Radio-diffusion-Télévision Française this past January. Pierre Dumayet sits down with Albert Camus to discuss the premier of his play, *The Possessed.* Khalîl's ears pricked up. And Hilal waved his hand at the same time, most likely signaling for him not to change the station. What a coincidence, he thought. He'd just been drinking *Camus and Soda*, and now he was about to hear the voice of Albert Camus himself. And leaving off his singing, he gave a chuckle and focused his attention. The two men seemed to find themselves on the same page for once. The winner of the Nobel Prize for Literature speaks to us today about his adaptation of the highly acclaimed novel by

Dostoyevsky, which premiered in Paris's Antoine Theater on January twenty-ninth of this year and was recently published by Éditions Gallimard. The play, which came last month to Venice's famed Teatro La Fenice, where the author was in attendance on opening night, is now embarked on a tour that will take it through several provincial capitals as well as abroad.

And to start us off, Albert Camus is going to give us a brief overview of the conspiracy upon which Dostoyevsky's work is based. In 1869, a student named Ivanov was killed by a small band of conspirators that was led by an individual who would later become a celebrated Russian revolutionary, Nechayev. Ivanov was exterminated for disagreeing with Nechayev's views. You might say it's the first instance of crime devised for use as political craft, it caused a great deal of uproar in its day. Dostoyevsky took this incident as his starting point for composing *The Possessed*. Note that this revolutionary did not take the life of some tyrant but instead killed one of his own confederates. Is this, in your opinion, a prophetic novel? I believe that it is, indeed, a prophetic novel. The writer coughed and cleared his throat, but immediately continued, his voice reflecting a mix of timidity and affectation. Because it speaks to the nihilism that comes to engulf even the most benevolent of ideologies, which is one of the central pillars of Dostoyevsky's own personal preoccupations. Who's this *Dostowsky* guy? Hilal asked. A Russian writer from the last century, Khalîl replied, his eyes flickering in the other man's direction with a tinge of contempt.

The worst of it wasn't that he didn't know who he was, or the tone in which he'd asked his question, but the fact that he wasn't even able to repeat the name he'd just heard. He was an idiot. Given the events that transpired after Dostoyevsky's death, there can be little doubt that *The Possessed* was a much more prophetic book than many others out there that were trying to pass themselves off as such. Do you feel that, inasmuch as it is a prophetic book, it's also a topical book? Absolutely. At some point, the prophecy becomes self-fulfilling. Is that what's happening right now? the interviewer interjected again. I like the way he talks, Hilal remarked. But the guy asking the questions is plain sickening. A worthless lackey. Khalîl burst out laughing. He was right. Just by listening to his voice, you could tell he must have one of those unctuous smiles, and lips like you might see on some page boy, itching to prove his worth with world-class obsequiousness but at the same time completely full of himself, perfectly capable of humiliating anyone who might let him get away with it. That may be, but you should know that for him, for Camus, and for Dostoyevsky, as well, it's we who are the demons. Or the possessed. Or a bunch of sick individuals fighting off one plague by spreading another.

He has to be killed, Hilal cut in sharply. Yes, all those who stand in our way must be killed, Khalîl replied. And then one day the world will be a desert. At this point, it's indisputable that the characters Dostoyevsky portrayed are very similar to ourselves, Albert Camus went on in that peculiar accent of his, dragging out his words slightly, especially the adverbs he used to open many of his affirmative responses, perhaps in the hope of being better able to calibrate the weight of each of his remarks. In what sense? the interviewer invited him to elaborate. In that they have a hollowness in their hearts, an incapacity to embrace any faith or belief, which is one of the premonitions from Dostoyevsky's universe that we see coming true today. Is this nihilism one of the reasons you chose this particular work? Absolutely. It's one of the concerns that I share, obvious differences aside, with Dostoyevsky.

Stavrogin's confession, normally published separately and not as a part of *The Possessed*—you've included it in your play, is that correct? Yes. I included it because, essentially, Dostoyevsky . . . Hilal was fed up, and starting in on his song again, he spun the radio dial around, blithely indifferent as to whether his partner might care to continue listening to the interview or not. *Hier au soir et zim boum-boum* . . . For his part, Khalîl decided to give in and converse with the man, in the interest of sparing his ears any further punishment. Let's get back to Operation Golan. We've got him in our sights again. The organization is arranging to plant someone inside his house. I've suggested Slimane, I think he'd be perfect for a mission like this. So no more hits for now . . . Hilal nearly applauded at that, but then he checked himself. The idea of working with Slimane again was none too appealing. What if they sent in a woman instead? Maybe he likes them as much as you do. A pretty woman could make excellent bait. As soon as he said it, he regretted it. Not only because of how Khalîl might react, but because he just then realized that if Slimane was working in the capacity of spy, he wouldn't ever have to get very close to the two of them.

Last night, in the city of Marseille . . . Leave it there. Leave it. Khalîl swatted Hilal's hand away and turned up the volume on the radio. Continued reprisals among North Africans, this time in the form of a café shooting in which at least six people lost their lives. It is believed that one of the gunmen, who fled before police could arrive on the scene, may be gravely injured. Several witnesses have reportedly come forward who may be able to provide information crucial for the composition of a police sketch of at least one of the assailants. Up next, we turn to sports. Khalîl switched off the radio. He'd already seen his face pasted up on thousands of signs all across the city. His face multiplied hundreds and hundreds of times over. There were almost as many posters of him as there would later be posters advertising the upcoming run of *The Possessed*. Camus himself would come down to Marseille to handle the preparations personally. Khalîl remembered the names of some of the actresses in the cast. Catherine Sellers, Nicole Kessel, Nadine Basile. The names conjured up all sorts of dreams for him. As did the names of the Russian characters they brought to life. Marya Timofeevna Lebyadkina, Dasha Shatova, Liza Drozdova . . .

No. There were more, a lot more, of the placards with his own face on them. They were hanging up all over the city. Khalîl from the front. Khalîl from the side. Khalîl in color. Khalîl in black and white. Khalîl with a scar. Without a scar. Khalîl smoking a cigarette. Khalîl at various train stations, down at the port, at all different bus stops, on every corner. And he smiled. But no matter, he immediately thought to himself. These people will never dare say a word. Tough luck. They'll never talk. And he turned his attention to the landscape. Driving along those seaside curves at dizzying speeds reminded him of a movie he'd seen a few years back, the first time he'd come to the metropole. The main character, a young, blond millionaire vacationing with her husband on the French Riviera, was driving a stunning convertible along a highway very like the one they were on now. Her hands gripped the wheel of a sapphire blue Sunbeam Talbot Alpine, and she had the most beautiful arms he'd ever seen in his life. But the actress had shortly afterward become the princess of Monaco. Bullshit prince, he thought. A swine. Mustachioed, flush with millions, and stuffed into some stage prop uniform. Turning slightly in his seat, he looked at Hilal.

His strong, dark-skinned arm, rough and hairy, clutching the steering wheel of a funeral hearse, made him laugh.

There was a reason he liked the cinema so much. Reality was crushing. Downright awful. Hilal must have noticed the hostility in his partner's gaze, because he stopped his crooning and asked Khalîl to go over the previous night's hit with him, every minute of the operation, every shot fired. Perhaps as some sort of homage to Rouget. Or maybe because he couldn't quite bring himself to accept the whole thing, since many of the victims had been Arabs. Muslims, like themselves. But they'd had their orders, and they had to follow them. They were trapped in the *nidham* of the FLN, an apparatus from which escape was impossible. Cell, division, group, *kasma*, sector, district, region, zone, *amala, wilaya,* Federation of France . . . And the Federal Committee in Düsseldorf. An infernal pyramid. The only way out for them was in a box, just like their victims. Just like Rouget, who was riding there in the back, in the coffin. Silenced forever. Hilal hadn't gone inside the café the night before, so he didn't know the details of the strike. Khalîl would have to tell him what had really gone down.

A matter of taxes, Khalîl thought to himself. It's always the same. The National Liberation Front forced most North African citizens living in France to contribute a series of payments depending on their profession. A construction worker or a day laborer would have to pay two thousand francs a month. A Muslim woman, five hundred. A taxi driver, eight thousand. A Muslim prostitute, or a European one with a Muslim pimp, five thousand. The business of trading women among different pimps was charged with sums ranging from one hundred thousand to five hundred thousand francs, depending on the value of the particular goods under exchange. A shop owner, ten thousand, although the figure might be higher depending on the status of the business. All professions were subject to similar taxes. In addition to these, there were donations, or dowries—in the case of weddings, for instance—fines for late payments, for tardiness or failure to attend organization meetings, for drunkenness, for smoking, for contracting mixed marriages, and for inappropriate behavior.

The FLN had a marked proclivity for prohibition. Individuals were not only prohibited from smoking, drinking alcohol, and gambling but also from keeping dogs. And dressing in the European fashion, although that was mostly applied to women, to men only on certain occasions, and never to the higher-ups. And from voting, in Algeria. And going to the movies. A few years ago, several bombs had gone off at the Olympia and Donayazad movie halls, in Algiers. An Arab-language film festival was taking place. All of the victims were Muslim women. A fine for smoking, Khalîd mused, and he took out a pack of cigarettes from his pocket. *Brune ou Blonde. Une Bastos affirme votre personnalité*, he read, then he slipped it back into his pocket. Being in the Hexagon was a treat. In his own country, people got their noses and lips chopped off for such things. Nothing escaped the organization's greedy grasp. When you came right down to it, it was no more than a business, and as such it had to be run carefully, because a lot of people were benefitting from all the money. Oodles of bills. And they, the custodians of collection for that entire *wilaya*, were in charge of punishing all those who fell behind on their payments.

We're fighting so that the French will withdraw from our territory. And after they've withdrawn, then what? We'll continue killing each other. That's what we're already doing, after all. Fighting is a common occurrence among Muslims. Among the chiefs of the different *wilayas* or power centers. Between Kabyles and Arabs. Between intellectuals and peasants. We're in the middle of a civil war. *Harkis*, Messalists, *caids,* army veterans, *bachaghas*, *moghaznis*, deputies, forest rangers, *ulemas*—we've got all of them in our crosshairs. The great traitors. Do you know who Napoleon was? he asked suddenly, swirling to face his partner. Hilal blinked at him in stupefaction, and Khalîd couldn't tell if it was because he didn't know who he was, because he thought it was just the name of a brand of Cognac, or because he did know who it was and couldn't believe he was being asked such a question. Whatever the case, he didn't feel like getting to the bottom of it, and he quickly lost what little desire he had to explain himself. If Napoleon had been at the head of the French nation right then, he thought, perhaps nobody would have felt like seeking independence.

It's not the same thing to have to submit to one of these de Gaulles as it would be to a man like Napoleon. The anti-colonialist Left allowed itself certain exemptions. As did the Arabs. Who could possibly be against Bonaparte? Forget it. Let's go over last night's strike. No more history lessons for Hilal. This guy's all about cars. Motorcycles. The owner of the café, which like so many others was a front for a brothel, had gone several months without paying his revolutionary taxes, thus securing himself a punishment that would likewise serve as an example to everyone else, and a warning to the following owner. At 22:36 the previous day, a man with matted, dyed-blond hair and a wool beanie pulled down to his eyebrows had come into the café, sat down at a table, and ordered a tea. The owner, an Algerian man from Constantine about forty years old, told him they were about to close but served him his drink. As he sipped at it, Slimane, for that was the name they'd given their prowler for the purposes of this particular operation, glanced around to see how many people there were inside the establishment. He had clear eyes and a lynx's gaze, and he used them to calmly survey each and every corner of the room. As he'd suspected, there was hardly anyone there at that time of night.

The owner was standing behind the bar, next to the cash register. Sitting at one of the tables were four men playing dominoes. You could hear the *click, click* of the tiles on the hard surface. A turntable up on the bar was playing, too. A woman's voice singing. Seated around another table, a couple of Arab prostitutes were finishing their dinner before heading back up to their rooms to sleep or go on with their work, as the case may be. There were two other women sitting with them that looked European. And a young boy. Maybe they worked there, too. As prostitutes, cooks, or cleaning women. The boy was probably one of the two's son. Up at the bar, but on the front side of it, stood a waiter. Slimane rose and headed for the bathroom, walking through a room with red rugs and cushions all over the floor. He checked that there wasn't anyone else there in the back. Then he returned to his seat and paid. At 22:44, he left the café.

Once outside, he'd adopted a slinking, feline gait. He was somewhat eccentric, but those thespian predilections, which at times might draw suspicion to him, were what made him such a fantastic associate, because, as Khalîl himself had once remarked shortly after making the man's acquaintance, they allowed him to move around with ease and great poise in any environment. Slimane had gone around to a side street, a dark one, where two cars sat parked with their lights switched off and their windows rolled down. A black Peugeot 403 and a gray Simca Aronde. Nervous knees, quick calves, and agile ankles. That was Khalîl's assessment as he watched him arrive. And in an admiring tone quite out of character for him, he'd added—Like a champion cycler. Slimane had approached one of the cars, leaned in at the open window on the driver's side, where Hilal sat, with Khalîd next to him, and given them a full rundown of everything he'd seen inside.

From the backseat, two more men had listened in carefully. A redheaded Algerian man from Oran, named Rouget, and a Kabyle man with light eyes, almost green, and fine clothing, a member of the OS, the Special Organization, who'd come to supervise the operation. Those guys were the elite, men trained abroad, in Morocco, Egypt, Iraq, and even Russia. They were paid generous salaries and could afford expensive clothing, a certain lifestyle. Even when they were in jail—the few times the police ever managed to catch them—they still drew their salaries. After detailing the situation inside the café, Slimane had left. He was only an informer. With slightly too odd a look about him to ever be taken for an Arab. Dyed-blond hair, a muscular physique, and strange attire like his were not common among them. He'd been born in Belgium, one of the countries where the Front had established itself most firmly. And if more than one Westerner had managed to sneak into the sacred city of Mecca, why shouldn't he, with his considerable interpretive gifts, be able to pass for just another random customer in that café?

He always seems like he's playing a role. He'd make an impeccable actor, Khalîl had remarked as soon as he was out of sight. He can calculate his effect on people with millimetric precision. Hilal had felt a stab of jealousy at that. In a flash, Khalîl and Rouget had stepped out of the car. Meanwhile, the door of the other vehicle had opened, as well, and two other men had stepped out. The only person left in the Peugeot was the driver. In the Aronde, there was Hilal, at the wheel, and the Kabyle man from the OS. The four other men, who'd already set out in the direction of the café, were dressed in either trench coats or long jackets. One of them posted himself at the entrance, a machine gun in hand. At 22:47, Rouget, Khalîl, and the other unit member, after kicking in the door, had burst into the café, pulling out guns from beneath their clothing and raising them quickly. *Click, click.* Khalîl, a Beretta. The other two, a machine gun each, a STEN and a MAT-49.

The light glinted off every curve, every line of my gun. The turntable cut off. The *click, click* of the dominoes cut off instantly, too. That's when we opened fire, guided by the information given to us by Slimane. With one of the machine guns trained on the bar, we took out the owner and the employee who was standing at one corner of it. The other was turned on the domino table, although at that moment there were only three men sitting at it, all of whom were quickly mowed down. Suddenly, the fourth man had appeared in the doorway that led to the back, and he'd raised a revolver and took aim at them, leaving Rouget seriously wounded. Khalîl had taken his automatic and felled the aggressor on the spot. It was written in the stars, Halil later remarked, with a swelling of self-importance. It was written in the stars. His shirt's been stained with red, and now we have to toss him into the sea. The air inside the place was heavy with the smell of gunpowder. Of chlorite. The floor, littered with 9 mm casings. The walls and the furniture, splashed all over with blood. After a few seconds of complete silence, we let the prostitutes, who were quaking with fear and cowering with their heads between their elbows, go and scurry away. They knew they'd have a new master soon enough, and they trusted the new one would pay the FLN.

They scampered for the door as if they'd just seen a rat. But before they could reach it, I leapt at one of the women and the boy who was with them. I shouted at them to turn around. Everybody up against the wall! You can guess who it was. I told you we'd run into them again eventually. The women obeyed. Only the boy refused. Resisted. He shouted in my face that he didn't turn his back on anyone. He wouldn't turn around, he raised his eyes to mine and held them there . . . Khalîl's voice faltered. The boy's gaze must have been stamped on his memory. Suddenly the parrot, which had apparently been hiding under the table, started flapping and screeching all over the room. I drew a bead on the moving target and shot it dead. Three single feathers floated very slowly down. I'd been waiting a long time for that moment, he said, turning to look at Hilal. I hate birds. Caged birds. Domesticated birds. Ever since the day that parrot did this to me. And once again, he raised a hand to his cheek. Hilal didn't dare utter a sound. And his partner continued the story. At that very same moment, as the parrot was falling to the floor, Khalîl had gone and knelt beside the café owner, who was gulping his last breaths of air. I took out my knife and I sliced his throat in a single, long stroke. Then I unzipped his pants . . . That was all that need be said. He'd emasculated him just as cleanly.

It was nothing but a meeting place for Messalist traitors, many of them railway workers, but the owner, in addition to being a member of the MNA, the Algerian National Movement, led by Messali Hadj, was a police informant. A Messalist pig. They'd dug out a sawed-off shotgun from behind the bar. And they made sure not to leave behind any of the weapons belonging to the domino players, either. I walked out of there clean, not a single drop of blood on me, Khalîl said. But they'd had to go back for Rouget, who they hoisted out one man on each end. It was 22:50. They'd made for the cars, slightly more slowly than planned. He knew the rest. At 22:52, each of the vehicles had taken off in a different direction. The Peugeot was parked back in another of Marseille's many neighborhoods, in the same spot where they'd picked it up hours earlier. They had a blanket, and they wrapped the wounded man in it. They left the keys inside a hollow space in one of the bumpers, and then they went their separate ways. In one direction, Khalîl and Hilal with the dying man. In the other, the Kabyle gentleman. A university professor would retrieve the car in the morning and drive it calmly off to work. The owner. And they'd arranged that in the event it wasn't in its spot, he was to report the disappearance as if it were a robbery.

All of them were using false names. Bashir, André, Baoualem, Philippe, Slimane, Rouget, Hilal, Khalîl. And they'd change them again. The next time, they might be called Sputnik, Tarzan, Moustache, l'Ange Blanc, Dada, Judoka, Petit Boxeur, White Teeth, or Lunnettes. They'd been brought together for that operation and that operation only. They knew they'd never see each other again, except the two partners. And now maybe Slimane, although he'd have to spend his time monitoring his target, so they wouldn't have much occasion to meet. The remaining members of the commando would follow other paths. They'd carried out their orders in military fashion—on short notice and with great precision. Hilal stopped the car on the shoulder of the highway. They stepped outside and pulled out the box with the dead man in it. They carried the coffin to the edge of the cliff and, after opening the lid, tipped the whole thing over slightly. The body slid out almost instantly and tumbled downward, toward the water. Now he really did look like a red mullet, with his bloodstained body, pink and slimy, encased in that makeshift sack. They'd stuck a few rocks inside so that it would sink as quickly as possible. *Die! We'll take care of the rest.*

144

And after smacking against several rocks jutting out from that otherwise sheer wall, the body sank into the sea, disappearing beneath the ever-widening concentric ripples created by his fall. Without ever opening their mouths, Khalîl and Hilal stood there watching those circles until the water's surface was once more still. Then they each kicked at the coffin to send it over next, and it, too, smashed against the rocks, splintering into pieces. A few bits got snagged by clumps of brush. The rest continued their downward plummet. Their ideally numbered three-person cell hadn't lasted long. But the two of them had already turned to face the highway again, bringing their hands up to their foreheads to shade their eyes from the blinding sunlight. There was no time for sentimentality. They'd already given him an A1 funeral. Killing Algerians to emancipate Algeria, Khalîl mused. Killing men to deliver humanity. What an odd cast of the light. And at that very same instant, there was a sound, and his eyes darted toward his partner's.

Had somebody seen them? They weren't concerned either way. If anyone was unlucky enough to catch them in such an act, they'd simply take out their guns and the unfortunate snoop, even if he happened to be a gendarme, would go the same way as Rouget. Khalîl slipped his hand into his jacket pocket and stroked the red swizzle stick. Her curly hair, the tips of her breasts, her legs, long and thin. That little redhead had become his good-luck talisman. A bullet had grazed him recently during a shootout, leaving no more than a slightly red line across his right temple. A few weeks and you wouldn't be able to see a thing. In the end, the only thing he'd have left would be that woman in his pocket, red and cold, unspeaking. He took her out for a moment and examined her closely. What an expression she wore. Tightly pursed lips, hooked nose, brow knitted over her eyes, her gaze aloof. His stirrer seemed perpetually angry, forever at war with the world. Once again, he'd allowed himself to be carried away by a first impression. He raised his eyes to look out over the sea, and for a moment he felt as if he were in his homeland, in Algeria. Why was all that—the sun, the sea, the fields in bloom behind him, the most simple and natural life, laughter, swimming, going for strolls—not enough? That almost animal life that holds within it something profoundly felicitous. Embracing a woman's body. Khalîl shivered. We are as nothing, his partner suddenly remarked. What a hackneyed thing to say, he thought. And yet, how true. But as he headed back over to the car to leave, Hilal, as if he'd been reading his mind, declared—Wherever you are, death will find you. And he slammed down the door of the trunk, which they'd left open earlier to take out the coffin. The tassels on all the curtains shook. Alcohol and gambling, idols and divining arrows, are but the filthy work of Satan, Khalîl answered back with another passage. Let's forget about the Qur'an, shall we? For a second, they locked eyes, sizing one another up, but then they quickly got into the car. They'd drop it in some random coastal city and steal another, a more discreet one, for the journey back to Marseille, their operational base. Hilal revved the engine and turned the radio back on.

Was it difficult to adapt *The Possessed* in this manner? Is the book too far removed from the theater? *The Possessed* is a novel that is very closely connected to the theater . . . You're kidding me. He's still talking? These guys don't just shoot off page after page of text, they yammer on endlessly, too. Maybe it was actually another station, broadcasting the same interview. Or maybe it was the same one. Maybe it really did go on that long. Perhaps writers, anxious to leave behind some trace of their passage through this life, have an even greater verbal incontinence than the rest of us mortals. Turn the radio off, Khalîl ordered. And after taking his cigarettes out of his pocket, he lit one. How strange it all is. And without realizing it, he said it aloud. Ever since they'd set out early that morning from Marseille, he'd had the constant, unshakeable feeling he was living a dream. As if Hilal and he were merely a pair of actors that were moving at the behest of a director, being guided through some oneiric sequence. That light, the hearse, the bottle shattering against the pavement, the coffin lurching around in the back, Hilal's crooning . . . We are but pawns on a giant chessboard. An invisible chessboard.

He inhaled deeply, stretched his arms a bit, settled down into his seat, and, leaning his neck back against the headrest, closed his eyes. They'd gone several days with almost no sleep. What if we just keep the car? Hilal asked suddenly. Not a chance. It's too conspicuous. You've had your fun with it. We'll drop it somewhere near Marseille, like I told you before, but first we'll find a nice, quiet beach and take a little dip to freshen up. Go swimming with that guy? The idea repulsed him. He'd inch away. Or just not get in the water. They had some clothes they could change into, and they'd burn anything with Rouget's blood on it. Or throw it into the sea. The sea cleanses all, Khalîl said to himself, as he pulled out the swizzle stick from his pocket again and brought it up to the level of his eyes so he could look through it. Woman-shaped sunglasses. And everything he saw was red. Or to be more precise, he couldn't see a thing. It was as if a gush or a sheet of blood were shrouding his sight.

Jacques opened his eyes, straightened up, and stretched his arms a bit. He'd fallen asleep on his writing table, and he'd dreamed again of the boy who'd written to warn him that a terrible menace was lurking on his path. I think you're in danger of being assassinated, he'd said. A man with falcon eyes and a scar on his cheek. What if it was all a bad joke? Or a mistake, one of those misunderstandings that crop up so often in life? How much stock should a person put in a letter like that? And what about dreams? A man's crooning voice outside shook him from his own dream state. Somebody must have been walking past the garden, out in front of the house. A perfume of flowers and breeze wafted in from the balcony. *Zim boum-boum: hier au soir et zim boum-boum, dans la rue Bab-Azoun et zim boum-boum, on a trouvé et zim boum-boum* . . . The same song as in his dream, and another voice, a very different one, unknown to Jacques.

AN IMPALPABLE MEMORY

And Jacques's father, killed at the Marne. What remains of that obscure life? Nothing, an impalpable memory, the weightless ash of a butterfly wing consumed in a forest fire.

All he had left was a photograph, a simple group snapshot. In order to see him properly, to adequately bring out that black-and-white figure lost forever in the midst of a regiment of men who like so many others had gone to fight in the French countryside only to be buried in mass graves, he'd have had to cut it out. To snip around or otherwise score the silhouette of that young man clad head to toe in the eye-catching uniform of the Algerian-born *tirailleurs*. The Zouaves. Their cropped, collarless jackets. Their sleeveless waistcoats. Their oversized, baggy trousers, fashioned from light-colored fabric. The *serousel*. And their woolen sashes wrapped around their waists. Their leather shin guards. Their fez-like hats with the tassel hanging from them. Or their turbans, in all different colors depending on where each battalion hailed from. Turbans cut from a cloth so long they sometimes used them as tents.

An entire detachment of men who'd been sent to their certain deaths all decked out in stunning regalia. Thousands upon thousands of men done up as if for some folk dance. The perfect target. The reds, blues, and whites of their raiment drew the focus of the enemy as a matador's magenta cape does a bull. Or his smaller red cape and dowel. They looked like fighting cocks, flaunting their plumage before an adversary they couldn't even see. They died before advancing more than a few steps. Jacques imagined the cries of the wounded, sprawling in the mud. Wait, what's this? Blood! Many of them had only just recently grown too old for play.

It was all he had left of him. That photograph and a chunk of the mortar that had killed him and that the government of France had gone to the trouble of having sent to his widow. His name was Lucien-Auguste Cormery. He was five feet, six inches tall. His hair and eyebrows were light brown. His eyes, blue. His occupation, according to his papers, driver. He'd been wounded at the Battle of the Marne and then transferred to the military hospital at Saint-Brieuc, where he endured a week of agony with a shattered skull. He'd died on October 11, 1914. That was pretty much all he knew about him. A few years back, Jacques got it into his head to visit his gravesite, which nobody in the family had ever been able to see. It was the grave of a stranger, but it made an enormously profound impression on him, because his father, when he'd died, was much younger than he himself was at the time. It was as if he were standing before the grave of his son.

Exhaustion was getting the better of him. He set the pen down next to his manuscript and leaned on the table. He was getting up every morning at around five and going for a walk out to the castle. After that, he got down to writing. And he wrote standing up. Like always. Or almost always, because he would sometimes set up out on the balcony. Or down in the garden. But he usually worked right there, at that tall, slightly slanted drafting table. He couldn't remain seated for hours on end. He needed to move. Not to mention the fact that he would almost immediately get a stiff neck, and then the pain would settle over the spot for days. He'd given himself eight months to make some good headway with his novel, and a substantial portion of that time had already come and gone. Rehearsals would start up at the theater soon, and then he wouldn't have much time to work on it. But for now, he left the table and went out onto the balcony.

That right there was the light of his childhood. A light, he mused, that not everyone has the good fortune to discover at such an early age, that many spend their entire lives looking for without ever finding it, perhaps because they don't even know they're missing it. That light, in certain landscapes, in certain people's eyes, that envelops us in a single instant of glory and teaches us what happiness is. He'd found that light as a child, he'd lost it when he left Algeria, and he'd never given up his search for it. He'd rediscovered it a few other times. In Greece, in Italy, and now here. In Provence. Jacques stepped over to the edge of the balcony. The butterflies there below him swished their wings languidly. Flitting over the plants in the orchard. And among the trees in each of the different gardens. Or fluttering from flower to flower. An Old World swallowtail had lighted on the stone balustrade and was now sitting so motionless it appeared as if it were injured. The cat, crouched at its post between the pots of roses and bougainvillea, stared at it with whiskers tensed. From the distance came the shrills of children racing through the town, the cool sound of water in the fountain. And every now and again, the bells rang out around him.

He liked standing there, gazing southward across that landscape, smoking his cigarette in the shade of the grapevines that grew along the eaves of the roof and wound their way down around the columns that supported it. Jacques recalled

151

an ancient Chinese proverb that stated that a butterfly's gently flapping wings could be felt on the other side of the world, a proverb closely resembling the theory according to which the slightest change in any one part of the planet might provoke large-scale cataclysms thousands and thousands of miles away. And what about distance in time? he wondered, and he began envisioning various series of absurd occurrences that might somehow be linked. In 1827, the governor of Algiers had thwacked the French consul in the face with a fly whisk. Then France—doubtless spurred by wounded pride and a desire for vengeance, one of the most ancient and deeply rooted of all impulses in the hearts of men and societies—had conquered Algeria. By the beating of a fly whisk . . . A billow of starlings set down in a fig tree just then, hopping along the branches and rustling among the leaves.

Jacques shifted his gaze back downward and looked at the small orchard spread out below him. Each of the houses along that edge of the town had its own plot of land out front. A very narrow path connected all the various orchards and gardens and their corresponding houses to one another. It was like an earthen trench or a secret passage, almost completely overhung with vegetation, and it skirted the entire southern portion of the town. Built into the outer wall of every house and in the fences bordering every orchard and garden, there was a little door. Down below, the afternoon sun lit up the lindens, the hundred-year-old olive trees, the bay laurels, and the fig trees, which always exuded a magnificent scent at that time of day. There was also lavender, in bloom, and mulberry, of course, and santolina bushes, almond trees, apricot trees, dracaenas . . . The pigeons, which in that region sported the same color plumage as the African gray parrot, cooed from underneath the shelter of the terracotta roof tiles.

Carina had gone down to water the plants and to feed Pamina, a jenny donkey that a friend had sent up to Jacques from Algeria. It hadn't rained a drop in a week, and the heat was oppressive, although the days were gorgeous and the sunsets even more so. Before night fell, the sky would take on a greenish turquoise hue that reminded Jacques of the sunsets in his own land. That scenery was what had convinced him to purchase the house, an old silkworm farm that smelled of wax and mold. And it seemed to him that if he but stretched out a hand, he could touch the African coast. Jacques drank in his surroundings. To the right, the castle. Across from it, a church. A little further on, the windmill, its blades now missing. In the distance, the foothills of the Petit Luberon Mountains, with their forests of Atlas cedars brought over from Africa so many long years ago. Straight ahead, to the south, the Durance Valley. And to the left, the tops of the cemetery cypresses. The swallows would be out in a few hours. Screeching, in pursuit of mosquitoes. They came out like that in the mornings and then again at dusk.

Jacques was convinced that when it came to art, one had to be realistic. Or rather, that one should strive to be, because he wasn't sure realism was indeed possible. Pure realism wasn't, that's for sure. People said photography provided an exact copy of reality, and that painting, on the other hand, picked and chose, but even the best photographs were a far cry from being carbon copies of reality. And even if you had a camera trained on a man day and night, filming his every most minute gesture, you still wouldn't have a faithful reproduction of his life. And this is because the reality of a man's life does not lie exclusively in the spot where he is. It resides in other lives, as well. In the lives of those he adores or abhors, but also in the lives of those who are complete strangers to him. All of a

153

sudden, the cat sprang up from where it had been sitting by his side and went over and stuck its head between the balusters. A man was standing at the entrance to the garden. He'd stopped there and must have been staring at Carina, who, as she often did, was lounging in the grass.

Jacques had asked her to go down there whenever she wanted a break. He liked seeing her lying there. Facedown, her sandals tossed onto the ground beside her. When she lay faceup, she would gaze at the clouds and rest her hands on her ribcage. But when she was facedown, as she was just then, with her head resting on her wrists, her eyes would scour the miniature world bubbling among the stalks and stems. A few feet above her, the blood in Jacques's veins simmered up, too. As he watched her. And he watched her often, admiring every one of her gestures, the naturalness of her movements when she didn't know she was being watched, as she in turn went about spying on all those scores of lowly creatures. There were ladybugs in their red, black-spotted suits. Bees, bundled inside their fur coats, shivering on flower tips. Beetles with glinting armor. Grasshoppers like camouflaged carpenters. Dragonflies copulating in bizarre equipoises. Aphids, ants. And myriads of miniscule, white-colored snails, speckled over almost every single plant like a sprinkling of flowers. They were dead, apparently, but they stuck fast to each shoot sprouting out of the dirt. There were thistles, too, so large they looked like magic wands crowned with stars.

Pamina would be munching carrots in the shed. The stranger set himself in motion. He didn't walk, he moved forward in curious, dancing steps, whisked along by the undulating rhythms of a melody that must have been playing inside his head. You could almost hear the music inspiring him to such a singular performance. The *darbukas*, the lute, the flutes, the tambourines. The movements of his body and the deftness and fluidity with which he traipsed through the bushes were exceedingly precise. All at once he was a statue, in silent equilibrium, as if the song driving him on were rippling itself out and had come right there to a standstill. He would gallop, slowly, and it seemed he sprouted horsehair. Or he'd flit like a fighter. That man was performing the dance of death. Of death? It looked more like a mating dance. Jacques didn't know who he was, although he'd spotted him a few times the last several days along some of the roads leading up to town. Continuing unabated his silent dance, on tiptoes atop lissome ankles, the prowler drew ever nearer. His muscles were like rubber bands. Carina appeared to ignore him, though she may have been following him out of the corner of her eye.

The stranger stopped again then lowered his head, raised and flexed his forearms, surveyed them, and kissed the muscles on each. First one, then the other. Jacques remembered the boxer Marcel Cerdan, the Casablanca Clouter, born in Algeria like himself and killed in a plane crash almost ten years ago. Just then, the intruder crouched down to pick up the jenny's blanket, which lay on the grass at his feet. He shook it out, pulled it taught and smooth, folded it carefully, and, one hand on his waist, executed a pass that nearly brushed right across Carina, who was lying there still. A long pass, from head to tail. Elegant, rhythmic, unhurried, gauging every distance. *Olé!* the man exclaimed, puffing out his chest, one leg planted behind him, red cap dangling, as if a bull had actually stuck its horn tips under the gathers of his cape and he'd sidestepped a goring by mere fractions of an inch and without so much as snagging the cloth. The impossible love of my life, he then spoke, his eyes focused on those incorporeal horns of air as he tossed the blanket aside and leaned over the body of the girl.

155

Carina lifted her head and blushed. A few, choice words were all it took to make her burn bright red, right down to the soles of her feet, which were now bare. The man regarded her from above with a hint of melancholy in his eyes, then he suddenly threw himself down alongside her on the grass, but in such a way that only their heads were touching. The man had blond hair, and he wore it pulled back in a small bun. Grinning, he appeared to be whispering something to Carina. Then a peal of laughter from her. Jacques had very good ears, and the silence at that hour of the afternoon was so absolute that he could hear their entire conversation without meaning to. I'm so close to you, the stranger was saying just then, that I've already left my scent on you. Oh, and what do you smell like? she asked. A little fox. A stray dog. He spoke with a wildcat's purr, and Jacques just barely managed to stifle a guffaw. Luckily, from down there, in the garden, you couldn't hear what anyone might be saying or doing up on the balcony. The swishing of leaves, the whirring of insects, and the flapping of birds formed a constant murmur. From above, though, you could hear every utterance and sigh issuing from down below, despite the fact that the balcony Jacques was standing on was a good fifteen or twenty feet off the ground. Nevertheless, he decided to light a cigarette, as a potential excuse in case one of the two happened to raise their head and look in his direction.

I'm going to fetch my suitcase and come to your house, the stranger was telling her now. I need food. And I have other needs. The girl made no reply, just smiled sadly, and he pressed on, unperturbed. I want to live with you at your house. I want to be by your side. That girl was like a magnet for the poorest of the poor, when she herself had practically nothing, barely more than her smile, a smile that had the power to heal, and a boundless desire to help all those who needed it. Remember today. One day soon, you'll be mine. The man would make an excellent actor. You could tell he'd learned to dissemble, to use his whole body to make himself understood, to change his voice as one changes a shirt. An arresting d'Artagnan, an intrepid Passepoil, battling foes, sword in hand. Or an unforgettable Robin Hood. And he seemed to be holding within him a veritable orgy of passions. To be following a rule book that, at the same time, not even he himself took very seriously, which gave him a certain air of innocence, as well. Of spontaneity. Or perhaps just the opposite, an air of premeditation.

Perhaps his gestures, his words, are merely the initial maneuvers of some skillfully constructed strategy, Jacques thought, and he moved back slightly. He felt an overwhelming impulse to modesty, but he didn't leave the balcony. He simply stepped aside from the stone balustrade a little and peered down from one corner. Like the cat. Being as he was so passionate about the dramatic arts, penning plays and adapting the novels of other writers for the stage, right down to coordinating sets and overseeing every last detail of a performance, he found it impossible to look away from a scene such as this. He felt like a director attending a premier after long months of effort and emotional expenditure. But now, unlike any director, who knows each line of text, who senses every clapped hand and every stomping foot that will cap the night's performance, and also unlike any headliner, for he himself had on more than one occasion stepped out on stage, treading the boards in a costume and mask, he was an intruder, spying from a makeshift box overlooking a most singular set, a spectator at someone else's play, a play that would be performed that one time only.

Speak to him about me, he heard the recently arrived character imploring. I want a part in his book. Some simple, sensitive character. A passionate man. Carina must have told him she worked for a writer. She was very proud of him. And she always took an interest in every minor, insignificant point he might share with her about the novel's progress. She'd ask him every morning. How many pages now? And as he gave his reply, she'd widen her eyes and repeat the number soundlessly, moving her lips, as if she were a mirror. As if whispering in admiration. She knew that Jacques, even in real life, was a man who was constantly assigning roles. And playing them. His daughter was the plague. His son, cholera. And Father? Jacques asked. Father is the victim, they answered in chorus.

With your own real first and last name, you mean? Carina now inquired of the man. Yes, yes. With my own real first and last name. And who would you like to be in the book? A good person? Or would you prefer your character to be someone who could kill a man? Being well-acquainted with the plot, she seemed determined to find the right spark of inspiration to continue moving ahead with the idea, but the pint-sized colossus was evidently displeased with the role she was offering him. No. I want to be a dramatic character, someone who's dying of love. Spanish girls always make me cry. But I'm the first one you've ever met. You said so yourself, she remonstrated, and a smile lit up her eyes. You'll make me cry, he answered. Carina's giggle emboldened her seducer. But if you like, I can be the assassin. Or split myself in two. Be the good guy and the bad guy at the same time. I can do impressions. All different accents. Carry on imaginary dialogues with up to four separate people, just by changing my voice. Or I could be your boss's bodyguard. Nobody looks at or lays a finger on my writer, he barked, using a deep, threatening voice, and with his right hand he readied a gun. Or I'll pump your brain full of lead.

Every actor finds his way to tragedy sooner or later, Jacques reflected. And seeing as how the man appeared to understand the fact that nothing is more serious than play and that he was, accordingly, going to persist with his amorous courtship, he decided to continue his eavesdropping no further and go back inside to work. The cat, on the other hand, stayed put, slowly tilting its head and ears to one side, as if tracking the scent of the two's laughter, as if their words were drifting through the air and it might be able to snatch them out of it. Jacques did not call the cat. He'd let it sit there until the act came to a close. Maybe the jenny was peeping around a corner somewhere, too. Or I could be the county gravedigger, he overheard the stranger saying. There it was. Once again. The desire for immortality. The actor's obsession with multiplying himself through the donning of additional fates. Anyone at all's, as long as it secured him a spot, at least in a novel. That desire was often a source of joy, but it could also bring about its share of evil.

Jacques dove into his work and forgot all else, time and space, the two of them down in the orchard. And when the girl came back up to the house by and by with her apron all rumpled and clumps of weeds clinging to the hem of her flowered dress, he looked at her with a mixture of amusement and severity, enquiring wordlessly. Carina blushed. His name is Édouard. Édouard Buysse. He's from Flanders. He was a matador, and he's appeared in rings all over the South of France, but he gave up bullfighting a long time ago. The last time, a bull caught him in the back, tore open his jacket, and cut a deep gash in him. His shirt was soaked through. That day's suit was brown and gold. He told me that the finely crushed rock laid out over the surface of the bullring was covered in blood and gold sequins that glittered in the late-evening sun. Like a trail of stars. Later, when he tried to go back to it, his wound reopened. He's never returned to the ring, except to watch other friends fight. He's lived as a wanderer ever since. He arrived in town less than a month ago and hasn't been able to find work.

Do you like him? Jacques asked. He could recognize love in a matter of mere seconds spent seeing two people together, but he wanted her to tell him herself. Modesty was becoming on her. As was love, apparently. Everything lit up inside her. Instantly. There was no need for her to respond. But nevertheless, with the self-possession of a child, she exclaimed—Of course! He was my birthday present. He came to town on the exact same day as my birthday. And she said this with the same innocent tone she might have used to declare that the man had simply plopped out of the sky or touched down from another planet. From some far-off star. I've never felt anything like it. Jacques felt a twinge of jealousy. And what about him? I mean to say, does he like you? Carina's face flushed even more brightly, and the transparent fuzz that coated her face seemed to stand on end and sparkle in the sunlight that was pouring in through the window.

Be careful. He's going to make you cry, Jacques heard himself say. And laugh, he added quickly. One Don Juan can spot another at first sight, especially when he hears him being talked about by a woman he himself loves. A Don Juan knows that there's nothing worse than losing this life, and as such, he does not tarry. And she too could be dangerous. Her beauty pierced the heart, and it was no easy task removing her from one's thoughts. He has no hope, Jacques added. He's like you in that sense. Carina looked at him in surprise. And like me, he went on. How could he explain to her that there was but one luxury in this life—namely, the chance to form

160

connections with other people? In ten years or twenty, we'll all be dead. Or long before that. Time flies by at lighting speed. Carina lowered her head and stood gazing fixedly at the floor. It looked like she was crying. Maybe she was just thinking. Maybe she already knew. Jacques regretted his words. Who was he to tell her to be careful? He of all people. And what were those clothes he was wearing? he asked, trying to draw Carina's attention away from the abyss she'd most likely just been staring into. That abyss containing just a single thought, the thought that at the end of everything, there is death. Lurking around the least likely corner. Is he a cyclist? Is he at all related to Lucien Buysse, who won the Tour de France in 1926? A tough race. The longest in history. He was Belgian, too, he added, noting that Carina still wasn't speaking a word. I don't know, she answered at length. But I do know that before his go at bullfighting, he tried to earn a living as a professional cyclist. His didn't fare much better there than in the ring. He says he was born too late. That he missed the boat on bullfighting. And on everything. That life is slipping through his fingers. That it's outpacing him, while death keeps running after him and nipping at his heels.

Jacques shook his head. What if he was just a braggart, a charlatan, a fraud, a fake? But then he remembered that the Belgian champion was called Little Buysse. A short man, possessed of incredible tenacity and strength. Just like this man. And endeavoring to bring his jealousy under control, he asked if he could meet him. He liked sports. And the people who practiced them. As he did all simple folk who earned their daily bread in time-honored trades. Those who spent their days out on rivers, catching fish. Those who kept watch over animals. And the fans who filled the stadiums. Boxing. Soccer. Bullfighting. And all those who hailed from Spain, where his mother's family had come from long before he'd been born, searching for some chance to avoid dying of hunger, where Carina had sallied forth from, as well. Where does he live? he asked. With the gypsies, at first, over near the castle. Now a painter in town has let him a room. It's very small, but it has a little balcony. He keeps his bicycle there. In his room. He says it's his wife. It's all he has.

Carina shrugged and smiled. He's got a clothesline covered in shirts, socks, and undershorts running from one end of the room to the other. There's a mattress on the floor, and he likes to sit there and look out the window, at the green and blue blinds of the other houses. And the rooftops, which he hadn't seen from indoors in a long time. He says it never rains inside there. And that it's much less cold in winter than it is outside, even though there's no heating. The rest of his clothes are piled in a jumble on the bed. He doesn't have a closet, and he sleeps on top of them all. At that point, the girl blushed. I sometimes bring him a little food, she added, no doubt in an attempt to justify this high degree of intimate knowledge. Then she proceeded to speak, somewhat shakily. One life passes and another begins, she said. Then that other life ends, too, and a third one begins, and afterward a fourth, and so on, unendingly. And each one cuts off as if by a scissor-snip . . . So she did know. Of course she knew. How could she not know? She, who had lost her brother at age thirteen, couldn't help but know. Better than anybody. And she would never forget.

Jacques knew that feeling. The feeling of embracing a person and knowing that any given day might be your last chance to do so. And yet how often we find ourselves lacking the courage, or worse still, the will, to make some gesture of tenderness, to speak any words of encouragement. Some days I'm scorched by his embrace. Others I'm frightened by his icy gaze, she suddenly confessed. Jacques gaped. Was she trying to make a martyr of him? He never dreamt he would hear such things issuing from the lips of that supremely delicate, timid girl, but she was clearly more comfortable around him now, and he got the unpleasant feeling that she suddenly thought of him as a family member, as someone older. He'd dreamt of kissing her again, not once but hundreds of times, so he was loathe now to imagine her in the arms of that strapping, smooth-tongued individual.

Tell him to come up. I want to talk to him. The girl spun around and hurried downstairs to the little garden. Jacques found himself questioning whether or not he actually enjoyed playing the role of spectator. As this most recent episode wore on, he was looking less and less forward to the outcome that appeared to be looming before him, despite the fact that he'd sensed from the beginning that Carina was not meant for him. Now it was time for him to switch on his own good sportsmanship. The girl returned a few short minutes later, dragging with her that hunk of flesh, who appeared unwilling to come into the house. This is your chance, my darling, Jacques heard him saying as they came up the final steps leading to his office. It's free, no charge. Because it's Tuesday. Give me a little cuddle. Actually, it's free every day. Just for you. Every day of the week. Hold on a second, she interrupted him. Your hair could use a comb. But I don't have a comb, he laughed, but as soon as he set eyes on Jacques, he fell silent, and with a gesture of the utmost seriousness, he made as if to remove his hat, even though he wasn't wearing a cap or anything else on his head.

Jacques approached him and saw that he had two large grease spots on his shirt, at chest height. The man lowered his head and moved to cover the stains, but Jacques stretched out his hand to him, and he, realizing that the attire of the home's proprietor wasn't in much better shape than his own, stepped forward and returned the greeting. His hands were strong, rough. Afterward, his eyes wandered calmly around the room, which was completely covered in books. The books didn't just line the shelves on the walls. They were piled up in little columns on every table, on every piece of furniture and every armchair. And even on the floor, rising in teetering towers at the foot of the walls. There were newspapers and magazines, too. And coffee cups, and ashtrays stuffed with cigarette butts, and a handful of drinking glasses. But despite the mess, everything was clean. There wasn't a single speck of dust on either the floor, the bookshelves, or the few inches of unoccupied space left on each of the various tables. Carina's handiwork, Édouard must have been thinking, because he turned and looked at her with rapture. He had pale eyes. And when the sunlight streaming through the windows hit him head-on, they turned blue, even though they were actually a clear yellow color, practically transparent. He had the eyes of a lynx. You almost couldn't see them they were so clear.

Jacques shook his hand. He had to admit it, his rival was nothing to sniff at. Monsieur Buysse, I'd like you to come work for me. The former bullfighter looked at him in surprise. Perhaps he wasn't accustomed to being treated with such instant familiarity, but Jacques suffered from a natural bias toward goodwill. That's why whenever he came across a new face, a little voice inside him would sound an alarm—Slowly now. Danger! And when the goodwill was strong, especially in those cases, he knew it was best to be on his guard. He'd experienced too many disappointments in the course of his life. The cat came into the room just then and padded over to the stranger. The Belgian man bent down to pet the animal, which then, after allowing its back to be scratched for a few moments, proceeded to rub its body against one of his legs. There's nothing to fear here, Jacques thought to himself, allowing his trusting side to take over once more, and he proceeded to enlighten the retired bullfighter as to what his job would consist of. I'd like you to work for me. As a gardener. I don't know the first thing about plants and trees, he replied with a matter-of-fact smile. The only flower I know . . . He didn't finish his sentence, he just beamed at Carina. A slight look of irony crept into Jacques's eyes. Then you'll be perfect, he declared. Just the person I was looking for. I don't want some prim, impeccable gardener. I prefer someone with an unkempt look. Well you can rest easy on that account, the ex-cyclist replied. I'll see to it personally.

When can you start? Right now. Or tomorrow, if that seems too soon, he replied, and letting out a chuckle, he slipped Jacques's arm into his own and took him for a turn around the room. Jacques was dumbfounded. By the way, he slipped in the question as soon as the man let go of him again, do you have any connection to the cyclist Lucien Buysse? Yes, of course. The Buysses are my father's cousins. Almost all of them are professional cyclists, although none of them are as good as Lucien. And I named my youngest daughter Luciana Estefanía. In his honor. The two men saw how the blood drained from Carina's face. How her body swayed a little, as if a gust of wind had swept into the room. Yes, yes. I have two daughters, Édouard rushed to explain, but I've been separated for a long time. And he smiled, flattered by the girl's reaction. He had a beautiful smile. Sparkling white teeth. Full lips. She inhaled slowly and seemed to recover her breath.

Jacques did some quick calculations. He must be about thirty years old, although he looked even younger, what with those cycling clothes, and that long blond hair he wore pulled back at the base of his neck, in a slightly matted bun, and the huge amount of physical exercise he must have done throughout his lifetime. And he remembered a photograph someone had snapped after one particular mountain stage. A storm had been raging, and little Lucien Buysse was posing next to his bicycle with his entire face and his legs and hands all covered in mud. He looked like a miner with coal-blackened skin. He wore two stacks of replacement inner tubes on his body, slung over his shoulders and looped around under his armpits. A race of titans, Jacques mused. Monsieur Terrasse, would you allow me to now ask a question of you? I know you're a famous writer. So, this Belgian guy was calling him that, too. Everyone in town knew he wished to remain anonymous and protect his privacy. And shortly after he'd arrived, they'd christened him with that name, a reference to his home's twin terraces, its two balconies stacked one on top of the other.

He nodded, inviting the matador to spit out his question. Go ahead, he said, seeing that he was having trouble summoning his resolve. Do you just write any old thing that comes into your head? Whatever you see happening around you? The burst of laughter Jacques let slip rang out even more richly than Carina's had down in the garden a short while before. He even threw back his head. I'd like to read one of your books, he added, perhaps in an attempt to excuse his forwardness. Jacques considered for a moment, but then he made a quick about-face and marched into the adjoining room. He returned with a cream-colored volume and handed it over to him. *The Stranger,* Édouard muttered, scanning the simple cover, unembellished except for the title, the author's name, and the name of the publisher in red and white letters. Looks interesting. Swelling with pride, Carina grabbed his hand and dragged him out of there. So, he liked reading, too. He was a chameleon. And she a fool for having thought that he might be illiterate. Édouard had been all over the place. He seemed to know a little bit about everything. Not to mention the fact that he had a different demeanor every day. He never seemed the same. Every time Jacques had happened upon him in town, he was unsure whether it was the same person. The first time he'd seen him, the man was sporting matted locks and a beard like Jesus Christ's, and he had a bare, sweat-covered chest and dark gloves that made him look like a boxer. Maybe he'd just come from a shift in the fields. Or some workshop in town. Another time, he'd spotted him with a multicolored kerchief knotted around his head in the style of a Russian peasant woman. Or a pirate. And another time wearing a wool beanie pulled down to his eyebrows. Or a cap with the brim obscuring his eyes. And once with a gigantic beret, even. And on those days when he was stuffed inside his multicolored headscarf or his hat like that, he would have such an intent and at the same time absent look in his transparent eyes and such a bitter cast in the area around his lips that Jacques felt sure he would have been incapable of uttering a single word. Possibly not even a passing grunt by way of salutation. And that stubborn silence had caught his eye. It was the mark of suffering. The pride, so often sterile, of the poor. Or was it more like resentment? Come on, Édou, said Carina. We all have work to do.

By the way, Monsieur Buysse, Jacques interrupted her. You'll have to feed the donkey, but make sure you don't wear orange gloves. Carina did that her first time, and the beast nearly bit off her hand thinking it was a bunch of carrots. And one other thing. Would you permit me to work in the garden? I sometimes like to go down there to write. Édouard leaned forward and gave a deep bow. Like an actor saluting his public at the close of a performance while basking in a fine round of applause. Or the most respectful of silences, because Jacques merely gazed at him in awe. He'd never seen anything like it. Not even in the theater. No trouble at all, said that expert matador. It occurred to Jacques that it wasn't going to be easy for him to concentrate with a guy like that wandering around the place, someone who would be constantly pulling faces and making jokes, acting out bullfighting passes, someone who would break into dance with no warning and no music playing, and who was sure to bombard him with countless questions about his work.

And he imagined Carina, too, tossing down little pouches of provisions to him from the balcony. Pastries, pieces of fruit, handfuls of candies folded inside some old handkerchief. Or little gifts to make his life more pleasant. A cake of lavender-scented soap. A comb. A pair of Jacques's socks. But he tried to console himself by thinking about all the potential for inspiration it would surely afford him. Just then, Édouard took Carina's hands in his and kissed them. First one. Then the other. God bless these hands, he whispered. She tugged at him again to get him out of there as quickly as possible. Jacques watched them go.

He was afraid that this erstwhile bullfighter, with his talent for putting on pantomimes and entremeses, would one day come to hurt Carina. The longer the man spent there, in his house, the more he would be able to find out about him. Now she would take him downstairs and show him what his tasks were and where the tools were kept. Meanwhile, Jacques returned to his desk, to take up his manuscript again in the same spot he'd left it off right before this new character stepped onto the scene. It's late. Too late, he thought. For several months now, he'd been getting the feeling he didn't have much time left. He had to hurry. He'd been working on it for thirty years, almost his entire life, ever since he'd spat up blood and been rushed to Mustapha Hospital at age eighteen. Jacques reread the last few sentences before moving on. Jacques's father, killed at the Marne. What remains of that obscure life? Nothing, an impalpable memory, the weightless ash of a butterfly wing consumed in a forest fire.

THE DANGER NO ONE SPOKE OF

They'd just gotten in to Sens. Throughout the ride, a fine white rain had scored the sky, making it look like a netting of spiderweb. Now the sun was out. You're scared, Michel said to him. Yes, he was scared, it was true, he couldn't deny it, but he was reluctant to say so out loud, because he didn't want it to thicken, didn't want it to spread to his friends. Come on now. I know this highway like the back of my hand, Michel reiterated yet again, trying to calm Jacques's nerves. You just had to look at his face. His somber mien, so different from his usual open smile, his quickness to jest. He experienced the same fear of death that often seized Jacques. Possibly ever since his youth. It was something they shared, as they did many other things. Like tuberculosis. His friend had even succumbed to deep bouts of depression on several occasions. But these past days, he'd seemed more scared. I'll go slowly, don't worry. I made you a promise. And I never drive fast when I'm with Anne and Janine.

Jacques put his free arm around his friend's shoulder, while the other he kept clutching the briefcase he almost never let out of his sight even for an instant. A black leather briefcase with fully expanded gussets, reinforced corners, and a lock he never used the key on. Sisyphus, always lugging his rock around,

Michel said to him, smiling. Inside that case, Jacques had the manuscript of his novel and the notebook he was still jotting ideas in. An unfinished novel is like a newborn baby. Like an ailing patient, or a dying man from whose side one must never stir even briefly, he thought as they made their way toward the entrance of the Hotel de Paris et de la Poste, an old colonial-style mansion that had been converted into a restaurant, where they were planning on having lunch. They'd telephoned a few days ago from the Lourmarin house and made a reservation in Jacques's name. After lunch, an hour or so later, they'd be in Paris. Janine and Anne walked ahead of them, trying to stretch their legs a little before sitting down to eat.

The car's backseat was so cramped that Jacques had insisted repeatedly that he'd be happy to give up his seat to Janine. But she'd refused his offer on the excuse that he had longer legs. Besides, that way, he could be closer to his friend. Floc tugged at his leash impatiently. He must have been hungry and a little tuckered out from the journey, despite having spent the entire ride staring constantly out the window, trying to see every last sight through the long curls of fur that fell in front of his eyes. He was a strange sort of dog. He liked landscapes. An adult dog, thought Jacques. In spite of his appearance and his playful demeanor. He was like a fuzzy, white ball. Children never exult in the sights nature or cityscapes reveal to them. Their interest wanes quickly, as does the concentration required to embellish and put into words their admiration of what they have before them, the way grown-ups tend to do. And yet the images perceived by children's brains are recorded much more vividly.

The wide space in front of the door leading into the establishment was filled with plants. There were flowers, and small palm trees with enormous fronds. Two hotel employees dressed in Moorish-style uniforms stepped out to meet them.

Wiry, olive-skinned, and approximately the same height as one another, they each wore a long, light-colored djellaba, leather slippers, and a red fez. Their assigned task—greeting customers—forced them to spend most of their time standing there at that large door, which was flanked on both sides by paper lanterns. Michel peeked out of the corner of his eye at Jacques. A discreet look of displeasure hung on his face. Why did the restaurant insist on keeping up that particular tradition? he was probably asking himself. But neither of the two said anything. Jacques listened to the flat sound of his steps on the cold ground and the rhythmic creaking of the handle on his briefcase. And when he'd drawn up face-to-face with the two employees, he addressed them in Arabic. They returned his greeting. *As-salaam alaikum.* And all three men moved a hand from their chests up to their foreheads, and then into the air. Peace be upon you. Michel turned his keys over to one of them, who went to go park the car. The other one took Floc by the leash and led him around back, to get him something to eat and drink. None of the vehicle's occupants were carrying any luggage. Only Jacques, toting his leather briefcase.

Just as they were entering the hotel, Jacques glanced behind him and saw two more Arab men, dressed in work overalls, heading for the spot where the Facel Vega was parked. The first one was carrying a bucket, a mop, and a handful of rags. The other, a long wooden-handled squeegee. Jacques stood there looking at them for a few moments, and his eyes locked with one of them, who had also turned back just then to look at the door. A handsome, youthful man. Although there was something unpleasant in his demeanor. The look in his eyes? Yes. And though it wasn't the first time Jacques had seen that particular expression, he felt a shiver run down his spine. It was the look of hatred. A person never gets used to that. And

173

he froze. Also, he'd seen that face before—but where? In a dream? He got the feeling he knew him from somewhere. Then again, he knew so many people without really knowing them . . . It was one of the many downsides of fame. He had to allow himself to be introduced to lots of people he would never see again. Shake their hands, exchange a few words. Sign the odd autograph. And so even strangers often seemed familiar to him. He got the feeling it wasn't he who was the public figure, but everybody else.

And yet, that face . . . And that scar, especially. That mark running across part of his nose and cheek. The man had turned his face, and now he could only see his profile. Maybe the scar was no more than a mirage. A few reminiscent features, a similar carriage, and a person could convince himself he was seeing the most distinguishing mark of whatever individual he had in mind. And yet . . . Yes, he was still getting that strange feeling. Like when a person spots someone walking down the street and believes he's standing before the incarnation of a character from a book he read ages ago. Even more than that, he reminded him of one of his own characters, although there were a few differences. His face was broader. His expression more hardened. And if running into a flesh-and-blood Raskolnikov or Myshkin or Ulrich walking down the street could make a reader stop and think, for a writer, stumbling across one of his own creations was bordering on madness.

What nonsense, he told himself. The whole thing was just a figment of his imagination. A phantasmagoria. If he went over and got a closer look at him, he'd see that not only did he not have a cut of any sort on his nose or cheek but that he looked nothing like him at all. But no, that wasn't something he could do, he had to be getting inside. His friends would be waiting for him. Turning back around, he went up the steps to the door and, once inside, headed for the dining room, although his mind was many miles away, lost in the remembrance of that feeling of constant danger he'd felt back in Algeria but that no one spoke of, because it seemed natural. An invisible menace that you could feel in the air, especially those evenings when a fight would break out. The hostility between Frenchmen and Arabs, those alluring yet disturbing men who often moved about in droves, making almost no noise. Just then, Janine signaled at him from the far end of the room.

He has the eyes of the sand men, Kassim remarked, his gaze fixed on the door leading into the restaurant even though Jacques was no longer standing there. Hadji noticed a certain sorrowful inflection in his partner's speech, and it worried him. There's four of them, he said. It's not just Golan and his friend Gilat. Another *rouget*. And two women, no less. One of them's very young, practically a girl. Kassim was stunned, too. They were so beautiful. He'd seen them get out of the car and walk into the place, and he'd hardly been able to take his eyes off those two moving figures. With their pencil skirts down to their knees and those never-ending legs, they looked like something straight out of a movie. He was indifferent to the fact that Gilat had red hair. He didn't believe in curses. They'd decided to call him that because he had a sunny face. In Hebrew, Gilat meant happiness. Petit Boxeur had described him perfectly. As for Golan, when he'd turned around at the last second to look at them, Kassim had held his gaze, allowing it to burn into his eyes. They're rich, he told his partner, well aware of what Hadji's greatest weakness was. Hatred of the rich and love of money mingled within his heart in equal measure. Tremendously rich.

There's no going back now. No, there wasn't. The faster his horse runs, he thought to himself, the sooner Death will overtake him. As for Hadji, he was certain Kassim was grappling with the same misgivings as he was, but he'd just about had enough. If it wasn't his silences, it was the man's fits of bad temper that got to him. Tell me the truth. Why him? Kassim, weary for his part of Hadji's constant questions, chose not to reply and fell into his customary silence. That man had attained something he himself never would. Immortality. It wasn't so much a question of material possessions but something much more important instead. Something he himself could never hope to experience. Even remotely. It was fame, the respect of thousands upon thousands of people, posterity. Reputation. He should be in with us. Because out there, he can do a lot of damage, even by doing nothing. Even by keeping quiet. There's such a thing as an accusatory silence. And he might speak up at any moment. Tell people what he's seen. Publish the list. With all the names on it.

The two Moorish-styled attendants were back at the building's entrance, but now whenever another vehicle arrived, only one of them moved from his post to greet the new customers. Hadji plunged the squeegee into the bucket then mopped it over the windshield. A wraparound windshield. Exquisite. Kassim opened the trunk and rifled through it briefly, though it contained almost nothing. Hadji stepped around to wash the back window. Kassim seemed put out. It must be in the briefcase he was carrying. We'll have to follow them, as planned, and then look for it again. Hadji moved back to the front of the car, popped the hood, and stuck his head in. That car was an absolute wonder. The box of wonders. He'd never seen anything like it. He would have loved to spend hours and hours going over every detail, examining every piece. He unfastened the air filter cover. Everything was right there at his fingertips. The carburetor, the dynamo, the gearbox, the starter, the dipstick, the cylinders. The heart of the beast. Three hundred and fifty horses. V-8. Just like the Cadillac Eldorado, he exclaimed. And underneath, the tubes for the hydraulic brake system, the steering, the transmission . . . The legs of the beast. And he started to sing. *Zim boum-boum: hier au soir et zim boum-boum . . .*

Jacques had now sat down at the table, between his friend Michel and Annouchka, across from Janine. It was a large dining room, decorated in the Burgundy style with a massive stone chimney, red embroidered tablecloths, and wood-paneled walls and ceiling. The large windows afforded a view of the many plants outside in the garden. They'd ordered the specialty of the house. Black pudding empanada with applesauce. And a bottle of Fleurie. It's so nice to see the two of you together like this, Jacques said, smiling knowingly. Even your eyes are sparkling. And see how you put your arms around each other and joke together. Jacques looked at his friend and smiled. The redheaded man let out a laugh that made his entire face light up, right down to his freckles. A veritable celestial chart. He loved the fact that Janine enjoyed seeing him enjoy himself. Jacques had never once known her to be angry, or even upset.

The restaurant's owner came over to the table to see how everything was going. She was a woman about thirty years old with piercing, blue eyes and medium-length blond hair. She wore a form-fitting Indo-Chinese-style silk dress in very light, metallic blue with tiny black spots on it. Michel and Janine went there often. They praised the black pudding empanada and Michel asked her for the recipe. Janine took out a piece of paper and a pen. You'll need a half a pound of black pudding with rice, and another half a pound with onion, one head of garlic, a large dollop of pork fat, a third of a pound of pastry dough, a pinch of cinnamon, cumin, nutmeg, and pepper. If the black pudding wasn't purchased already without the skin, you'll have to remove it. You melt down the lard and sauté the onion until it's cooked through. Am I going to fast? Janine looked up and smiled. No. I'm used to taking things down quickly.

All right. Then you add in the black pudding and the spices, and you let it cook for about five minutes. You put the entire mixture through a grinder until it's all very fine, and then you check it for salt. You grease an empanada pan with some lard, line it with the pastry dough, and top it with the black pudding mixture. You cover the whole thing with another layer of pastry, which can be decorated however you like. You put it in the oven on high, three hundred and fifty degrees, until it's browned, and you serve it warm, with a garnish of very smoothly pureed apples. Your friend sure doesn't eat much, the blond woman said suddenly, and she smiled widely at Jacques. It's because he's planning on living to be two hundred years old, Michel explained. And keeping himself fit as a fiddle. Moreover, he's so scared of death, he might even suspect the pudding of being poisoned. Not to worry, he added, winking at his friend. This woman right here is the best cook in the world. The owner laughed in satisfaction and excused herself in order to attend to the other customers.

Without a doubt. Everything was exquisite, although Jacques ate only a little, and slowly. He was not a particularly voracious man when it came to eating, and the same was true with alcohol. He never had been. And places like that intimidated him. He preferred taverns and alehouses, wooden chairs and tables worn with use, peeling walls, checkered tablecloths, mismatched plates, and heavy glass tumblers instead of these balloon-shaped goblets. A bit of cured meat, some cheese, and some bread. Or a little vegetable couscous. What really mattered was the company, the conversation. And he thought back to the restaurants in Algiers, dirty, noisy, filled with Arabs and construction workers, with prostitutes. I want to go into the theater, Anne remarked suddenly. Michel objected. I don't think it's a good idea. You're very young. You still have to study more. Janine said nothing. She didn't want to get involved, even though it was her own daughter. Michel was only Anne' first cousin once removed and now the man of the house, but Anne had just turned eighteen the day before, and she had to learn to stick up for herself, to fight for her ideas.

Jacques intervened on the girl's behalf. I'll help her get started, on the condition that she keep up her studies. Maybe she can even give me a hand with my next project. I want to write a piece about Julie de Lespinasse, to flesh out the theory of dual love. Dual? he checked himself immediately. Dual, triple, or multiple, he added, thinking about the many women he'd fallen in love with. The temptation of tenderness. And if I do end up managing my own theater and she can prove what she's capable of, she could work for me directly, be my right hand. Janine thanked him and squeezed his left forearm, warmly. I see you've been taking notes, too. Are you planning on whipping up an empanada for yourself? Jacques smiled and shook his head. A few days ago, I was out driving, and this gendarme pulled me over and asked to see my identification. When he saw what it said under "profession," he asked me what kind of books I write. Novels, I answered. Romance or crime? Faced with these alternatives, I had no choice but to tell him half and half. So, since my books don't have any elements of crime fiction in them—although they don't have any romance in them, either—I thought I could stick in a nice dinner recipe, like crime writers sometimes do.

At that exact same moment, a waiter came up to the table and very quietly, almost in a whisper, told Jacques that there was a telephone call for him. That it was urgent. He stood up, excused himself, and walked out of the dining room and over to the glass-walled booth where there was a handset, he was informed, that would connect him. It was Francine, his ex-wife. On the line from Paris. When she told him what was going on, all the color drained from his face. He could see it in the glass. His own face reflected like a corpse. He could hardly speak. He'd never mentioned his fear to her, nor did he do so now, because he didn't want to alarm her more than she already was. Édouard had been found in the Petit Luberon Forest, his body beaten and battered. Apparently it was very serious. He'd lost almost all of his blood by the time a shepherd had come across him and run to the nearest village for help. From there, he'd been transferred to the hospital in Aix-en-Provence. Everyone was amazed he hadn't died. Carina was with him now.

Jacques recalled the girl's sad face when he'd left town. She seemed to move as if in a trance, like a sleepwalker. And when he saw her, he thought for a second that she'd come to work in her nightgown. She looked as though she'd just gotten back from a tour through Limbo. It was obvious that some bad dream had kept her up a good part of the night, although she'd calmed down somewhat as the day wore on, as she puttered back and forth among the various rooms of the house, repeatedly bumping into furniture and stumbling on the steps. She'd even dropped a few things, which wasn't at all like her. Meanwhile, he'd been gathering up his papers and trying to bring some sense of order to his office. And her nightmare must have disappeared from her thoughts entirely, only to float back up to the surface of her memory the instant she heard the car honk. His friend, who'd docked his boat at Cannes after one of his crossings, had just pulled in. Carina, peeking through the window, had seen the car parked down there next to the big wooden door that led from the street to the lower portion of the house and the surrounding patio. She'd stifled a scream and buried her face in her hands. Two coffins, she'd said. And then she'd fallen silent. Jacques had gone over to see what the matter was. He'd seen his friend's car before, but when he looked down, his heart froze. Black and gleaming, Michel's Facel Vega looked like a hearse, despite the luxuriousness it oozed. Or perhaps because of it. And from the height where he stood, his own car, also black, and relatively new, although dirtier and more outmoded, might easily have been a funeral buggy. Or a casket. Michel had already stepped out of the car. Anne and Janine were making their way over from town on foot. Whistling, his friend had glanced up and spotted the two of them at the window. Carina had jumped, exclaiming in fright—A redhead! Even his eyelashes are red! Jacques had looked at her quizzically. It's supposed to be bad luck for a redheaded person to come into your house. Don't worry, I won't let him come up, he'd assured her with a laugh. But . . . Carina trailed off. Jacques, smiling, encouraged her to speak whatever fears were on her mind.

But the Devil will also take any person who crosses paths with a redhead before undertaking a journey. Oh, heaven help us. Round men of red beard or hair, beware. That's the saying. Such locks ne'er found on cat nor hound. And following that strange recitation, she'd withdrawn again into her trancelike state. It was as if a trembling light were radiating inside her and its shimmerings had welled up into her eyes. Delirium is contagious, Jacques reflected, and he'd felt an initial urge to rid her mind of such notions, but then it occurred to him they must be fairly deeply rooted, and he was running short on time. He'd do it when he got back. As soon as he returned from Paris, he'd sit her down and they'd have a serious talk. You didn't need the presence of a redheaded man or woman for terrible things to happen. Accidents and disasters happened for other reasons. He'd speak to her about chance. About the power of nature. Or the power of the ill will of others.

Did you have a bad dream? was all he'd asked, trying to play down his own apprehensions, even though he wasn't superstitious. How did you know I had one of my nightmares? she'd replied, raising up a hand, as if to shield herself or dismiss a bad thought. Don't worry, you don't have to be frightened, he'd told her. Carina had regarded him silently. And Jacques had read in her face all her agonizing misgivings. He'd seen the thought that her mind was working to banish flutter across her eyes. And she lowered her eyelids and swept him with several fleeting glances. Don't tell me what you dreamt last night, he begged her at last. Don't tell me. I don't want to know. And in an effort to refortify his rationalist upbringing, he told himself it didn't matter. That Carina might dream something terrible any old day. Even every night. And that didn't necessarily mean anything. And yet . . .

Yet he'd still believed it was he who was in danger in her dreams. It hadn't occurred to him to think that it might be someone else. And least of all Édouard. That's how spooked he was at the thought of his impending drive to the capital. All on account of the threats he'd received over the course of the last several years, and which just a few days before leaving Lourmarin he'd found himself being inundated with yet again. Although it was also the idea of returning to Paris, of being back in those intellectual circles he so detested, in that city that had become over time so acutely inhospitable for him. When they bid farewell, Carina had lowered her eyelids once more, and her black lashes had sparkled curiously, like a night sky whose thousands of stars had lit up all at once. Perhaps she'd just been crying and they were still damp. Perhaps she, too, was thinking it would be him, not Édouard.

In the end, the girl managed a smile, but Jacques was shivering, unable to shake the feeling that the smile lighting up her face was a death sentence. Even though he knew that any time she said goodbye to someone she cared about, even if it was only for a day or a few hours, Carina always cried inconsolably, and that always made her break into laughter, knowing how absurd her own sentimentality was. I'm such a goose, she'd say, laughing and crying. Far from it, Jacques would assure her. It must have been the idea of death that was making her cry. The deaths of others, not her own, which she seemed untroubled by, like one who believes himself to be immortal and realizes only with age that the same irrevocable ending that's coming to everyone is awaiting him, too. As if she didn't have time to think of herself. Or it hadn't occurred to her to do so. Yes, perhaps she thought herself immortal. And he liked the idea of someone like Carina being immortal.

Jacques thought back to the afternoon when she'd told him of Édouard's resolutions. It was just a few days earlier. Or rather, his plans for the new year, she'd explained, taking it upon herself to clarify the Belgian man's words. And that she was included in those plans. She hadn't ventured to ask him then what they were, but a few days later, she did. She asked him. And he told her that he was going to ask for her hand in matrimony and begin a new life. Even the iron was gushing all over itself. Those were the words Carina had spoken to Jacques. The iron spat out torrents of water all over the table and she'd burst out laughing. That's how she herself had described it to Jacques. She was funny when she spoke. And she'd assign human attributes to objects, to landscapes. Like so many writers and poets. For them, trees tremble and receive the fright of bees, flowers stalk faces, wind speaks. And like the pure-hearted characters in those same writers' books, that girl understood everything, or at least she tried to. She would more readily believe that someone was enduring unbearable suffering or even some serious malady than that they were a bad person. She always endeavored to find a reason not to hate, to understand what it was that had made another person act a certain way. Almost nobody in town liked him anymore. Liked Édouard, she'd told him recently. They say he's a savage, that he's off his rocker. Because of his shifting moods, because he's unpredictable. Because of that crazed look he sometimes gets. Lots of days, he doesn't even answer when people pass him on the street and say hello. And he can go a whole week without ever uttering a single word, just scowling. Some say he might be dangerous. That he has the look of a killer at times, when his eyes shine even more clearly and he stares off into nothingness. They're calling him *Monsieur Danger*, and they're wondering if he might not have escaped from some jail somewhere. Or a mental hospital.

Luckily, most people are still treating him nicely, she'd said, because other times he makes them laugh. When he found out they'd nicknamed him that, Monsieur Danger, he went and fashioned himself a set of wings out of pigeon feathers, white ones, gray ones, sepia colored ones, a few green and purple ones from around the neck, feathers he'd found in the garden or along the nearby roads. He spent several days putting them together, and one afternoon he stuck them on his back and went walking all around town, with an olive branch clenched between his teeth. The children went wild with glee and applauded him, begging him to let them have that grand

184

furbelow off his man of peace ensemble. I know he's out of his mind, Carina had told him, but I'm still convinced he's a good man, incapable of doing anything bad to anyone. He just seethes with anger, with pain, occasionally. And so he goes from constant joking to uttermost seriousness, as if one of the strings that had been allowing him to live life as a game up until then had suddenly snapped inside him.

I'm just going to get away from the flu that's going around, Jacques had told Carina as he took his leave. As a joke. In eight days, I'll be back. She'd kissed him goodbye. He could still see her lips moving toward him. Then he remembered what had just happened to Édouard. And he imagined the scene of the crime. The previous day's rain had stopped, but the forest was likely still sodden and windy. He saw the tops of the trees rustling in rapid waves, their trunks creaking right down to the roots, and the clouds, low, threatening, coursing after one another across a chill sky. A mournful midday. A backdrop befitting of a duel like those of old. Only in this case, there were no rules to abide by. No selection of weapons, no counting out of steps before the pulling of the trigger. Out there, in all likelihood, several individuals would have fallen upon just one, whom they'd have taken to that spot against his will, possibly bound at the wrists or even gagged, there to unleash their onslaught upon him.

But assuming he hadn't been bound, Édouard would surely have done everything in his power to defend himself. Let's give a warm welcome to His Majesty, Pain, he'd have muttered in rage through gritted teeth while protecting his face behind both fists. It was just the type of declaration he might make, and one he could have spoken not only to himself, in reference to his situation at that precise moment, but could have directed at his attackers, as well, undaunted as he most assuredly was at the prospect of taking on two or three men at once. And springing into a boxer's pose, his feet planted a little more than shoulder width apart and his body ducked slightly behind his fists in order to protect his face as much as possible, he'd have landed several solid punches on the men who'd dragged him all the way out there. It was better to imagine him that way. Fighting to the finish. I can see the departed, Carina had told Jacques one afternoon as she lay on her back in the garden, gazing skyward. They're the clouds. They play together, kicking up puffs. They embrace. They chase one another. Sometimes they put on colorful dresses, when the sun hides behind them. Yellow ones, blue ones, green ones, purple ones, red ones, orange ones.

Might they have tortured him, depriving him of the chance to even try anything? Jacques shuddered. That was one of the greatest affronts that could be committed against a human being. And he suddenly recalled one afternoon when he'd been turning out sheet after sheet down in the garden. He'd gone into the house for a minute to look something up and grab a pack of cigarettes. When he peeked out at the balcony for a moment before going back down, he'd spotted Édouard there, rifling through his papers. Maybe he'd even read a page or two, trying to find any passages he might make an appearance in. That's what Jacques had thought at the time, anyhow. He was constantly asking about the progress he was making on the new book . . . As was Carina. How many pages have you got now? The two always seemed deeply impressed by what little he told them. And when Jacques had returned to the garden that afternoon to dive back into his manuscript, Édouard had winked at him. I can feel the fear. I can smell it, he'd said, making the sign of the cross in the air in front of his face and falling to his knees. Before him.

Afterward, laughing, he'd stood back up and walked away from the table Jacques was writing at in the garden, to go get his rake. When all of a sudden, flipping it over in his hands, he'd fired off an invisible barrage, using the long wooden handle as a machine gun. *Rat-tat-tat-tat-tat*. He'd given over the entire remainder of the afternoon to one of his face-pulling, pirouetting displays, executing menacing sequences every time Jacques raised his head and looked away from his manuscript. He'd no sooner pretended to whip out a pistol and pull the trigger than he was bringing his hand up to the level of his neck and tracing the movement of slitting a throat. First slowly, without pressing down. Then clean through. Jacques was not at all amused by this little number of his. It wasn't the first time he'd seen him act out similar mime routines. Those out-of-the-blue performances in the middle of a workday were a frequent occurrence. Neither was it at all out of the ordinary to hear the man talking to himself. Or with the flowers.

When he wasn't saluting with his pruning shears or the little trowel he used for planting bulbs and digging in the dirt, rotating his body very slowly around with his offering held high in one hand and his arm outstretched as if he were standing in the center of the bullring, waving his endless thanks to a nonexistent public, ladies and gentlemen, mothers and fathers, boys and girls, grandmothers and grandfathers, loyal republicans and not-so-loyal republicans, he was snarling at a tree in the middle of pruning it. This is going to hurt, he'd say, with a voice so gravelly it reverberated deep inside his throat. Jacques didn't know if he was doing it to express his profound respect for nature in a moment when he had no other choice but to harm it, or if he was simply seizing an opportunity to give free rein to his fury, because other times he'd wave his scissors rapidly around in front of a flower and say—I'm gonna break those little legs of yours. And one afternoon, he'd heard him threatening some bushes he was supposed to be fumigating, too. If any of you give me any trouble, I'm taking you all downtown. Although he'd stepped back a second later and exclaimed, grinningly—Not to worry. I'm only taking the girls. Look out, flowers!

It was easy enough to ignore any single one of his outbursts, which were almost always outrageous, but Jacques was beginning to grow tired of the man's natural flair for the dramatic. Silence is death, he'd muttered under his breath at him on another occasion. No, he'd come back at him decisively, since he was having trouble concentrating on his work that day anyway. Silence can be death. But it's also a form of happiness. What if he'd let his tongue get away from him at some point? Édouard likely rubbed elbows with a lot of unsavory, underworld sorts. Was that his real name? Did he really belong to that family of champion cyclers? He'd worked for a spell down at the docks in Marseille, apparently. And he knew every single hole-in-the-wall in all the poorest districts of the city. The brothels and the cafés, Arab and French ones alike. Maybe someone knew he was working for him. Maybe he'd been offered money and had yielded to temptation. The thought had crossed Jacques's mind for a few brief instants that afternoon when he spied him sniffing around his papers behind his back, but he'd done his best to put it out of his mind. The children were crazy about him. It wasn't just Carina. Or the cat. And yet . . .

Fame had its share of downsides. And dangers. They'd already had a woman working in their house in Paris for a time that had turned out to be a journalist just snooping around for juicy tidbits to feed her readers. What if Édouard was a spy, an agent on the payroll of some terrorist organization? Might they have threatened him and forced him to reveal crucial information? What if he'd refused to say a word, and that's why they'd tried to kill him? In the last several years, it wasn't rare to come across a piece in the papers explaining how some Algerian man, although it was occasionally a Frenchman, too, had turned up dead in a forest or another out-of-the-way place with writing scrawled across the palm of his hand in blue ink—*By order of the FLN*. No, no. That was impossible. If that were the case, Carina might be in danger, too. And his ex-wife. And his children. Not just Édouard. Not just him, Jacques, who'd felt for some time now like a dead man walking. Like a prisoner who's just eaten his last meal and is replaying his existence in his mind during his march out to the gallows. He might have only a few hours left to live, Francine had remarked.

It seems the police officer in charge of the investigation had said that there wasn't anything surprising about the case, that a career such as that man's was bound to end as it had. What a stupid way of speaking. What a slew of simplifications from the first parting of a person's lips. I've never stolen anything, Édouard had declared one day while he was brushing the jenny and Jacques was writing in the garden. It had never occurred to Jacques to think that he might have. I've never snitched on anyone, he'd continued. Then Jacques supposed that he must have been speaking for Carina's benefit, because he'd gone on to add—And I've never been unfaithful to a woman. The girl had burst out laughing. Just the same as if he'd up and announced that he, a thirty-year-old man, was still a virgin. It was clear that she didn't believe for a second that last proclamation, the one about his having never been unfaithful to a woman. And as for the first two, perhaps she'd found them too serious. Too dramatic. *Excusatio non petita,* thought Jacques, who'd gotten the feeling that Édouard was attempting to confess something more than a straightforward act of infidelity.

In order for a person to escape from himself, from the judgment of others, from the life he's been leading, it's not enough for him to change his name, or his city, or his profession, he recalled him having said shortly after that. And Jacques felt the weight of all the threats he'd been receiving of late pressing down on him once more. The ones he'd been bombarded with on his last visit to Algiers, because nobody, or almost nobody, seemed to agree with his proposal to seek out a third way, a conciliation between the different peoples inhabiting the country, in order, hopefully, to forestall a rise in the number of victims, especially innocent women and children. Red Cross morality, they'd spat at him with derision. Beautiful soul, with a sneer. And there were those other, more absurd ones, too, from so many long years ago. The ones he'd received from a handful of Oranians for having described their city in one of his books in terms they hadn't appreciated. People don't like for anything bad to happen in their city, even when it's only in the pages of a novel, despite the fact that in reality, evil is ever present. Anywhere in the world you look.

All those oaths and curses had been swirling around inside his head for days. And in the end, he'd decided not to take the train back to Paris as he had previously planned. Michel had telephoned him after he'd already bought his ticket, and he'd accepted his offer to go up with them in the Facel. Jacques recalled certain words set to paper by one of his old friends, he who was hailed by some as the be-all and end-all of contemporary and possibly even the whole of twentieth century writing in France, he whom Jacques had, after an intense falling-out, nicknamed Monsieur Néant. The King, the Pope, the Supreme Judge. The Grand Inquisitor. The alpha and omega for so many countless dupes who prided themselves on having no religion at all, though they did just the same. Boy, did they, along with all the same defects and all the same virtues as everyone else, and perhaps they had no God, granted, and perhaps no true love of man, either, but they did have a Church, one that was willing to wield the power of excommunication and seemed, ultimately, to have just one single commandment: Thou shalt lie.

It was several years ago at that point. An apparently hollow remark buried in an extremely lengthy open letter that had come to constitute the final break between the two. Car brakes can fail . . . The words were right there, stamped on his mind. And he sat there inside the telephone booth, paralyzed. Jacques could call up paragraphs and paragraphs of the text by heart. Its personal, insulting, threatening, smug tone. If you'd taken a few minutes to reflect on how other people think, he who was supposedly still his friend at the time had written, you would have observed that a brake cannot be applied to liberty. What could possibly apply it? And what need is there to check it? Car brakes can fail, because they are built to have them. But liberty has no wheels. Neither has it hooves nor jaws in which to put a bit . . . Was it just a stupid, insubstantial remark? It was the remark of a cynic, a cynic cloaked in the guise of some infallible philosopher, who sees Marxism as a science with which to dominate history. The remark of a man who's convinced that history is a bear, and that his own doctrine is the ring to be shoved through its nose. It was almost enough to make him laugh.

Then again, eight years had passed since that whole affair. At the end of his letter, Monsieur Néant had invited him to continue writing in to his journal, although he'd warned him at the same time that he would not reply to him further and hoped that their silence would cause the polemic to be forgotten. And he'd kept silent on the matter, yes, but not out of a sense of obedience, not out of fear, but rather out of pure weariness, out of desperation. Because one doesn't argue with the gutters, he thought. And because he'd made a private resolution not to lash out at anyone. And even for that they'd reproached him. For keeping silent. Somebody rapped on the glass wall of the telephone booth, startling Jacques from his reverie, and he shrank back with a jolt, as if right there at that very instant there'd just been an explosion. He felt a steely cold behind his ears, like a man on his way to the guillotine, being turned out for the final act and feeling a pair of scissors swipe their way across the back of his neck. But it was only Michel.

Then he realized he'd been sitting there for quite some time, thinking, even though he'd hung up several minutes ago. Jacques stepped out of the booth, apologized for taking so long, and walked out with his friend to the car. They'd all finished eating. Janine, Anne, and Floc were waiting outside. The two women smiled his way, and the dog came up to him wagging his tail. You're shivering all over! Everything OK? Jacques flashed him a less-than-convincing smile, but Michel, probably thinking he was having some sort of trouble with his ex-wife and not wanting to talk about it, clapped him on the shoulder and held the door open for him to climb into the car, which was sparkling brightly, freshly scrubbed.

AN INVISIBLE MENACE

As soon as they were all inside, Michel turned on the engine and drove away from the restaurant. The damp, dark morning, all shrouded in rain and mist, which had made the world seem like a stage set done up in gray scale, had gradually been giving way to the light and all its colors. The sun was still half-hidden behind the clouds, but the heavy white curtain had been slowly drawing aside, and little by little, the green of the fields, the brown of the earth, and of the tree trunks, and the blues of the still-wet rocks started peeking through. Jacques, however, remained immersed in his memories. For a good while now, he'd had the unbearable feeling he was creeping toward some unknown catastrophe, a catastrophe that would destroy everything around him and within him. The tapping on the glass wall of the telephone booth had transported him back to Algiers, four years ago. He'd gone there seeking a truce, in the hopes of sparing civilian lives, both Arab and French. And he'd done it despite the fact that a trusted acquaintance of his had made urgent entreaties for someone to talk him out of going. Because they were going to kill him, he'd said. It was feared there might be some sort of attack, and so security measures had been stepped up. Afterward, a friend had written to him in a letter—Everyone wanted to kill you.

It was four thirty in the afternoon, and the hall was full. When he came in, flanked by two of his brother Lucien's friends, he'd introduced them with a joke, the idea being that he would crack all those serious expressions on everyone's faces, including his own, even if only for a few seconds, saying—These are my bodyguards. Meanwhile, just outside, a throng one thousand strong had rallied around the place, clamorous. They hurled slogans to send the whole lot of them up against the wall. And death threats, as if they were still in the Middle Ages. Some naming him outright. The hate-filled cries were calling for his and Mendès France's heads on a stick. He hadn't gone there to divide people but to unite them. He'd wanted to speak to both camps and to put himself forward as someone who was unaffiliated with any particular brand of politics, but in Algiers, everything was politics. Jacques rested his head against the glass of the car window. It was ice cold, though it seemed to him like fire. Maybe because his head, for some time now, had been feeling like it was burning. He was convinced that in order to arrive at a community of hope, there had to be dialogue, and, therefore, a civilian truce.

Locked in bitterness and hatred, he'd said, each side finds it impossible to listen to the other. Every proposal, regardless of the spirit in which it is made, is greeted with suspicion, immediately twisted beyond recognition, and ultimately rendered useless. We find ourselves increasingly entangled in a web of accusations old and new, escalating acts of retribution, and endless bitterness, as in an ancient family quarrel in which grievances and discord pile up and are passed down from one generation to the next. We resign ourselves to fate too easily, he'd gone on to say. We too readily believe that, ultimately, there is no progress without bloodshed, and that the strong advance at the expense of the weak. Just then, rocks began to fly against the glass windows of the hall. There was a sudden scramble to close the blinds. Jacques's face had gone pale, but he'd continued with his lecture. It wasn't safety that worried him, his own personal safety, but the thought, the very same thought he'd been struggling for some time to dispel, that the door he was so firmly convinced could lead to a possible solution was being sealed off for good.

He concluded with a discussion of free men, those who refused both to employ terrorist tactics and to endure them. Those who did not wish to live as either victims or executioners. The audience had given him a round of applause, but deep down he knew that no one had liked what he'd had to say, though that wasn't really the point, the point was to speak the truth. To bring about a conciliation, above all else. To try to save lives, even if just a single one. That day, although unbeknownst to him at the time, several members of the National Liberation Front had been on hand, and armed, to safeguard his own life. Politics is a macabre, paradoxical game, Jacques thought to himself. Among French Algerians, there were many who believed he was just another advocate for independence, while a like number of Arabs considered him a defender of colonialism. For some, he was a naïve humanist, a Leftist who'd turned his back on his country and deserved the penalty of death. For others, a reactionary, an adherent of slavery. Those were the paradoxes of war. In an effort to unite, he'd made himself the enemy of all sides. The Communists accused him of serving the cause of American imperialism. And the Gaullists, of being in the service of Russia.

How much time has to pass before a person can stay in a country, before it becomes his own, before he's no longer considered an outsider? he'd asked himself almost angrily. More than ten years ago, the leaders of an Arab nationalist movement had made it known to him that their most hated enemies were Frenchmen like him. The mediators. The proponents of dialogue. Much worse than the colonialists, they'd explained, because your type weakens us in our will to fight. Whose side are you on? You're not on the side you should be. The question and the accusation were ever present. And if you didn't play the game, that made you the enemy of both sides. A deserter. Jacques stared at the glass windowpane. It seemed to him that all the glass in the world would one day shatter into a million pieces. And he was forced to roll it down. He needed to breathe.

What could Édouard possibly have read? Had he really had time enough to dig up something damning? Perhaps some code name, although he wouldn't have been able to understand it. The initials most likely wouldn't have told him anything. But what if that wasn't the first time he'd done it? What if he'd found some other occasion and had copied out the list Jacques had compiled with the names of a wide range of people connected to the Algerian terror cabal, individuals who'd pledged themselves to a cause whose full implications they were only vaguely aware of, who bullheadedly refused to acknowledge the more than likely consequences of an overly hasty independence movement and insisted on supporting means that could not, in any conceivable sense, justify the ends, and all while simultaneously turning a blind eye to the massacre of so many innocent Frenchmen and Arabs?

They were mostly names of French citizens. From the metropole. Names of artists, of intellectuals, of women as well as men. Lots of women. Jacques knew of professors, journalists, historians, lawyers and judges, ministers' and generals' sons, union bosses, actors, seminary students, and even priests and monks who were on the FLN's payroll. Seventy-five thousand francs a month for the most heavily involved. At the beck and call of O.B., the Kabyle man who came over in June of 1957, was mocked for his garish form of dress, and now ruled them all with an iron fist. Jacques had been similarly derided on more than one occasion for his humble origins, for resembling a Mediterranean street urchin, as he'd been called, with one part affection and two parts disdain. That Kabyle man, handing down order after order, only stooped to speak with F.J., the network's boss, when he decided someone in their inner circle needed to be taken out. And they were finding it harder and harder to free themselves from that tangle of ideas.

F.J., the mixed-up philosopher, and H.C., the capital-hating financier, of course, but also J.D., his own J.D. And also O.T., F.T., F.S., with his Jaguar, S.S., Fathers D., U., B., S., and C., A.M., P.M., E. and P.B., P. and C.CH., F.M., J-M.D., A.F., G.S., and a lengthy et al. And there was S.R., his S.R., who let them use his film studio. And J-P.S. and S. de B.? Maybe, perhaps. Although he wasn't a man of action. His area of expertise was thought. Or his perversion, rather. That afternoon, he'd discovered that the sheet he'd listed them all out on—just one record of the many he was using as documentation for his novel, and which he planned on destroying once he was finished with it—was out of place. He thought he must have moved it himself without realizing. It didn't occur to him to ask him about it, and then he'd forgotten all about it. He didn't give it a second thought. It was only just then that he'd begun turning it over in his head, after learning what had happened to Édouard. And now he kept running mentally back through the list, which he knew by heart. There were also J.V., C.M., E.B., R.B., R.D, and, naturally, D.D. And the Keeper of the Seals, yes, the Minister of Justice, E.M. And his adviser, G.G. And the mayor of Algiers, J.CH.?

197

An entire organization set in motion to arrange forged documents, transportation and housing, border crossings, legal and medical coverage, cash and weapons provisions, and prisoner support, and also to arrange for the generation of propaganda to be distributed through underground linotyped pamphlets or large-run newspapers, but with money laundering and revolutionary tax collection at the top of the list. The financial lung of the FLN. Five hundred million francs a month, collected from among one hundred and fifty thousand contributors for whom threats were the main incentive. The Front had succeeded in setting up a bona fide parallel state in France, with its own courts of justice, its own military zones, or *wilayas*, and even its own version of a Social Security system. And it had made sizeable inroads in Germany, Switzerland, and Belgium. All thanks to those sacks of bills with a smell so rank it was enough to make their couriers retch. Thousands upon thousands of bills, groped by so many hands it was sickening. Fuel for terror.

And there it was again, one of his recurring nightmares. The one with his own execution. Always a different rendition, but always the same. In one of them, not long ago, he'd swiveled around to see himself marching toward his punishment in the company of several other prisoners, among them Scotto Lavina, a friend of his from Algiers that he only ever saw very rarely these days but for whom he nevertheless felt a great deal of affection. Scotto whispered into his ear—My wife told me about X. and Y. yesterday. Jacques warned him—No first names. Whatever you do, no first names. And immediately, in a sugary voice, as though he were speaking with someone who felt unwell, his friend apologized—Oh, do forgive me. Someone in the group of men, which was surrounded on all sides by guards, asked Jacques why, and he, just as he was reaching the bottom step of that daunting staircase, replied—I want to stick to generic names. He'd repeated that phrase over to himself later, and it gave him a certain sense of peace. Then he saw his children at the top of the staircase he'd begun to make his way up, his hands tied behind his back, moving very quickly, aware at all times of the feeling of someone pushing him forward from behind. Jacques hugged the two of them and cried, for the first time. They said goodbye to him as usual. Or that's how it had seemed to him, at least.

No. Jacques wasn't looking to finger anyone. The supreme goal of art is to confuse the judges, to strike down all accusations, he told himself, recalling a few of his own words. He just wanted to write something strongly rooted in truth, a violent, barbaric reality that generated nothing but suffering and injustice. His task was not to accuse, not to condemn, but to try to understand. Both sides. To make mutual understanding possible. But no. Édouard hadn't said anything. Maybe he'd worked at some point for the FLN, maybe he'd even wormed his way into his home for that purpose, but the time he spent with Carina and with Jacques himself must surely have made him change his mind. Perhaps that was why they'd tortured him. Carina couldn't possibly be wrong about him. But what if Carina . . . Jacques felt unable to breathe, felt the hair on the back of his neck and his forearms stand on end.

What if Carina had been their go-between? What if she knew, and that's why she'd behaved so strangely when she'd said goodbye to him? What if she knew something might happen to him, and not because of some presentiment but with certainty? In that case, was everything she'd told him about herself false? And the story of her brother, too? Had she made it all up to gain his trust? Had she been drawing from that song about the little white horse struck dead by a bolt of lightning?

Was she simply a skilled actress? An imposter? No. Not Carina. How could she fake her blush? No. She couldn't possibly be mixed up in something like this. But what if something really did happen to him? Then he'd never have the chance to find out the truth. Just as with so many matters in life that touch on us in some way or another without our ever even imagining them. Nevertheless, that new suspicion, though it had only crossed Jacques's mind for an instant, left behind an aftertaste of bitterness and a feeling, a torturous feeling, of guilt.

No, no, he told himself, trying to banish such ghosts. Both of them are innocent. It's I who am doing them wrong. And he remembered some of the words he'd spoken when he'd been awarded the prize. Words and phrases, even the simplest ones, cost their weight in freedom and blood. For that reason, a writer must learn to wield them with restraint. That's why he'd decided long ago to lapse into silence, to refrain from making any public statements, and to stick to narrative works. No newspaper articles. No speeches, either. He'd wanted to remove himself from politics forever. But words in works of fiction could also end up spelling death. Those words, too, could prove jeopardous. He'd get rid of a few pages. He'd tear them out. Maybe he could get away with erasing a couple of paragraphs. Or taking out an entire chapter. He'd do it. As soon as he got to Paris. He was anxious. Now suddenly he was in a hurry to arrive, and he was almost tempted to ask Michel to step on it. He'd have been stunned.

Although, perhaps . . . Yes, if something did end up happening to him, perhaps someone else would do it for him. Someone else would handle the ripping out of those pages. One of his enemies, whose ranks were growing by the day. Some of them were very powerful. Others were vicious enough to wipe him, and not just a manuscript, from the face of the earth. Or maybe his ex-wife would do it. Maybe it would be she who would eventually tear out those pages. To protect him. Or some friend, frightened by what Jacques had written to him. Or someone on the police force. Or even someone belonging to the highest echelons of power. Every time he thought about the whole thing, a bomb seemed to go off inside his head, and thousands of papers swirled around him. So then he wasn't wrong? He did have cause to be afraid? So then those two guys in the work overalls, back at the restaurant . . . *What would you do if you were invisible?*

And the letter that kid had sent him from Marseille . . . Suddenly all the doubts he'd always had about Saddok came flooding back to him. And about so many other people he'd thought of as moderates and had turned out to be with the Front, as well. Seeking independence at all costs, without recognizing the deadly errors such a policy would lead to . . . Perhaps he should speak with Maurice Papon, the prefect of the Paris police. No, I've lost my mind, he told himself. How could he possibly go and speak with that man? And yet, he imagined Georges Loubet, André Malraux's chief of staff at the Ministry of Cultural Affairs, or his deputy, Paul Maillot, or indeed any representative of the French government, shut up for hours and hours, pouring over evidence inside some room at a city hall in any given small town along the route from Lourmarin to Paris—although it would be somewhere much nearer to the capital itself at that point—that small town being the place he would have met his death barely an hour earlier.

The gendarmes would take all of his belongings, everything they could find on his body or scattered around it. His black leather wallet with his passport inside it, a few personal photographs, the manuscript of his novel, his journal, and the two books he had on him at the time. A school edition of *Othello* and *The Gay Science*. A shiver ran down Jacques's spine, as he imagined each and every detail of his own death. And while Francine and his closest friends were being informed of the bad news, he thought, while she was making her way down there and checking, just as he'd asked her on so many occasions to do, that he actually was dead, that he wouldn't be buried alive, whatever high-level government official it was would not be reading the Nietzsche or the Shakespeare. He'd have read them long ago and would probably even be able to cite a few passages from memory. Or perhaps not. In any case, he may not have the slightest intention of ever reading them at all.

No. That man would concentrate his reading efforts on the manuscript. Even then, there was a chance that most of his new book, *The First Man*, which would remain unfinished, might be spared the spoilage. Maybe they wouldn't take any pages out, or almost none. Or maybe they would, maybe a lot of them would be lost. Especially from the latter portion of the book. And the notes. A large number of them were sure to disappear. And that was assuming that all those papers, after his death, didn't just end up scattered all over the countryside, among the trees, along some random highway. The mud would soak them, the wind would toss them to and fro, and they'd eventually rot in the rain. One way or another, he felt certain that if something happened to him, his book would never come to be published. Not even some mutilated version of it. In the best of cases, it would take years and years for it to resurface. A lot of things would have to change before that could happen. There was no one who stood to benefit from the whole thing coming to light. Nobody seemed willing to make the slightest effort. To not lie. To speak the truth. To avoid generalizations. The impossibility of speaking in a world where it wasn't exactly silence that reigned was increasingly painful to him.

Sooner or later, my intellectual executioners will become my physical executioners, thought Jacques. Those who attempt to know and control everything end up killing everything. Francis Jeanson, Monsieur Néant's intellectual flunky, had gone on to become Omar Boudaoud's hatchet man. He'd made fun of him for remaining so steadfast in his defense of a third way, for being convinced of the need for non-violence, and for having always believed that the Left could not possibly position itself against such a notion. Jacques had been an idealist, he'd been naïve. Yes, they were right. And they were powerful, too powerful, and they would continue to be powerful for a long, long time. Perhaps they'd never cease being so. They'd managed to turn him into a pariah of sorts, even though the abuse he'd suffered was so far only verbal. And he'd thought that he'd left the worst of it behind him by withdrawing as much as possible from public life and abstaining from writing in to newspapers, but now suddenly he was seized by the notion that the worst of it, the real violence, some act of physical aggression, something beyond mere threats, might yet befall him. And that it might affect others besides. Not just himself.

A person who thinks, with no sense of compunction whatsoever, or with so little that it surely wouldn't be long before he'd have it printed up under his own signature, that Communist-led violence is not only necessary, inasmuch as it represents "proletariat humanism," but also worthy of admiration . . . That practice of goading people on in their antagonism of one another, instead of acknowledging the suffering of both those who die and those who kill, was absolutely abhorrent to him. Every time he recalled one of those remarks he'd heard issuing from the lips of his friend way back, remarks the latter then began publishing, untrammeled by any process of due consideration—normally so essential to a writer's task—that might have persuaded him not to, he shook all over with sadness and disgust. Killing is necessary in the early days of a rebellion, he'd heard him say in reference to the very type of drama unfolding in countries like Algeria. To kill a European is to kill two birds with one stone: you're eliminating the oppressor as well as the oppressed. When it's over, you're left with one dead man and one free man. He'd heard him make that argument more than once, and with that monumental self-satisfaction of his, he'd probably end up publishing it, as well. Prudence was not one of his virtues.

Jacques's head had been aching for a good while now. And he felt shivery in his gut and feverish in his forehead. He attempted to get comfortable in his seat, and he turned to look at his friend. Michel sat at the wheel, alert to every last detail of the road, happily engrossed in the driving of that machine that seemed to give him so much pleasure, and completely unaware of the terrors, quite beyond his well-known fear of speed, that were currently wreaking havoc within Jacques's head. I'm not cut out for politics, he thought. I never have been, and I never will be, because I'm incapable of desiring or accepting the death of my adversary. Michel must have sensed his friend's eyes on him, because at that same instant, he turned ever so slightly and winked at him. What's with the death-row sulk? We'll be there soon enough, he smiled at him. Jacques did his best to return the smile, resolved not to come unglued, not to lose his grip on reality, not to alarm the others.

Was he losing his mind? His blood seemed to be thumping furiously in his temples, his skull felt about to explode. He lit a cigarette and breathed in deeply. It wasn't long before he was enveloped in a cloud of smoke, and he felt a little better. In the end, if something happened to him, if he lost his life on that trip—or on some other trip, because it could just as easily happen any place at all, or any other day; it was no more than a hypothesis, after all, and equally valid as its counterclaim —they'd say the cause of his death was unimportant. But if it happened now, on that trip, in that car, he thought, then maybe they'd blame the redhead. They'd say he was driving too fast. Or that he'd been drinking. He wouldn't even put it past them to come out with something completely fabricated, even something utterly stupid, leaning on whatever half-baked excuse they could come up with, like a black cat having crossed the car's path.

It was a straight stretch of road, someone would say. The pavement was dry. And the whole highway, deserted. It was fate! There'd be talk of outrage, of the abolition of the order of man by inhuman forces, they'd say it was an unforeseeable death, completely out of left field. That there was an unbearable absurdity about it. Others would insist that it was written. In the stars. That it was fated to happen, when perhaps somebody had caused it to happen with their own two hands, by guiding the course of history.

THEY WERE COMING FOR HIM

More than five minutes had gone by since the Facel Vega had pulled out of the restaurant's parking lot. Now it was making its way along the Route Nationale 5, a good, wide highway nearly thirty feet across. The terrain was flat. There was no one else on the road. And the hour being now past midday, the pavement had dried in the timid sun that had followed the morning's mist, a fine, frozen rain that Jacques had at one point even imagined might outlast him. As for the visibility, it was crystal clear. And the speed at which the vehicle was traveling, moderate, despite its being such a powerful car. A 1958 FV 3B, with a French chassis and an American engine that did perfect justice to its magnificent form, a Chrysler V8. Eight cylinders arranged in V formation. The second that car had crossed into town on its way to Jacques's house, the whole place had flocked to it. There was an instant swarming of children and men. Truly, that car was a star.

Jacques looked down and focused his gaze on the keychain. The Chrysler star jangled around in the middle of that clutch of metal. Vega, or Alpha Lyrae, is a first magnitude star, he thought. And he remembered that its name came from the Arabic *waqi*, meaning "that which falls." His own Citroën was like a banged up old sardine can next to that machine. It was strange, not to say ridiculous, to cross the country in a car like his friend's at such a pitiful pace. More than an automobile, it was like an ocean liner, plying its way carefully through the ice fields of the North Pole. Or like the Norwegian whaling ship of the same name, *Vega*, on its plodding return journey now eighty years since, months after cracking open the frozen Northeast Passage.

Hey, hey, what's the rush? Jacques exclaimed every time he felt his friend pressing down lightly on the accelerator. From the back, Janine and Anne kept their eyes on the speedometer inlaid on the metal dashboard that was hand-painted to look like elegant walnut wood paneling. Root wood, which has more burls. Every Facel Vega was distinct from all the others. The control panel alone would have made it a one-of-a-kind. As soon as he'd laid eyes on it, Jacques was reminded of Meursault's mother's coffin in *The Stranger*. And a shiver had run down his spine. A coffin painted with black walnut powder, a dye made from the husks of the nuts and used as a varnish to make any other wood look like walnut. He'd always been surprised at the luxuriousness of the coffins most people chose to bury their family members in. Or themselves. Often spending ruinous amounts on them. With their crucifixes and their silver fittings, their fine woods and their soft, satiny fabrics lining the insides. When the only thing they were good for was rotting and rusting away beneath the earth. Yet another ridiculous ostentation. Then again, weren't they all?

Before setting out on that trip, he'd recited once more— There is nothing more scandalous than the death of a child, and nothing more idiotic than dying in a car crash. He'd said that to his friend Emmanuel Roblès, too, on a trip to Sidi Ferruch, and asked him to drive more slowly. There's nothing more idiotic than dying in an automobile accident. And this coming from a man who was convinced that everything in this life was absurd. But as soon as he said it, his friends would lay off the accelerator. Don't worry, Michel had promised him. We'll take it slow. We'll make the journey in two legs. We'll stop to sleep, grab some lunch, have dinner, and we'll celebrate Anne's birthday. We'll get in on Monday, a low-key day, after the holiday weekend. Jacques could find no reason to object. It was all very reasonable. But his fear was not. And Anne, Annouchka, who was almost like a daughter to him, had turned eighteen just yesterday. They'd celebrated over dinner, at the Chapon Fin de Thoissey, then gone to bed early. Now he rode along in silence. He was thinking about Édouard. About whether he should turn back around as soon as they got to Paris.

There were just a few miles left to go before they got to Fontainebleau. He'd try to get in touch with Francine again. He could catch a train and make his way to Aix-en-Provence. He had several appointments set up in Paris, but he'd cancel them. It was a simple matter of making a few phone calls, wiring off a few telegrams. I can't leave them all alone, he thought to himself. Over and over. He turned to the window and saw his face reflected in the glass. The color of his skin had changed. Fear acts as an acid, he thought. Out of nowhere, Michel started talking about a life insurance policy he'd been wanting to take out. As if in his friend's silence, in the look on his face, he'd read the thoughts darkening his spirits. He, too, often thought about death. Jacques remarked that his own lungs were so full of holes, he'd have a hard time finding anyone willing to write him a policy. But Michel's were pretty well shot, too. I want to die before Janine, he confided, glancing at her in the rearview mirror at the same time. Because I couldn't live without her. I, on the other hand, she rejoined with a smile, want to go on living. With you, of course, but without you, too, if that's how it has to be. Don't worry, Jacques told her, turning around. They can embalm both of us and stick us in your living room to keep you company. And he laughed. What do you say, Michel? I'd move to a new house, shuddered Janine, who couldn't stand the idea of seeing a dead body.

What would work better? An embalmer or a taxidermist? No idea, Michel replied. Although a taxidermist is only for animals. And finding a good embalmer these days can't be easy. In ancient Egypt, they'd pull your brain out through your nose with a metal rod, Jacques explained with sudden animation. They'd take your guts out, too, your intestines, lungs, and liver, and store them all in jars. Stop, stop, Janine protested. No, I want to hear about it, Anne pleaded. Maybe a taxidermist would be better, Jacques continued. They probably make good hairstylists. And instead of setting us up in the middle of the living room, you could prop us up in the entryway with our hands facing palm-up so you could set your keys on them when you got home and be sure to grab them when you left. Like a couple of hunting trophies. Janine didn't bother replying. Jacques quickly became lost again in his gloomy thoughts, in that unbearable feeling of drawing nearer and nearer to some unknown catastrophe. On the road behind them, without anyone noticing it, a succession of shimmering drops trickled out onto the dry asphalt, like dark blood, a long, oily constellation. The blood of the beast. Tick tock, tick tock. Like a liquid timepiece, silent and thick.

Were human beings always turning tail and flying from death only to then run smack into it? He remembered when they'd left Paris ahead of the Germans' arrival twenty years ago. They'd fled the Gestapo on bicycles. Pierre, Michel, and

Janine had brought him along with them, because he'd been involved in running a Resistance paper. Back then his name, to his comrades, was Bouchard. Some of his writers had been shot. After that, he'd been provided with false documents. Under the name of Albert Mathé. They'd taken up refuge in the countryside. The three of them had swapped turns carrying Janine on their handlebars. His turns were shorter, because he often had trouble breathing. The tuberculosis that had nearly killed him back in '31 had been flaring up again. He wasn't sleeping enough. He wasn't eating well. And he was constantly smoking. But he liked carrying Janine, catching whiffs of her hair and her skin out there among the rural scents.

She'd married Pierre shortly afterward, and they'd had Anne, but the marriage didn't last long, and after their separation, Janine had gotten married again, this time to Michel, Pierre's cousin. Were all three of them in love with her, then? And she with all three of them? Back then, Jacques was happy. Now the vim and vigor of those youthful legs pedaling through the fields had been replaced with the horsepower of a luxury vehicle. And Pierre with Anne, Janine and Pierre's daughter, another lovely-smelling woman. He'd promised to help her, so as soon as they got to Paris, they'd get down to work. In his head, Jacques ran over all the meetings he had lined up there. With María. With Catherine. With Mi. Before leaving Lourmarin, he'd written a letter to each one. He owed many of his deepest emotions to women. Women, he said to himself, are the true luxury. At least they were to him. Love and friendship. Though there were also his children, the sun, the sea. And the stars. Jacques revealed to his friends that he was convinced he'd made all the women in his life happy, even when he'd loved them all at once. Michel smiled. Janine didn't have to speak a word. She was completely sure of it.

Death is the only certainty, Jacques then said to himself. That's why people didn't need to bother swearing anything. Not even love. Just go out and love. Love boundlessly. Right then, the highway began running alongside an enormous, open field that was crowded with carts and wagons all strung together by lines hung with clothing in a kaleidoscope of hues. It was a vast, sprawling gypsy camp. It put Jacques in mind of what people down in Lourmarin called the curse of the castle. During some renovation works at the castle, when a cultural foundation it was hoped would rival that of the Medicis in Florence was being created and the site was being prepped to become its headquarters—the same foundation that had previously recruited a teacher of his, Jean Grenier, and with which he himself had ties—several gypsy families that had been living there for years and years among the ruins had been kicked out.

All those who have dealings with the castle shall die a horrible death. At least, that's what people said. They said the gypsy queen had uttered that curse against the historian who'd purchased the castle and decided to restore it so that painters, sculptors, and writers might flock to it every summer. He'd died five years later, in a car crash. He'd smashed into a watering trough. Or so they said. When people make up their minds to feed a superstition, they're not only willing to believe anything they hear, they'll sometimes make it up themselves. And in town, all the talk was about those who'd gone after him. One, shot. Another, found floating in his bathtub. A third, heart attack. And another, killed in a second car crash. Completely run-of-the-mill deaths that people were determined to find some mystery in.

Not only was Jacques not superstitious, he found it illogical that so many people in the twentieth century, in Europe, still were. Yet he couldn't prevent a shiver from running down his spine when he saw all those people milling around among the clothes. The world was full of poor people. And it always would be. And these ones here didn't even have the sun and the sea that had afforded him happiness in the midst of the most extreme poverty. But perhaps they did know love, just as he in his life, thanks to his mother, had known it. A silent love, almost entirely lacking in outward intimations. A girl of about six paused to watch the car as it drove past. She was standing next to a horse, clutching a bald-headed, dirt-covered doll under one arm, and her black hair fell down to her waist. Suddenly she raised her hand, grinned, and waved goodbye to them. Jacques rolled down his window and returned the farewell. *Le petit cheval blanc*, he reminisced. *Mais un jour dans le mauvais temps, un jour qu'il était si sage, il est mort par un éclair blanc. Tous derrière et lui devant . . .*

Janine and Anne had turned around to look. The girl was waggling her doll in the air and bouncing up and down with glee. You see? He's a charmer, Janine remarked. Irresistible. Even the youngest of girls go crazy for him. He's not just good-looking. He knows how to listen. And that intent concentration is one of his most attractive qualities. That, and his carefully reasoned passion for life. His contagious amicability. His perpetual good humor. His uprightness, and his equanimity, much gentler and more just than that of any Solomon. His love of freedom. Enough, enough, Michel protested. I don't think that little girl could have possibly seen all that. Jacques breathed a little easier seeing his friend rush to his defense like that. No. It's so Anne starts getting an idea of how to spot a good man. Gee, Mom. That's going to be tough, the young woman joked. And that sad look of his, just like his smile, Janine insisted. Jacques attempted to flash a smile, but his thoughts, ever more somber, pulled him away again.

He'd run up against the scythe. He just remembered that he'd left one of his friend René's books on his desk, open to the page containing a poem entitled "The Raised Scythe." Save for here, no place, disgrace is everywhere. That was the last line. René had come by to visit him a few days before he'd left for Paris. They'd discussed a book they wanted to publish together. A book about Provence. With photographs of various places accompanied by texts written by each of them. When they'd said goodbye, Jacques had asked him to be sure, whatever might happen, to see the project through. Arching his eyebrows, René had placed a hand on his shoulder. Your old marked-for-death syndrome back again, is it? he'd asked. Back again, Jacques had replied. Don't go to Paris. Stay here. I have to go. Among other things, I've got a meeting to see about the theater. He was supposed to have a shot at being put in charge of a national theater, and the entire company was anxiously awaiting the outcome. If they gave it to him, they'd have more freedom to do things their own way from then on.

Yes. Nothing got past René, despite so much time having passed since their last meeting. His old marked-for-death syndrome was back again. He was the only person he could talk to about it. René was the only person he could converse with freely about his fear. Left-leaning by nature, like himself, he was one of the rare few that were able to perceive the beam in their own eye. And to acknowledge it with all the courage one would expect of a man. Jacques always cracked up at his dislike of Monsieur Néant. Of all of those tin-pot prophets, those café intellectuals, many of whom bore aristocratic names. And suddenly the accident he'd had at the end of '48 sprang into his mind. His wife and two children were with him. Bidasse and Mandarine were just three years old at the time. He'd had a febrile seizure brought on by his tuberculosis, although he'd thought at first that it was just a flu. It was raining buckets, and he lost control and veered off the road, in the other Citroën, the first one he'd had, which was also black. Luckily, they'd all been fine.

Jacques rooted around in his jacket pocket, pulled out a packet of Gitanes, and leaned forward to reach for the lighter on the Facel's dashboard. He took a long, deep drag, and before exhaling, he rolled down the window so as not to bother the others with his smoke. Michel went to turn on the radio, but Jacques reminded him there was a strike. There'll be nothing but music and news flashes. Several fantastic chords rang out. Mozart. It was the Requiem, the most tearful passage, and Michel quickly spun the dial. An unfinished funeral piece, he'd likely have thought. Not the best choice for cheering up his friend. Breaking news. The death toll in Algeria continues to rise. Don't change it. Leave it there. And as he moved his hand to stop his friend from changing the station again, a sprinkling of ash fell onto Jacques's pants. The mayor of Changarnier and his wife were assassinated this morning in the Djelfa Province. In Kroubs, in the Constantine Province, a grenade went off in a local shop. One person was killed and thirteen were injured. This rabid nationalism has been out of control for far too long now, Jacques said. Ever since it turned against the dispossessed on both sides, not even caring that these are their own people.

They heard a caw. Perched on a stone cross, a black, glossy bird stretched its wings and took flight. An entire horde of crows, which had been huddling low against the dark earth until that very instant, rose up behind it. The silence in that spot was so absolute and the hum of the engine so smooth that they could hear every last rustle of feathers. And soaring in circles through that dirty-white sky, all the birds began to cry out at once. The poverty almost everyone lives in over there

215

is downright scandalous. Jacques felt a need to speak. And he continued his train of thought out loud. It was years ago that we let what might have been our last chance of securing some sort of peaceful coexistence slip away. And we've been stuck in this never-ending cycle ever since. Revenge, that deep-rooted desire to punish the other, is at best nothing but a waste of time. Jacques thought back to the anti-French broadcasts on the Cairo radio, inciting against those they still considered colonists. Kill them all. Spare not a single Frenchman . . . The Egyptian prime minister had made a declaration to the effect that they were merely reprising what a significant chunk of the French population had been saying about them. Such rhetoric was all too familiar.

And once again, he reflected on just how necessary a revolution still was. The revolution of souls. But how to bring it about? He knew all too well that every revolution ended up becoming dangerous, so perhaps it was more appropriate to talk about the revolt of souls. A constant, unremitting revolt, with not a moment's pause. Then again, yes. Perhaps the only revolution that was truly possible was just that. The revolution of souls. The radio was discussing the death of Fausto Coppi. He'd succumbed to a tropical disease just a few days earlier. An asymmetrical man of humble origins, like Jacques. Two different women had fought over the leading role at his funeral, just as they'd fought for his heart in life. Seeing the cyclist standing alongside his brother Serse's coffin, nine years ago, had made a deep impression on Jacques. Two identical brothers. One living. The other laid out in his casket. The same face. The exact same expression. The same body stuffed into the exact same jacket. It was like looking at a lifeless version of yourself in the mirror. An impossible occurrence. Like describing your own death in a book.

They say celebrities are particularly prone to suffering horrible fates. That was Janine speaking. From the backseat. There it was again. Fate. Always lying in wait. In this instance, with the cyclist, in the form of malaria. Jacques felt the urge to break things down. Couldn't it be that when it's a poor person, almost nobody realizes or seems to give it a second thought? Who, except Carina and his wife, Jacques's ex-wife, that is, was going to care about what might happen to someone like Édouard? Maybe the man's two daughters back in Belgium, although their mother might decide not to tell them. It was possible they'd never find out. It wouldn't even show up in the papers. He couldn't leave them all alone. He had to go back. His head had been hurting for a while now, and his neck was starting to seize up. He couldn't clear his head of those whirling thoughts. The image of Édouard, beaten, injured, possibly on the verge of death. And Carina at his side. He should be with them. And out of nowhere, he remembered back to the horoscope reading Max Jacob had given him. When he was very young. He'd foreseen for him an untimely, ruthless death. Oh no, no. He wasn't superstitious. And yet . . .

Jacques ran his fingers over the train ticket he hadn't ended up using but still had in his pocket. He'd been afraid. He'd felt a hunch he shouldn't make that particular journey, he, who didn't believe in the autocracy of the stars. His suitcase was on that train, on its way to Paris. He'd sent it on ahead of him, because the trunk on the Facel Vega was tiny. He had to think about something else. He was suffocating. He rolled down the window again to breathe in a little good, clean air. He felt as if he were being forcibly shuttled along, like a man lying inside a coffin in a state of suspended animation, unable to move or scream, but knowing he's being taken to be buried.

Or a death-row inmate, weighted down with chains, being transported inside a prison van to the Conciergerie, the palace housing the old Paris prison, where in a few hours' time, he'd have his head chopped off. Crowds would swirl around the car. Scores of people would peer in curiously, trying to catch a glimpse of him as if he were some rare insect. He had to get out of that infernal automobile.

Car brakes can fail, he repeated to himself. The dialectics of Jean Paul and Francine, J-P.S. and F.J. And he thought back to those two men he'd seen servicing Michel's car at the restaurant they'd just eaten at. What if they'd sabotaged it? What if they'd tinkered with the steering or the brakes? Why was he suddenly flooded with such dread? His dread was recurring, it surfaced whenever he was confronted with the unknown, and especially at the thought of death. An old friend who'd rushed at him every evening since he was a boy, advancing just as swiftly as the darkness devouring the light and the earth. But at that time of day, it was completely absurd. It was just coming up on two in the afternoon. It was an hour of light, despite the sky being white and thick, like a closed door. *He never saw the Spring arise to gild the dreary landscape o'er. He never saw the sunny skies, either behind or before.* Jacques looked in the rearview mirror. He got the feeling there was a car following them. But he didn't see anything. What a sense of impotence and isolation, being unable to speak to his friends about what was frightening him.

He glanced around. The rain had petered out hours ago. The pavement was dry. The highway, straight as an arrow, ran between two rows of trees standing beautifully in their austerity, not a single leaf on their branches. They were plane trees. Panthers of winter, he'd written in the book he was preparing with his friend René, next to a photograph of a tree trunk straining its every last muscle to reach the far-off sun. A desiccated rime sweat had crusted into all the various creases of his skin. Just then, the air lit up again with a timid smile of the sun. And finally, with the coming of that light, he was able to forget everything that was worrying him, and he lost himself in an imagined contemplation of Mi's back. He brushed his hand across her neck, sweeping aside her blond hair, her straight, gleaming hair, and moved slowly downward until he arrived at her waist, where he lingered, running his fingers over the cluster of freckles there on her skin in the shape of the seven-starred constellation that guided sailors from its spot in the heavens. Suddenly the car made a thumping noise. Shit! Michel shouted, and the vehicle lurched.

Jacques remembered when he was still a child and, clinging to his uncle Ernest's back, he'd glided away from the coast. He still didn't know how to swim. You're not scared, are you? his uncle had asked him. Yes, he was scared, but he didn't say so, he was spellbound by all that solitude, suspended there between the sky and the sea, each equally vast. And when he glanced back, the beach seemed to him like an invisible line. An acid fear gripped his stomach, and with the first prickings of panic, he pictured beneath him the immense, dark depths into which he would sink like a stone if his uncle were to ever let go of him. Then the boy would squeeze his arms more tightly around the muscular neck of the swimmer, who immediately said—You're scared. No, but go back. The car veered off the road, and through the glass window, Jacques saw not his grandmother, with her long, black prophetess dress, warning him once more that he was going to end up on the gallows, but his mother, who smiled at him, the same way she had once a year when she'd ridden the tram with him to attend his school's annual promotion ceremony.

And at that same exact instant, Jacques recaptured space and light, as the car glanced off a plane tree on the left-hand side of the road and plowed into a second one, some forty-two feet past the first and on the opposite side, ramming straight into his door. Was it a nightmare? That recurring dream where they were coming for him, to chop his head off? Or reality? He tried to remain attentive to what had been transpiring inside the car over the last several seconds. Michel's attempts to regain control, Janine and Annouchka's screams from the backseat, each of the points of impact with the trees, but an invincible fatigue was creeping over his entire body, and he finally closed his eyes. There was almost no movement around him. Just a single wheel spinning in the air and the body of the car creaking every so often, as if it were old and groaning. But Jacques could no longer perceive any of that.

A few seconds later, there was a squeal of brakes, and another automobile stopped a short distance away from where the Facel sat, split in two. The dashboard, the entire nose, and the two front doors lay some fifty feet ahead. The rest was wrapped like a snake, or a gigantic wad of gum, or a boomerang, around one of those bare-branched plane trees lining the highway. On the other side of the road, beyond the thirty feet of asphalt, the spectacular engine sat alone, looking every bit as absurd as some urban sculpture. One of the wheels had flown off, too, the front left one, taking with it part of the control arm, which had been yanked clean off. A man stepped out and went running over. Another man followed him a few seconds later. Neither of the two went to the aid of the driver, whom they spotted lying crumpled on the ground a few yards in front of the vehicle, in the middle of a pool of blood, or the two women, passed out in the mud on the side of the road. Next to them, a dog whimpered, its body flattened into the ground.

The man in the passenger seat had flown backward against the rear window, and his head had shattered the glass, but his body remained trapped inside the car. One of the two men approached the corpse and looked at it. His neck was broken. His skull, fractured. But not a single drop of his blood had been spilt. The line running across his forehead was clean. A dark, unbroken line. A decisive stroke, a long strike-through. As if a bolt of lightning had come down from the sky and burned everything inside him. Kaddour stared at the dead man for a few moments. An intense wave of emotion washed over his entire body. He'd come to admire that man, after having read some of his writings, a series of articles in which he'd discussed the misery of the Kabyle people, the need for peaceful coexistence between Arabs and Frenchmen. What if he was right? He recalled something doctor Rieux had said: You have to try to cure as much as possible. To avoid absolute condemnation. He felt himself flushing in the face of that new victim, but Hishâm quickly shook him from his trance. Do you have it? Only then did Kaddour lean over the body, to locate the briefcase. It's not here. It has to be around here somewhere. The car's been torn in half, and almost everything inside it's flown out.

The Skye Terrier, wild with rage, began barking and charged in their direction. It planted itself, snarling, baring its teeth, a few inches from where Kaddour stood. Hishâm pulled out his gun. Don't even think about it, Kaddour shouted at him, but at that same instant, the dog leapt at the man, sinking its teeth into his calf muscle. Hishâm shot it. You idiot! It's nothing but a big, furry rat. You could have just kicked it. And now what are we supposed to do? What if someone heard the shot? There's a gas station right nearby. Pick it up! We have to get it out of here and dump it somewhere, quick. Let's get moving. I hear a car. Someone's coming. Pick it up! he shouted again. They're still going to suspect something. Dogs never leave their masters' sides in these kinds of situations. Hishâm appeared unable to move. Pick it up, or I'm going to kill you, Kaddour threatened, already rushing back to the car. Hishâm bent down to pick up the dog and rushed after him. What about the briefcase? We can't waste any time looking for it now. Then we did all this for nothing, Hishâm lamented. Not for nothing, no. Now we have one enemy fewer. Hishâm stuck the animal's body in the trunk. And they jumped hastily back into the car.

Anyhow, Kaddour said, Petit Boxeur saw him dropping off his suitcase at the Avignon station, bound for Paris. Maybe the document's in there. If that's the case, our brothers will have gotten ahold of it. Hishâm had already started the engine, and they took off. By the way, that's one quick finger you've got there . . . Look who's talking. The arrogance in Hishâm's voice and eyes were galling to him. He was no doubt referring to the boy he'd run into again in that café back in Marseille. I didn't kill him. I just shot his parrot. I respect intelligence and valor. Kaddour liked to think that a little ingenuity and courage were all it took to derail fate, to turn it around, flip it upside down. The way he saw it, the moment a brave man stood up and rebelled against something, he became invulnerable in a sense, no matter how precarious his victory. But realizing he was being overly explicit, he went on the offensive. What are you, stupid? Don't you know how to count? In the report we heard on the radio, it said there were six people dead. And besides, do you really think you're so lily-white? You killed this one, and I'm not talking about the dog. With those skillful hands of yours. With your mechanical expertise. And most likely another one of them will end up dying, too. Maybe all of them.

Hishâm shot back at him. Yeah, well, you're going soft. You didn't finish off Slimane, your Petit Boxeur. And you wouldn't even let me do it instead. Kaddour stared at him fixedly, but then he smiled when he saw the bruises on his face. The punches Slimane had let fly at him back in the forest had served only to sharpen his ears and his feeling of bitterness. Kaddour slipped his gun out of his pocket and pressed the barrel into his partner's belly. As they continued to put distance between themselves and the scene, a truck pulled to a stop beside the remains of the car. The Facel Vega's clock had slowed to a halt a few minutes earlier. It read 1:55, when in fact it was 2:00 in the afternoon on Monday, January 4, 1960. The speedometer had rolled back over to zero, and that's how it was later photographed, in the center of a control panel run strangely aground in an expanse of cropland. The crash site would soon fill with cars and people, who would begin milling around the area, ogling the remains of the Facel, which lay in pieces. There were so many different fragments that people thought at first there'd been several cars. Or that there'd been an explosion.

Gendarmes, residents of nearby towns, and doctors and nurses would throng together under those trees. And they'd all get down to work. Each to his own task. The police would begin gathering up everything they could find scattered across a three-hundred-foot radius, a space the size of several football fields. A purse, a couple of shoes, items of clothing flung outwards like the contents of a piñata, several small suitcases in unusual shapes, made to match the Facel's contours, the steering wheel, a camera, and a toiletry bag all lay dotted about the field, among the strewn wreckage of two tons of metal, plastic, and leather. And a dark-colored briefcase with documents, a notebook, a manuscript, and a couple of books inside. And loose leaves of paper, which looked like stars sparkling all around in the middle of the sodden earth. Or like those myriads of miniscule, white-colored snails back in Lourmarin, speckled over almost every single plant like a sprinkling of flowers.

Two reporters would arrive on the scene very shortly after the accident. They would be the ones to spread the alarm. The dead man, lying there in the passenger seat with a single fine wound line running across his forehead, was a celebrated figure, a writer renowned the world over. A Nobel Prize winner. It would take them hours to remove the body from the wreckage. And in the meantime, the authorities would arrive. It makes no sense. What if it's an assassination? If you look at the skid marks on the road, they don't appear to have been going that fast. My men have found clear signs of sabotage. In the brake and steering systems. The envoy dispatched to the scene by the government of the republic would stare fixedly at the head of the local gendarmerie. Not possible, he'd declare, and then he'd shake his head from side to side. Not possible. Keep Papon away from all of this. And General Salan, too. Neither the prefect of the Police of Paris nor the commander of the Tenth Military Region were to start poking their noses around. And not a word to the families of any of these people. It was an accident, plain and simple. The cause? A blown tire. Excess speed. The fact that they were doing a hundred and ten, or better yet make it less, ninety is plenty, and mention that that's what the reading on the speedometer was. A scientific fact. It's reading zero, sir. What are you, stupid?

Maybe the pavement was damp. It rained this morning. And it will rain again soon, he'd add. The envoy dispatched by the government of the republic would look up. The sky would be overcast, but not dark, just a sad, thick, white color, with no source of light behind it. No doubt about it, he'd assent stonily. However you want to do it. You can even come up with some whole big theory if need be. Say a mouse or a rat climbed inside the engine looking for a nice, warm nest and gnawed through some of the wires. It's feasible enough. Rodents always get in everywhere. Especially in winter. And they eat everything they touch. I don't care. Whatever you like, however absurd you want to make it. Sir, the brakes on this car are hydraulic . . . What does that mean? They don't work with wires. Fine, so blame the driver. Say he was drunk. Or he fell asleep at the wheel. He got sick and passed out. Or blame the car. The tires. A blowout. They're extremely dangerous, you know. Blame it on speed.

Pick one. Or pick all of them. But it has to be clear that this was just an accident. I'll take full responsibility. After relaying these instructions to his go-to man on the police force, the envoy dispatched by the government of the republic would then hurry away, lost in thought, entirely indifferent to the question of whether the pavement at the time of the crash had or had not been dry. If the tires were worn or, precisely the opposite, if they were in fact practically new. He had other priorities. The last thing they needed was a martyr that could become a potential rallying point for the French Algerian cause. The echoes of de Gaulle's voice, speaking that past September, still resonated loudly. As for the reporters, they already had a juicy enough story to work with. They didn't need anything more. The truth must never come out. Was this really, he would wonder to himself, another assassination? He was confident that it was.

Shortly thereafter, Paul Maillot would shut himself up for hours and hours inside a room at the Villeblevin city hall with all the papers that had been found scattered around the car, including the manuscript of the novel that Jacques—Albert Camus's alter ego in the book—had lately been working on and that had been discovered completely intact inside his leather briefcase in the vicinity of the crash. Meanwhile, the writer's body would eventually be laid to rest inside a simple coffin, unadorned by any cross, a wooden coffin that would be placed in another of the rooms inside the city hall of that small town, a drab, austere room, with a cold, checkerboard tile floor, whose sole decorative touches were a portrait of Marianne, the personification of the French Republic, on one wall and a small bouquet of Sweet Williams set atop the casket. Little by little, family members, a handful of important personages from the world of French culture and politics, and more local residents would start trickling in. Then would come the wreaths. A few feet down the hall, Maillot's world would come crashing down around him as he realized the magnitude of the responsibility he'd just taken on, the full scope of which he'd never even imagined.

There before him, in that very manuscript, he'd find the names of some of the *porteurs de valise* that had been assisting Algerian terrorist efforts in France, a discovery that would later allow the government of the republic to dismantle their setup in just over a month. The author hadn't had time to cover his tracks, to mask some of the people in his novel behind false names, to destroy the list, to tear out a few of the more compromising pages himself. When the police got down to work on the matter, Jeanson would make good his escape. His cohorts would not. For their part, the French Algerians, feeling General de Gaulle had betrayed them with his recent recognition of Arab Algerians' right to self-determination, would waste no time in mounting their insurrection. And shortly afterward, thousands of men, women, and children would be gunned down or have their throats slit. *La valise ou le cercueil.* The suitcase or the coffin. Those who could, would get themselves out, with their trunks and their baby carriages stuffed with belongings and their hastily rolled up mattresses in tow. Or with a simple bundle stuck under one arm. They'd cram the airport departure lounges, the wharf-side piers. Others would flee on foot, overland across one of the country's several borders. The exodus that's being forever and continually played out at one point or another on the planet.

Car brakes can fail, but liberty has no wheels . . . Jacques had always wondered whether books like most of the ones he'd published could rightly be written, if he shouldn't have merely composed an ode to love and friendship. What would now become of his wife, his children, his mother, illiterate, old, and deaf, back in Algeria? He'd left them all alone. Just as his book was now forsaken. Even my death will be contested, he'd written a few years earlier. And yet my deepest wish today is for a silent death, one that would bring peace to those I love.

DOCUMENTARY APPENDIX

LE FIGARO, *Tuesday, January 5, 1960*

ALBERT CAMUS KILLED IN CAR CRASH NEAR VILLEBLEVINE (YONNE)

The car being driven at a high speed by Michel Gallimard crashed into a tree, apparently as the result of a blown-out tire. The driver is in critical condition. His wife and step-daughter suffered minor injuries.

[Courtesy of our special correspondent] Sens, January 4. The great writer Albert Camus, 46 years of age and winner of the Nobel Prize for Literature, met his death at approximately 2:00 p.m. this afternoon in a grisly automobile accident that took place on a highway running between Sens and Montereau, near the Yonne and Seine-et-Marne county line. Michel Gallimard, his wife Janine, and the latter's 18-year-old daughter are injured and have been taken to a hospital in Montereau . . .

COMBAT, *special edition, January 5, 1960*

The car was traveling at over 110 mph on the Route Nationale 6, between Sens and Paris. It would appear the back left tire blew out . . .

L'HUMANITÉ
Central Committee of the French Communist Party,
Tuesday, January 5, 1960

WRITER ALBERT CAMUS KILLED IN CAR CRASH

The writer Albert Camus, who was awarded the Nobel Prize for Literature in 1957, died yesterday in an automobile accident on the Route Nationale 5, not far from Champigny. He was 46 years old.

FRANCE-SOIR, *Tuesday, January 5, 1960*

The writer Albert Camus (Nobel Prize recipient) died in an automobile accident in Petit-Villeblevin (near Sens). He was 47 years old. Michel and Janine Gallimard, nephew and niece of the well-known publisher, were injured. Their daughter Anne was not hurt.

PARIS-PRESS, L'INTRANSIGEANT,
Tuesday, January 5, 1960

Nobel Prize Winner And The Most Brilliant
Spokesman Of The Postwar Generation

WRITER ALBERT CAMUS KILLED IN CAR
CRASH NEAR SENS

Sens, January 4. The writer and winner of the Nobel Prize for Literature, Albert Camus, met his death this afternoon in a car accident that took place in Petit-Villeblevin, near Villeneuve-la-Guyard (Yonne), on the Route Nationale 5.

The vehicle in which Camus was traveling was being driven by Michel Gallimard, nephew of publisher Gaston Gallimard, who was accompanied at the time by his wife, Jeanne Gallimard, and her daughter from a previous marriage, Anne.

For reasons investigators have not yet determined, the vehicle—a Facel Vega—veered off the road on a straightaway and struck a tree. It was 2:10 in the afternoon.

Albert Camus, who was in the passenger seat, died instantly. Michel Gallimard, 42, director of the La Pléiade collection, was seriously injured and taken to the Montereau hospital. Jeanne Gallimard and her daughter Anne, 18, suffered only minor injuries.

The novelist and his friends were returning from the *Midi*, where they had spent the Christmas holiday.

Albert Camus was 47 years old.

LE MONDE, *Wednesday, January 6, 1960*

A strictly private
MEMORIAL SERVICE FOR ALBERT CAMUS
TO BE HELD IN LOURMARIN

The remains of Albert Camus, fatally injured Monday afternoon in an automobile accident, will be laid to rest in Lourmarin, on the right bank of the Durance, at the foot of the Luberon Massif, near his home. Michel Gallimard, who was driving the vehicle, was seriously injured, although his condition was said Tuesday morning to have improved . . .

LES LETTRES FRANÇAISES,
No. 808, *January 21-27, 1960*

DID MICHEL GALLIMARD KILL ALBERT CAMUS?

BY ÉTIEMBLE

On January 4, 1960, at 2:00 in the afternoon, a Facel Vega had a sudden blowout on the Route Nationale 5, not far from Sens, near Petit-Villeblevin. The body of Albert Camus, who perished instantly, was pulled from the wreckage of the vehicle, which had collided with a plane tree. In the adjacent field, three people lay injured, one of them in critical condition— the driver, Michel Gallimard, who, following an operation to remove his spleen, died of an embolism in Paris in the early hours of the morning on Saturday the 9th, two hours after a medical examination had pointed to an improvement in his condition.

Since January 5, in a display of one-upmanship based on insinuation and slander, the majority of newspapers and radio stations have been characterizing Michel Gallimard as the assassin of our dear Nobel Prize recipient. One broadcaster claiming to be in the business of reporting "facts" has announced that the driver will most likely be charged with reckless homicide. Such a serious affront requires justification. And they go all out to provide it. One points to the "worn" tires that would, it seems, explain the accident. Another, possibly the same one, notes that the "hot rod" was traveling at "terrifying" speeds. More hypocritical still are those who would seek to somehow excuse the driver—a person with a "serious illness" can, as I'm sure you'll understand, have an unexpected fit. Hearsay informs these details, it embellishes them. Someone told me that Michel Gallimard was driving

234

at 93 miles an hour on a wet road. That he'd taken Camus to Lourmarin against his will. Because Camus detested traveling by car, and he'd already bought a train ticket. And that's not all, I heard they covered the distance from Lourmarin to Sens without stopping once. Others then point out that the accident took place right after they'd stopped for lunch, *if you catch my drift*. After a few days, grant you, the tone of the conversation changes. The entire affair becomes "inexplicable" or "banal." As if those who spread the initial lies, having become aware of their blundering, were now attempting to bring the catastrophe back down to its proper size, a catastrophe that is, indeed, exceptional, and not just because it involves the death of Camus.

We cannot accept either the insinuations of those first days or these more recent excuses. You have said too much, gentlemen. Show us your evidence, or if not, you can start by announcing your apologies in all the papers, on all the radio stations that attacked the honor of a man who suffered such a terrible blow that he can now no longer defend himself. Michel Gallimard is dead, and no one will ever know how this expert driver might have explained the accident. But his friends mourn, because they, too, will be unable to live long in peace until justice is done. Why am I getting involved? Because it is my duty. I've known Michel Gallimard for thirty years. I was his mentor for seven of them. Every summer, I spent several months living in close quarters with him during vacations. Afterward, we remained friends. And I hope you'll excuse this declaration, which does have some bearing on the matter at hand: I became a member of his family, a collaborator, in some small way, on his Far East classics collection, a project in which he always gave me his full support. I am quite well acquainted with his ideas, his character, his preoccupations, and his quirks.

I formed him, in a certain sense, I loved him dearly, and I admired him just as deeply. It is necessary that I speak.

Without seeking to prejudge the verdicts of the relevant experts and counter-experts, I can provide the following testimony based on several certainties.

Let us first turn our attention to the tires. Those knowledgeable about such matters will ask the journalist who described them as worn if he's seen them up close. He has not seen them, no, but he *is* recounting word for word what he's been told. After I wrote to *France-Soir* that as of just a few weeks ago, Michel Gallimard's tires had clocked less than 6,500 miles, and most likely somewhere between 4,000 and 4,400, another newspaper chimed in to say that I'm crazy and a wise guy for thinking I could make an on-the-spot evaluation that the good men at Dunlop and Michelin wouldn't be able to put out themselves until after a thorough investigation of the dismantled wheel. Did I ever say I'd evaluated the wear on the tires "on the spot"? I only said what I knew to be true, because I'd spoken about it with Michel Gallimard: a few weeks ago, the Facel Vega's tires had less than 6,500 miles on them. Further, don't think for a second that Francine Camus is going to believe your accusation that the driver put his passenger's life at risk. Would Michel, who is so passionate about his cars, who has the expertise of the Gallimard fleet's mechanics behind him, have allowed not only his own life, which he knew to be his sole life, but also his wife's, his step-daughter's, and that of one of his in-house writers, who was, moreover, like a brother of his own choosing, to be put in danger? He was so careful, so meticulous, that he always carried a complete set of replacement tires with him, to be able to swap his out at the first sign of wear. And given that those who have seen the tires in question with their own eyes have attested to them being in excellent condition, some other explanation will have to be found.

So speed, then? The car's speed has been described as "terrifying." It's being described as a "hot rod." Some say 81 miles per hour. Others say 93. The speedometer read 90, alleging assassination. A slight wiggle of the needle, as everyone knows, can significantly affect a speedometer's readout. Who can look me in the eye and tell me that in the moment when the control panel was wrenched from the vehicle, the needle remained in the exact same position it had been in just before the accident? Let us suppose that, at the moment of the car's fragmentation, it was traveling at 90 mph. It does not follow that I must accept as fact that at the moment of no return, it was also traveling at that same speed. In short, and most especially, 90 mph in a Facel Vega, and on a straightaway—only a demagogue would call that an unsafe speed. There has been a lot of talk concerning the testimony of a driver Gallimard is alleged to have passed on the road at a "terrifying" speed. A good driver, when passing another car, should do so as quickly as possible. Is the man piloting a Porsche as he overtakes a 4 CV, which can leave a 2 CV in the dust, a dangerous driver? The dangerous man is the driver of a 2 CV who gets it into his head to pass a 4 CV, or a 4 CV driver who gets into it with an Aronde, in short, the guy who overtakes others for the sake of Sunday driver bragging rights. Those who imagine themselves to be actively participating in the class struggle by overtaking a vehicle with twice the horsepower as their own are deluding themselves. That being said, what almost always occurs is the following: piqued by some impertinence he feels himself to be the victim of, the driver of the 4 CV will, as soon as he draws up even with the driver of the 2 CV, floor the accelerator and speed up to 65. The village tribune, which is to say, the guy in the 2 CV, responds in kind, in a display that, despite appearances, has nothing remotely socialist about it and always reminds me of that scene in *The Great Dictator* where Hitler and Mussolini take turns raising up their barbershop chairs in order to sit a little higher than the other. Let us imagine that a powerful car then comes around a bend in the road. If the driver happens to be Michel Gallimard, our two imbeciles are safe. If not, tough luck for them. Their slowness is terrifying, indeed, and how! When a Jaguar passes me, whether it's a 403 or even a 2 CV, I slow my Grand Large in accordance with the rules of the road. And if misfortune has it that one mile later I come across the wreckage of the car that's just "left me in the dust" strewn all over the highway, I don't believe, even for a second, that I would stoop so low as to avenge myself by telling the gendarmes that those madmen at the wheel deserved their accident. We must do away with this somewhat naïve notion of democracy according to which our sense of justice varies in inverse proportion to an engine's horsepower. Armand Salacrou confessed to me the other day that he drives a fast car. Does that make him a fascist? I very much doubt that all the millions of morons voting for Pierre Poujade are driving around in Alfa Romeos.

Furthermore, from the moment we begin manufacturing and importing sports cars, can we reasonably demand that those who purchase these machines wait patiently as they travel from Paris to Cannes behind a long line of small cars? I'll go one step further. It is precisely out of a sense of precaution that practiced drivers, as soon as they find themselves in possession of the necessary means, purchase these machines that more demagogic circles are writing off as "hot rods." When I asked him not long ago if he could still justify the purchase of a Facel Vega given the state of congestion on our highways, Michel Gallimard replied, "Yes, exactly, a vehicle like this allows me to pass people in a completely safe manner. With no risk to others, or to myself, I can, on a nice, clean straightaway, overtake three, four, or even five or six of those cars that always crowd so close together and thus prevent me from passing them one by one. It's the main reason why I remain faithful to large-cylinder engines, even to this day."

Everybody whipping up all this anger against Michel Gallimard is forgetting that speed, in cars, is not an absolute concept. At 90 mph, a Porsche can, if driven well, be less dangerous that a 4 CV that's being kept under 60. All that should be asked of a man sitting behind the wheel of a so-called hot rod is that he knows how to control it. Just as heavy vehicle licenses are required of truck drivers, permits should be issued for "over 60" driving. For all intents and purposes, Michel Gallimard earned this license at the age of twenty. He drove more than 620,000 miles without a single accident. Camus, as we know, disliked traveling by car. But he himself was quick to add—Except with Michel. I'm never scared with him. I, for my part, have traveled a great deal with Michel Gallimard. I've experienced a blowout with him. I've never been scared. A blowout at 90 mph, or even more, could not have rattled a pilot of his experience, one with twenty-five years under his belt driving extremely fast cars.

But what about tiredness, illness? After his tubercular kidney was removed, this "seriously ill" man always functioned impeccably. Ask his doctors. Tiredness doesn't explain anything, either. They'd left Lourmarin in the middle of the morning on Sunday, stopped for lunch in Orange (55 miles) and for dinner in Thoissey (155 miles). And as he always did when he knew he'd have to drive, Michel Gallimard had gone to bed early, at 10:30 p.m. On Monday morning, at 9:00

a.m., they left Thoissey. Three and a half hours later, they stopped in Sens for lunch. Let's run the numbers: 190 miles in three and a half hours, which yields an average of 53 mph. Is that a "terrifying" speed when you're in a Facel Vega? Do not make insinuations by saying that they'd dined richly. A full meal accompanied by a glass or two of wine had, over the years, become the driver's standard fare. He'd been joking with Camus, nimble and alert. From the instant the car veered out of control, during that brief sprint toward death, his wife and step-daughter saw him physically struggling against that fate. Those who know the invincible horror aroused by death can imagine just how much extra fortitude the thought of it would have injected into his experience as a pilot.

Neither the alleged wear of the tires, nor the (made-up) speed of the vehicle, nor the incompetence some dare to assign him, nor tiredness, nor illness, nor a rich meal are good enough explanations of this catastrophe for me. No. Michel Gallimard did not kill Albert Camus.

Why, then, this slanderous campaign? Why, then, these spurious explanations? What is so seductive about the thought of a rich boy killing the son of a poor man? Is it because, in an affair such as this, people require a victim and an executioner in order to draw an accurate portrait of Camus? In fact, at the same time as they are jockeying to appropriate the Nobel Prize winner, to drape him in the guise of a "Christian who doesn't realize he is one," the almighty press is fashioning him into a demigod, into the god of French letters, even. Now, gods, as everyone knows, take pleasure in sniffing their victims' scents, but Camus's entire being rejects any finale that would see Michel Gallimard suffer. "What a fiasco," one of Albert's friends said to me on the day of Michel's burial. That's the word for it. On January 4, on the Nationale 5, two fraternal corpses lay lifelessly, two victims *ex aequo*. It is not yet known to what extent their deaths are inexplicable and whether this whole "fiasco" really is so banal. One gets the impression, rather, that whoever killed Michel Gallimard and Camus is trying to bring dishonor upon the former in order to excuse himself for having assassinated the latter. What I mostly see are people who altogether unscrupulously, under the pretext of venerating the god Camus, are serving some mere avatar of the god Mammon. Perhaps the day will come when that avatar can be called by its true name. I doubt it's *the Absurd*.

The true cause of the accident in which Albert Camus and his friend Michel Gallimard lost their lives has not yet been resolved. The stretch of road where the incident took place was described as being straight, wide, dry, and deserted. Floc, Janine Gallimard's pet dog, was never found, nor was the writer's suitcase, which he himself had checked onto the train to Paris. Like the man himself, his suitcase would never reach its destination. Paul Maillot, a government envoy, spent several hours at the Villeblevin city hall in possession of Albert Camus's belongings, including his manuscript of *The First Man*.

Little by little, the controversy surrounding the incident died down, and the following description of the event was all that remained: Albert Camus, recipient of the Nobel Prize for Literature, lost his life on January 4, 1960, in a freak car accident that occurred in a place called Petit Villeblevin, somewhere between Sens and Fontainebleau.

Following the incident, almanacs would continue compiling information:

On February 3, 1960, the insurrection of French Algerians that had begun with a student protest on January 24 was quelled, thanks in part to a widely broadcast speech delivered by de Gaulle.

On February 20, the FLN support network coordinated by Jeanson (author of the "review" published in *Les Temps Moderns* of Camus's *The Rebel*) was dismantled and the majority of its members jailed. The trial, which examined the topic of torture in greater detail than it did the topic of terrorism, constituted the culminating victory of propaganda efforts in favor of Algerian independence. In January 1961, French ultras founded the OAS (*Organisation de l'Armée Secrète*), whose subsequent bombing and assassination campaign left the French and Arab communities even more sharply divided.

On March 20, 1962, France recognized the independence of Algeria. Following the killing of colonists that took place in the face of inaction by the French army headquartered in the region, one million French Algerians fled their homeland and were received with hostility by France. Meanwhile, the *harkis*—Algerians in favor of establishing a peaceful coexistence with the French—were massacred.

Total number of attacks on French soil officially attributed to Algerian militants between January 1, 1956, and January 23, 1962: 11,896. With a balance of 8,813 wounded and 4,176 killed. Of those killed, 3,957 were Algerian and 219 were European. Not included in these figures are the numbers of the missing or the victims of incidents police were required to describe as accidental.

Although the figures are still the object of some dispute, it is estimated that in the eight years of the Algerian war (from November 1, 1954, to March 20, 1962), some 300,000–400,000 people died in the North African country, of whom roughly 30,000 were of European descent. Among Muslims, approximately 100,000 perished at the hands of the FLN.

In the 1990s, a new, undeclared civil war broke out in Algeria, which at that point had been independent for thirty years. The Islamic Salvation Front (FIS) rose up against the military government that had inherited power from the FLN. More than 200,000 Algerians from all walks of life died in the crossfire of terrorism and repression.

AUTHOR'S NOTE

The opening and sometimes closing passages of several chapters (the first, third, fifth, seventh, eighth, and ninth), those in which the protagonist is writing, are transcriptions of paragraphs taken from Albert Camus's posthumous novel *El primer hombre* (Tusquets, Barcelona, 1994; Spanish translation by Aurora Bernárdez), as well as from two of the notes appearing in the appendix of that same book. As are the excerpts appearing on the following pages: 44-45 (the paragraph in which he is describing the execution attended by his father) and 219 (when he talks about being a boy and going swimming in the sea with his uncle). There are several other passages that are readily identifiable, as they are described in each instance in the text as being the work of the author himself.

Most of the chapter titles are likewise drawn from sentence fragments appearing in *The First Man*. The others are taken from articles of Camus's and from his essay *The Rebel*.

BERTA VIAS MAHOU
Monday, January 4, 2010

TRANSLATOR'S NOTE

Writers from several language traditions are quoted in this novel. As translator, my foremost guiding principle when determining whether to borrow from previously published English translations or to compose new versions of my own was that these quotations should be readily identifiable to those familiar with the various authors' works while simultaneously blending in well with the overall flow and tone of the novel. I deemed this consideration to be more important than rigorously extracting from a single translated version of each work.

The Camus and Sartre quotes posed the greatest challenge in this sense, as the book contains, quite simply, more and longer excerpts from these two writers than from any others. Generally speaking, for the shorter one-liners of theirs that are sprinkled throughout the text, I chose to make use of well-established English translations, occasionally introducing slight changes, for example to punctuation, in the interest of editorial consistency. Thus, I have to thank Stuart Gilbert for the novel's epigraph and the line "There weren't no rats in that house," both taken from *The Plague*, as well as his rendition of *The Stranger* for the phrase "Paris is a dingy sort of town"; Ellen Conroy Kennedy's translation of *Lyrical and Critical*

Essays for "Poverty kept him from thinking that all was well under the sun and in history, while the sun taught him that history wasn't everything"; Philip Thody for the oft-quoted "I know of only one duty, and that is to love," which appears in *Notebooks 1935–1942*; David Hapgood's version of *The First Man* for "To you who will never be able to read this book"; Arthur Goldhammer and Robert Zaretsky for their restating of Camus's response to a question posed during a lecture at the University of Stockholm, "If that's justice, then I prefer my mother" (for a succinct discussion of the controversy surrounding the original transcription and translation of Camus's remarks, see the Columbia Journalism Review's article "Joining The Chorus"); and Justin O'Brien's translation of Camus's Nobel Prize acceptance speech for "Words and phrases, even the simplest ones, cost their weight in freedom and blood." However, the translation of Sartre's comment on Billancourt is my own.

Similarly, the titles of the third, fifth, seventh, and ninth through eleventh chapters are borrowed, again, from David Hapgood, the titles of the fourth and eighth chapters from Anthony Bower's translation of *The Rebel*, and the title of the sixth chapter from an editorial of Camus's dated May 17, 1945, and translated by both Alexandre de Gramont and Arthur Goldhammer. All other chapter titles, as well as the title of the novel itself, are my own translation.

In the case of longer excerpts from Camus's and Sartre's writings, I almost always chose to produce a new translation from scratch. This was done, as mentioned previously, in order to avoid any mismatches of tone and at times also to ensure a more seamless connection to the novel's plot and structure. For these fresh versions, I worked from the original French texts side by side with the Spanish edition of this novel. This two-sourced translation process was necessary, I felt, not only in the interest of having the English conform, at the most basic level, to any structural or syntactic changes to the original French that might be required to fit the passages into the surrounding text, but also to ensure that the meaning and spirit of the two writers' French works as well as Vias Mahou's Spanish take on them were both reflected as faithfully and harmoniously as possible.

In a few instances, however, a previously published English translation of a longer segment of text suited the novel's purposes perfectly. This is the case of the opening passage from the seventh chapter, which is once again taken from David Hapgood's *The First Man*, as well as two extracts from the tenth chapter—namely, the description of the "constant danger" Jacques had felt in Algeria, for which I turned to Hapgood once more, and the fragments of Sartre's "Reply to Albert Camus," beginning with the statement "Car brakes can fail," for which I leaned heavily on the translation by Benita Eisler in *Situations*.

Apart from these Camus and Sartre extracts, a variety of other sources are quoted in this novel. Paul Fort's "Lament of the Little White Horse," which begins "He never saw the Spring arise," is from a translation by John Strong Newberry. "Receive the fright of bees" is an excerpt from René Char's poem "Youth," translated by Denis Devlin and Jackson Mathews. A fragment of a second René Char poem, "The Raised Scythe," is borrowed from Robert Baker's translation of *The Word As Archipelago*. Citations from the Kabbalah, the Qur'an, and the Bible, as well as from Cervantes and Kierkegaard, are standard translations. The FLN communiqués mentioned in the novel are my own translation, working from both the original French and Vias Mahou's Spanish versions.

And finally, the translated extracts from Dostoyevsky's *The Possessed* and Sergey Nechayev's *Catechism of a Revolutionary* are my own and were based on this novel's Spanish renditions in simultaneous comparison with a variety of differing and at times contradictory English versions. Many thanks to Al Lapkovsky for helping me to decipher the original Russian, and to Guillermo López Gallego for his assistance with some of the trickier nuances of the French.

Cecilia Ross
October, 2015

ABOUT THE AUTHOR

BERTA VIAS MAHOU (Madrid, 1961) is a Spanish author and translator. She has translated the works of renowned German-language writers such as Joseph Roth, Arthur Schnitzler, and Goethe. She has published short stories, an essay on the role of women in literature, and four novels. She is the winner of the Premio Dulce Chacón de Narrativa and the Premio Torrente Ballester de Narrativa, two prestigious Spanish literary fiction awards.

ABOUT THE TRANSLATOR

CECILIA ROSS is an American translator and editor who has spent nearly the entirety of her adult life abroad, residing for the bulk of those years in Madrid, Spain. She has been an editor at Hispabooks since 2014, and her published works include the first ever translation of the poetry of Dorothy Parker into Spanish, *Los poemas perdidos* (Nórdica Libros, 2013, with Guillermo López Gallego). Her translation into English of Beatriz Espejo's *The Egyptian Tomb* is included in a forthcoming anthology for Words Without Borders, and she has also translated a work of nonfiction by the award-winning Mexican investigative journalist Lydia Cacho, *Memoir of a Scandal*. When not working, Cecilia can be found enjoying life, the universe, and everything with her husband and two Spanglish-fluent children.

Lightning Source UK Ltd.
Milton Keynes UK
UKOW01f1001110416

272007UK00001B/1/P